"I've just thought – a whole week in France with Simon!"

At the end of her first term at the Central London School of Music, Lizzie is picked for an Easter holiday trip to France. Her best friend Laura is going too – and of course Simon. But is Laura really to be trusted? And is Simon as nice as his good looks suggest? In the term that follows Lizzie faces a lot of ups and downs before she learns who her real friends are.

In this absorbing and often hilarious sequel to *Lizzie Oliver*, Lizzie continues her own story with characteristic wit and honesty.

Dedicated with much affection to the children of Rydal Preparatory School; past, present and future.

Lizzie's Luck

by
Catherine Robinson

Macdonald Children's Books

Cover illustration by Julie Dodd

Inside illustrations by Liz Roberts

Text copyright © Catherine Robinson 1989
Illustrations copyright © Liz Roberts 1989

First published in Great Britain in 1989 by
MACDONALD CHILDREN'S BOOKS

Set in Raleigh Medium by Leaper & Gard Ltd, Bristol, England
Printed and bound in Great Britain at
The Guernsey Press

Macdonald Children's Books
Simon and Schuster International Group
Wolsey House
Wolsey Road
Hemel Hempstead
Herts HP2 4SS

BRITISH LIBRARY CATALOGUING IN PUBLICATION DATA
Robinson, Catherine
    Lizzie's luck.
    I. Title
    823'.914 [J]

    ISBN 0-356-16806-9
    ISBN 0-356-16807-7 pbk

CONTENTS

Good News	7
Percy's	19
My First Public Appearance	30
Laura	44
Quarrels and Concerts	59
Simon's String Quartet	72
The French Trip	86
Boarding	100
Marmite	113
The Pact of Silence	127
The English Family	139
Seven Rowan Place	155
Seadrift	171
Simon Takes a Swim	185
The Mozart Concerto	199
Facing the Music	211
The Concert	223

1

Good News

As I watched the dinginess of London in March turn gradually to the softer suburbs, one word kept going through my mind. Sausages, sausages, sausages, sausages – it fitted the rhythm the train wheels were making on the track. Daddy had asked me that morning what I wanted for supper; as it was my birthday, he had said I could choose whatever I wanted. Big deal, I'd replied; I usually choose anyway. *AND* I cook it, more often than not.

"Oh Lizzie, you fibber!" he'd replied mildly. "Wendy always cooks supper now; you know she does."

It was true; she did, and it was usually healthy things that are really good for you, like chick pea stew or vegetarian lasagne. Yuckerama. She and Daddy had been married for almost a year, and she was taking her wifely responsibilities very seriously.

"I know she does, but I've been doing it ever since she's been in hospital," I pointed out, collecting up my things for school. "Will you do it tonight? I do think you might, as it's my birthday."

"Of course I will, sweetie," he said. "I have tried to help out but it's been difficult, what with visiting Wendy and the baby twice a day and all this work I've got on at the moment. You don't mind, do you?"

"Have you seen my pencil case?" I asked him. "Oh, there it is. No Daddy, I don't mind, but I didn't think I'd have to do everything instead. What happened to sharing the chores, like we agreed?"

"OK, OK, point taken," Daddy said hurriedly. He didn't like doing things around the house – I'd even caught him making a cup of tea in a cup I'd had cocoa in the night before, just to avoid doing any washing-up. He is disgusting sometimes; how I managed to turn out reasonably hygienic I don't know.

So he agreed to cook the supper, and asked me again what I wanted; "You choose, as it's your special day," he said. "Is there anything in particular you fancy?"

"Oh, brill!" I said immediately. "Sausages."

"Sausages?" Daddy repeated, raising an eyebrow. "I give you the opportunity of having whatever you like, and you choose sausages? Not fillet steak, or Dover sole?"

"We haven't had sausages for ages – Wendy's convinced they're full of poisonous E numbers, or something," I explained. "Besides, even you can't ruin sausages."

"Don't you believe it," Daddy said cheerfully. "Right then – sausages it is. I've got to go in to town this morning, so I must remember to pick some up on the way home. Want a lift to the station?"

So that's why I was sitting on the train, going home, thinking about sausages. Big fat juicy brown ones, sizzling in the pan, along with chips and baked beans. It was just as well Wendy wasn't going to be there, I thought: all that cholesterol, she'd have a fit. I was just mentally wiping out the frying pan with a piece of bread (unhealthy white) and eating that too, when the train stopped suddenly, with a jerk, jolting me rudely out of my sausage-dream. There was no hint as to why we'd stopped; we were nowhere near a station. The man sitting opposite me lowered his newspaper with a cross rustle.

"Not again!" he exclaimed, to no one in particular. "That's the third time this week! What are they playing at?"

The lady next to him smiled sympathetically. She had a tired, kind face and about ninety million shopping bags on her lap. "I shouldn't worry, duck – just sit tight. Ain't nothing you can do, anyway."

"It's too bad," the man said with a loud sigh. "My wife is getting fed up with having to keep supper hot for me because I'm late home. I really do think they should send the guard round with an explanation." And he shook his newspaper angrily and jabbed at it with a fountain pen, pretending to do the crossword.

Everybody else in the carriage ignored him, hiding behind papers and books or staring out of the window. I leant back in my seat and watched the two small children sitting across the aisle from me; one was crumbling crisps on to the floor, while the other was busily engaged in trying to stick chewing gum on to the trousers of the schoolboy sitting opposite him, who was swearing under his breath and trying to edge away. The children's mother was gazing through the window, chewing cow-like on toffees and ignoring all three of them. What brats, I thought; the new baby – my half-sister – had better not turn out like that if she wants to see *her* fourteenth birthday.

"This really is insupportable!" The newspaper man was off again. "When you consider the amount one spends on a season ticket! I shall complain to the Commuters' Club – to British Rail!"

The lady with the shopping clucked her teeth and offered him a large piece of Fruit & Nut which he accepted, slightly mollified. She offered me some too, with a smile, and I took it and smiled back. I realized that was the first time a stranger had smiled at me since we moved to London. It was one of the things I had found most difficult to get used to about London, the millions of people all milling around and all ignoring you. There was no way everyone would sit silently on a stationary train in Cornwall; mind you, in Cornwall I'd probably have known everyone on the train anyway.

"I expect we'll be off again in a tick," the lady said soothingly. "Besides, if you get too bored I daresay this young lady could give us a tune on her fiddle! It is yours, isn't it?" she asked me.

I nodded. "Yes, it is."

"Just fancy," she said, admiringly. "A little lass like you, playing the fiddle!"

"It is a violin then, and not a machine-gun?" the businessman enquired, smiling faintly at his wit. I've been playing the violin for years and have heard the machine-gun joke millions of times, and each time the person thinks they're the first one who's ever said it. I gave up trying to think of clever replies ages ago. So I just smiled politely and didn't say anything.

Just then the train started up again, with a shudder, and a sarcastic cheer went up from the back of the carriage. The lady offered me another piece of chocolate and started telling me how she once bumped into Princess Diana in Selfridges: "She was in disguise, of course, but I knew it was her. It was her eyes, see."

She was so nice and so interesting I hardly noticed the train slowing down, until I saw the name of a station slipping past – B-A-R-N-E . . .

"Heavens!" I said, jumping up and pulling my violin and music case from the luggage rack above our heads. "Barnes! That's my stop! I didn't realize we were there already!"

The man with the paper held the door open for me while I struggled with all my belongings. I managed to get everything together and practically fell out of the door on to the platform, just before a very bad-tempered looking guard came stomping up to bang the door shut.

"What's the hold-up?" he grumbled. "Come along girl, you'll make the train late."

I pulled a face at him as he blew his whistle in a very self-important way. What a cheek! The train was already half an hour late, Daddy would be wondering where I was. I was starving; I hoped he hadn't burnt the sausages. Hurrying home across the Common, I could almost smell them. I could hardly wait.

I ran the last few hundred yards to our back gate, which opens on to the Common, and swung my violin as I walked up the path to the back door. It was locked when I tried the handle; strange, I thought, I wonder why Daddy's locked it. He's almost always in when I get back from school because he works at home – he's a writer. Usually if he's going to be out it doesn't matter because Wendy's there, but of course she was in hospital with the baby. I knocked on the back door, loudly. Rufus immediately began barking: if anyone ever broke in he would probably lick them to death, but you'd never guess that from the way he woofs at people.

It was beginning to dawn on me that Daddy wasn't in. It didn't really matter because the spare key is kept under a broken flowerpot hidden in the front hedge, but I was cross. There was I, worrying that *he* might be worrying, and he wasn't even at home. He might have told me he was going out; it was my birthday, after all. He might have been there to welcome me home. I was starting to feel hard done by.

Rufus stopped barking as soon as I turned the key in the lock. By his doggy reasoning, burglars don't have keys. He wagged his way up the hall to greet me, grinning in that particular way retrievers have, and looking round for a present to bring me. He couldn't find a ball or a bone or a slipper, so he picked up a dead leaf that had fallen from the geranium on the hall table, and carried that around proudly instead.

"Good boy!" I said, patting him on the head. "Where's Daddy then? Daddy!" I called, thinking he might possibly be upstairs, but it was a bit of a forlorn hope. There was no reply. "Rotten old Daddy," I said sulkily, kicking the kitchen door open. So much for cooking me sausages, I thought.

"He's probably even forgotten it's my birthday," I grumbled to Rufus, opening the fridge door and pouring a glass of milk. Fishpaste immediately jumped down from the Aga and wound himself around my legs, miaowing loudly.

"You can't drink out of a glass," I told him nastily, "Go away." If I was going to be neglected, so was he.

I wandered out into the hall and drank my milk half-heartedly. Fishpaste came after me, still miaowing, followed by Rufus, complete with dead geranium leaf in mouth. I didn't like letting myself in to an empty house; I didn't like the implications. I shall turn into one of those latchkey kids, I thought to myself; I shall hang around the streets after school instead of coming home. I shall become a vagrant, unwanted, a. . . .

I suddenly noticed an envelope propped up against the geranium pot. LIZZIE, it said, in Daddy's handwriting. I reasoned it must be for me – I'm bright like that – and tore it open.

Happy Birthday Girl.
No, I haven't forgotten you, or the sausages! What I had forgotten, however, was Wendy and the baby; I'm due to be bringing them home from the hospital today. So I must fly, sweetie, or I shall be shot !!

Lots of love, Daddy.

The word 'shot' was underlined about five times. I sighed

heavily. It was typical of Daddy to have forgotten something as important as fetching his wife and baby daughter home. To say he is absent-minded is a bit like saying the Royal Family is quite rich, or Terry Wogan is on TV rather a lot. (Or even the other way round.) I don't know how Wendy puts up with him sometimes.

I felt a bit better now I knew Daddy hadn't forgotten me after all. And I was looking forward to having Wendy home again. And the baby; when I saw her in the hospital, the evening after she was born, I had been quite overcome by her; her smallness, her pink perfection. I wondered if she was destined to be called The Baby for evermore; she was already a week old and didn't have a name yet, mainly because Daddy had been convinced that she was going to be a boy. He'd managed to convince Wendy, too, with the result that they'd thought of lots of boys' names, but no girls'.

I screwed the note into a ball and threw it at Rufus, who promptly started shredding it to pieces all over the hall carpet. Then I finished my milk, and went upstairs to change out of my school uniform. I had just pulled my sweatshirt over my head when I heard the front door slam.

"Lizzie!" called Daddy's voice. "We're back! Are you home yet?" yet?"

"No," I called back, "I've run away. Did you get the sausages?" I thrust my arms through the sleeves, pulled it down and started down the stairs. "Hello Wendy. Are you all right, how's the baby, can I see her?"

Wendy and Daddy were standing at the foot of the stairs, holding a dark blue carrycot between them (blue for the boy they were sure they were going to have). Daddy was beaming. Wendy looked serene and very, very tired.

"Let's just get her into the nursery," Daddy said, taking the carrycot upstairs.

"The nursery!" I said. "It was just called the spare room yesterday."

"Well, it's going to be called the nursery from now on," he said firmly. He set the carrycot down on the floor, next to the crib full of white broderie anglaise draperies. "Come on downstairs, and leave her in peace," he whispered.

"But can't I hold her?" I said in my normal voice.

"Ssh," hissed Daddy. "She's asleep – you should never wake a sleeping baby."

"You sound just like the night sister," said Wendy with a laugh. "For heaven's sake, Jamie, let Lizzie hold her! She won't be asleep for much longer, anyway – she's just about due for a feed. Come along my little sweetheart," she said lifting the shawl-clad bundle from the carrycot and handing her to me.

The baby screwed up her eyes and munched up her mouth with little muttering sounds. She looked sleepy and cross, and just like a little old man.

"Oh," I breathed. "She's so sweet. She looks different already to when I saw her."

We all stood around for a bit looking at her and not saying anything. I felt a big lump in my throat. I don't know why; it was weird. She was just so little, and so helpless. Then I gave her back to Wendy, and we all went downstairs.

"It's nice to have you back," I said to Wendy. "We've missed you – even the animals." Rufus was practically wagging his tail off with pleasure.

"So it seems," said Wendy, looking around the hall with a grin. I followed her gaze. My empty milk glass was still on the hall table, where I'd left it, and the remnants of Daddy's Rufus-chewed note were scattered across the carpet.

"And your sweatshirt's on inside-out," she said.

"Oh, Lizzie," said Daddy with a frown. "I spend all afternoon cleaning up, and you're home for five minutes and the place is a tip."

"Huh!" I replied, aggrieved. "You can't talk! Do you know," I said to Wendy, "he didn't wash up once while you were away. Not once, *and* he forgot you were coming home. . ."

"All right, all right," Daddy interrupted quickly. "Let's all have a nice cup of tea, shall we?"

We sat drinking our tea as Wendy fed the baby.

"Have you decided what you're going to call her?" I asked, taking another biscuit. "After all, you can't call her 'It'. Or Edward James," I added. That's the boy's name they'd finally decided on.

"Flora," said Wendy, rubbing the baby's back.

"*Flo*-ra?" I said.

"Flora Angharad," said Wendy. The owner of the name gave a loud burp.

"Good grief," I said weakly.

"What do you mean, good grief?" Daddy demanded. "They're perfectly good names. Wendy's favourite grandmother was called Angharad; she was Welsh."

"Oh," I said "But what made you choose Flora? Makes her sound like margarine. Why not Stork Angharad, or – I know – Golden Churn Angharad!" I laughed loudly at my wit, and took the last biscuit.

"Ha, ha," Wendy said equably. "We liked it, that's why. And now I must change your nappy, little Flora Angharad. Oh Lizzie," she said from the doorway. "I never wished you a happy birthday. Have you had a good day?"

"It was OK," I shrugged. "Nothing special."

"Oh well," she called from the stairs. "There's still time, isn't there? It's not over yet."

"What does she mean, it's not over yet?" I asked Daddy, puzzled. "What's going to happen?"

"She must mean these," Daddy replied with a big grin. He took a white paper packet from the fridge. "Ta ra!" He sang a fanfare.

"Sausages!" I shrieked. "Oh Daddy, you didn't forget after all!"

* * *

But Wendy hadn't meant the sausages, although it was the end of the evening before I found out just what she did mean. After Daddy had cooked the sausages, and we had eaten every last one – E numbers and all; they were delicious – and Flora was bathed and changed, and tucked up asleep in her little white crib, Daddy lit the fire in the sitting-room and the three of us sat round it, drinking coffee.

"Ah, it's good to be home," Wendy sighed, kicking off her slippers and holding her feet out towards the warmth of the flames. "It feels like I've been away for a year, not just a week. Hospital beds and hospital food – yuck. Did you like your present?" she asked me, changing the subject suddenly.

For a moment, I didn't know what she meant. "Present?" I said blankly. "What present?"

Daddy clapped a guilty hand to his mouth, and Wendy shook her head and tutted softly. "Oh Jamie," she said, half-laughing. "Don't say you forgot to give Lizzie her birthday presents! Honestly, you are the limit."

"It's been an odd sort of birthday," I confessed to Wendy, as Daddy hot-footed it upstairs to get my presents. "Not like a birthday at all, really, what with school and you not being here and Daddy in a tizz and everything. I had some cards this morning, but that was all. To tell you the truth, I'd forgotten all about it being my birthday until coming home on the train." I paused, and couldn't resist adding a dig, "I suppose not having any presents had something to do with it."

Wendy sighed. "Your father is truly beyond the pale sometimes. Although to be fair he's had a lot on his mind; becoming a father again is pretty exciting for him."

I was just telling Wendy how I'd had to organize him when Daddy reappeared with assorted parcels.

"Here we are," he said, setting them down. "Meg and Charles sent money with strict instructions what to buy you, so you'd better open theirs first of all. It's from the children too, of course." Meg and Charles's present was a new music case; I sniffed the leather appreciatively and reflected how odd it was that my sister always knew exactly what to give me.

Then there were assorted small presents from Rufus and Fishpaste, and a turquoise silk blouse from Flora. "Isn't she clever," I said, holding it up against me, "knowing what size I am?"

Then finally there was the present from Daddy and Wendy. It was large and box-shaped, wrapped in snazzy foil paper and topped with a large red bow.

I tore the paper off eagerly. "What on earth is it?" I asked. "It looks like a coffee table without any legs."

But it wasn't a coffee table. It was a box. And inside the box was a new violin case, leather-covered, and lined with silky crimson velvet plush.

I was quite overcome. "Golly," I gulped, stroking the inside. "Isn't it lovely? Nobody will recognize me at Percy's now, with all my posh things." I went and gave them both a kiss.

"Am I forgiven, then?" Daddy kissed me back, and grinned. "For all the chivvying along I needed?"

"Oh yes – it's whizz, Daddy! Mega thanks!"

"We thought your old one looked a bit past it," Wendy explained. "Anyway, you can't go to music school and not have all the proper bits and pieces, can you?"

Daddy and Wendy exchanged raised-eyebrow glances, and then Daddy nodded slightly.

I pounced. "What is it?" I asked suspiciously. "Why are you looking at each other like that?"

"There is another present," Daddy said, slowly. "Although you'll have to wait a bit longer for it. But I can tell you about it now."

"Tell me about it?" I queried. "What d'you mean – tell me about what?"

I must have looked worried, because Daddy gave me a reassuring smile. "It's all right," he said. "Nothing horrid. The fact is, Wendy and I have been discussing it for some time – since she was expecting Flora really, but mainly since she was born – and we know how much you fought against the idea of moving up here . . ."

Wendy interrupted him with a sigh. "You do waffle," she told him. "I've never really thought London is a good place for children to grow up in – and as your father said, we've always been concerned at how much you seemed to hate the idea of living here," she said to me.

It seemed to me they were *both* waffling. "And?" I prompted. "And?"

Daddy laughed. "We are making a meal of it, aren't we? Poor Lizzie, desperate to know – although I think you've already guessed. We're going to move back to Cornwall." He looked at my incredulous face, and laughed again. "It's true. I've been around all the estate agents, and they're sending details to me. You're going back, sweetie – you're going back home."

2

Percy's

7th March.

*D*ear Diary,
What an ace, brill, seriously MEGA-WHIZZ birthday – or rather, what an ace, ditto ditto ditto birthday present. Moving back to Cornwall! – I can still hardly believe it. When I came up to bed I suddenly thought about this time last year – my thirteenth birthday – with Daddy and Wendy just about to get married, and bringing me here to see this house, and me absolutely hating the thought of moving away from Penwithin to London. And when it actually happened it was just as awful as I imagined it would be. I wonder when all that changed? – when it stopped being awful, I mean. I can't remember; it all seems such a long time ago, now. Just goes to show how life changes without you even noticing . . .

Anyway, I don't have to think about that any more, because we're going back; even though I'm more used to London now it'll be just brilliant to be living in Cornwall again. Although of course I'll only be there in the holidays, 'cos I'll be boarding at school. Boarding school. Will it be like Enid Blyton, I wonder? – Mallory Towers, all midnight feasts and pushing the school bully in the swimming pool ("Crikey! Gosh, Felicity, what jolly rotten luck".) Can't see it, somehow;

I'll have to ask Laura. Can't wait to see her face when I tell her – she's always going on about poor old day-pupil me missing out on all the best bits at Percy's.

"Will you try and buy the cottage back?" I asked Daddy the morning after my birthday, as we ate breakfast.

"I don't suppose we'll be able to," Daddy replied, pouring himself his third cup of tea. "The folk who bought it from us were very keen on it – I doubt they'll be looking to sell it again so soon after moving in. Anyway, it'd be too small for us now, what with Wendy and Flora as well as you and me."

"I suppose so," I said. That took the gilt off the gingerbread a bit; although I'd seen the estate agents' blurb that morning, somehow it hadn't registered, and I'd been imagining moving back to our old cottage, with life the same way as it had been before we moved away. Of course, it couldn't possibly be. The thought made me somehow sad.

"Oh well," I said, sighing. "Never mind – I expect we'll find somewhere nice. It will be Penwithin though, won't it?" I said anxiously.

Daddy looked at me with an expression of real tenderness. "If I can possibly help it, sweetie, it will be Penwithin. Anyway, if we're going to move all that way I want to be near Meg and Charles again."

"Have you told them yet?" I wanted to know.

"I did mention it – Meg was thrilled to bits. She's never liked the idea of us being so far away."

"She's not the only one," I muttered into my toast.

Daddy covered my hand with his. "I know you were miserable, Lizzie – I know you didn't want us to move, and life was pretty awful for you when we did. But you are happier now, aren't you?"

"Oh yes," I said honestly.

"And you like it at the CLSM?"

"Percy's," I corrected him, automatically. "Yes, I do – it's brill."

"I can never understand how you manage to get 'Percy's' out of 'the Central London School of Music'," Daddy said, looking baffled.

"*You* can't call it Percy's," I told him airily. "Only people who go there can call it that. It's called Percy's after the man who started it all off – you know, the . . . " I waved my arms around, fumbling for the right word.

Daddy obligingly supplied me with it, "The founder."

"That's right," I agreed. "The founder. Sir Percival Chalstrey. In seventeen hundred and something."

"Aha!" said Daddy, light dawning. "All becomes clear at last. So you don't mind starting to board?"

I shook my head. "No – I'm quite looking forward to it, actually. I'll really belong then. When d'you think I'll have to start?"

"After the Easter holiday, I imagine, all being well – we're aiming to move some time in May. Although come to think of it," he went on, "I suppose you could always go back to your old school in the village; that would save me a bit of money . . ."

"Daddy!" I said, outraged. "You can't mean that! You know how I . . ." Then I saw his face.

He laughed. The pig; he always knows how to get me going. "Only teasing," he grinned, looking at his watch. "Though if you don't stir your stumps and go and catch your train, they'll kick you out for being late."

"I see," I grumbled, "no lift this morning."

"Don't be lazy," said Daddy. "I must help Wendy with the baby; I can't leave her on her own." He yawned, and fisted his eyes. "Oh dear, I think I'm getting a bit old for this Nappies at Dawn lark."

"Yes," I said unhelpfully. "I heard Stork Angharad this

morning; what time was it? Three o'clock? I didn't get back to sleep for ages."

"There's more where that came from." Daddy yawned again. "Go on now, off you go to school."

As I turned in to the entrance of Percy's I thought about my baby half-sister. She's very sweet, I reflected, but three a.m. really is a bit early. Anyway it'll be good when she's a bit older, then I can teach her the violin, and we can play duets. I imagined myself as an old lady, a world-famous violinist of years gone by, and Flora as a brand-new sensation after having given her début recital. Then I remembered she was only fourteen years younger than me, and amended my day-dream hurriedly. I was a *middle-aged* world-famous violinist of years gone by, having had to give up my career tragically early, and Flora was a late developer.

"I taught her everything she knows," I croaked tragically.

"She is a wonderful person," Flora gushed. "I owe her such a lot. She had to give up her career so tragically early . . ."

"Careful, Lizzie!" said a male voice. It was Mr Hadleigh; he teaches history, and all the senior girls fawn round him disgustingly. Some of the not-so-senior ones, too. I went red as he put his hands on my shoulders to steady me. "Where's the fire?" he enquired mildly.

"Sorry, sir," I muttered, looking at my feet. I suppose he is quite good-looking. If you like that sort of thing. I was cross at myself for going red, though. "I'm late for registration, and Mrs Maxwell goes bonkers if you don't get there on time."

"Well," said Mr Hadleigh, looking amused. "Don't let me keep you."

Idiot, I thought, opening the door to my classroom. He knew jolly well why I was hurrying. I can't stand these men who think they're God's gift to females.

"Hi, Lizzie," said Laura, not looking up from the magazine

she was reading. "Late again?"

"What do you mean, again?" I asked hotly. I was still strangely unsettled from my encounter with Mr Hadleigh in the corridor. "It's the first time I've been late for ages."

Laura looked up in surprise. "What's bitten you? I was only joking. Anyway, old Maxwell's away today. We've got Mr Hunky instead, yum yum."

I had this suspicious feeling. "Mr? . . . you don't mean Mr Hadleigh, do you?"

"What's up? Don't *you* think he's hunky?"

Laura considers herself to be something of a connoisseur of older men, despite being the same age as me, and wouldn't have understood. I wasn't entirely sure I understood myself; why should bumping into a teacher have made my feet feel so large, my hair feel so untidy, and the spot on my chin feel so enormous and beacon-like? I wouldn't have felt like that if it had been Mrs Maxwell and not Mr Hadleigh I'd walked into, I knew that. What's more, he'd known how I'd felt; he knows all girls feel like that when he talks to them. I hated the thought of turning into one of the silly simpering band of third years who hang on his every word. At that moment I envied Laura her composure, her easy discussion of Mr Hadleigh's hunkiness.

I didn't tell Laura what I thought of Mr Hadleigh. "I think it's going to be one of those days," I said instead, sighing.

Things improved, however, when I remembered at break to tell Laura the good news about Cornwall. We were mooching around in the day-room, as it was pouring with rain outside.

"Does that mean you'll be boarding?" asked Laura with interest.

"Yes," I said, "probably after Easter."

"Whizz!" Laura said, eyes sparkling. "Lynne Brown's leaving at Easter, so there'll be a space in my dorm. Mrs Nightingale might let you have it, if I ask her."

Mrs Nightingale is the housemistress of the girls' boarding house. She's motherly and friendly; I thought she would probably agree.

"That would be great," I said. I still felt a bit of a new girl, and the thought of boarding was a little bit daunting; it would be nice, I thought, to have Laura showing me the ropes again. She had been the first person to befriend me at Percy's when I arrived at the beginning of that term from Oaklands, my old school.

Emma Nash was standing over by the notice board. "Hey, come and look at this," she said, thoughtfully. "I've always wanted to go to France."

"What're you on about, Mouse?" demanded Laura. "What do you mean, France?"

"Come and see," Emma urged.

There was a new, important-looking notice pinned up in a prominent position, with a pink cardboard arrow stuck next to it.

"Looks like one of Sporanti's," I remarked. Signor Sporanti is the Head of Senior Music, conducts the Symphony Orchestra, and is famous at Percy's for two things; his explosive temper, and his habit of attaching pink cardboard arrows to his notices, marking them out as important.

I read the notice out loud.

MIDDLE AND UPPER SCHOOL INSTRUMENTALISTS – EXPAND YOUR HORIZONS!
We have been invited by the Société Culturelle Française to take a Chamber Orchestra to various concert locations in France. This is to take place for one week during the Easter vacation of the Central London School of Music. Anybody who is interested should sign below by 10th March, 12 noon, when this notice will be removed.

"Good grief," I remarked, "he doesn't give us much time, does he? The tenth – that's the day after tomorrow!"

"If it's anything to do with Sporanti, I'm not going," Laura said decisively. "It's bad enough having to put up with him at Orchestra, let alone in the holidays as well!"

Emma produced a chewed-looking fountain pen from the depths of her skirt pocket. "Well, I'm signing," she said, adding her surprisingly neat signature under the dozen or so already there.

"So'm I," I decided. Like Emma, I'd always wanted to go to France. "Lend me your pen, Mouse."

"It's a bit inky, I'm afraid," Emma apologized. "I think Deefer must have got hold of it."

"Who's Deefer?" I enquired, drawing a line under my signature with a flourish.

"My dog," Emma explained. "It's my Dad's idea of a joke – you know, Deefer Dog."

For some reason this struck me as hilariously funny, and I snorted with laughter. Emma started laughing too. "Stupid, isn't it?" she giggled.

"When you've finished having hysterics," Laura said loftily, "perhaps I can borrow the pen."

"I thought you didn't want to go?" I said.

"I never said that," Laura protested, adding her name under mine.

"Yes you did," Emma said mildly, pushing her glasses up her nose. "You said, if it's anything to do with Sporanti, you're ..."

"Well I've changed my mind. There," Laura interrupted, screwing the lid back on to the pen. "Oh God, Mouse, look – I've got ink all over my hands."

"I did say it was inky," said Emma. "Sorry Laura. Look – you can borrow my hanky to wipe them."

"Won't your mum go mad if you go home with ink all over

it?" I asked, watching the spotlessly white handkerchief turn blue.

"Oh no," Emma reassured me. "She's used to me."

"Wendy would go bananas," I said. I was just telling Emma and Laura about Wendy coming home from the hospital with my brand-new half-sister, when the door to the day-room opened and a boy with very blond hair came in.

"Hello fans," he said, raising his arms in Caesar-style greeting.

Laura snorted. "We're not your fans," she said. "Well, Lizzie might be, but Mouse and I aren't."

He came over to us. "Are you my fan, Lizzie? How sweet."

I felt myself going red. "Shut up, Laura," I muttered. I was furious with my face for making me look stupid for the second time in one morning.

"Have you seen the noticeboard, Simon?" Laura asked him, losing interest in who was a fan of whom. "Sporanti's organizing a trip to France. We've all signed up."

Simon wandered over to the noticeboard. "Cool," he said approvingly. "Hey, this looks really whizz." He started whistling "I love Paris in the Springtime" under his breath as he added his name under our three. Laura suddenly giggled.

"Remember Marina Gillespie?" she asked Emma.

"Who's she?" I asked.

"You mean you haven't heard about Marina Gillespie. She's a Percy's legend," Simon informed me solemnly. "She was a barmy Australian who used to go around doing mad things, like standing up in the middle of concerts and yelling 'What about the Aborigines?' Emma and Laura were actually here with her."

"I remember her," Emma put in. "I could never understand why she was so interested in the Aborigines."

"She was socially aware," Simon explained. "She wanted to make people think about the Aborigines' plight."

"Never mind the Aborigines," I said. "What about Marina Gillespie?"

"She got kicked out eventually, I think they got fed up with her," Laura told me. "She used to say Sporanti was a Fascist, and whenever he put one of his notices up she used to sign it Mussolini."

"Who is Mussolini, anyway?" said Emma.

"He was a Fascist," Simon told her.

"Oh," Emma said. "What's a Fascist?"

"Oh Emma," Simon groaned. "Don't you know anything?"

"Not much," Emma admitted cheerfully.

"What *is* a Fascist, anyway?" I asked, not feeling as stupid as I might have done if Emma hadn't admitted she didn't know.

"It's a – sort of – well, you know," Simon said lamely.

"Like Sporanti is," said Laura helpfully. "Wouldn't it be funny if we added some spoof names on the bottom of the list!"

We all looked at Signor Sporanti's notice. All that blank paper did look awfully inviting.

"I don't think it would be funny," Emma said decidedly. "I think it would be silly."

"Don't be such a spoilsport!" said Laura. "Come on Mouse, lend me your pen again."

Emma did so, with a sigh, and watched as Laura wrote 'Donald Duck' and 'Mrs Thatcher' under Simon's name, in careful block capitals.

"Who else shall I put?" she asked.

"Here, let me have it," said Simon, writing 'Madonna' firmly. "I'd go twice if she was going. And how about – let's see – Princess Diana."

Emma sighed as she put her pen back in her pocket. "Pointless," she remarked.

Just then, the bell went for the next lesson. Laura and I

were still giggling as the three of us collected our books and walked down the corridor.

"Honestly, can you imagine Madonna playing in a Percy's chamber orchestra!" I snorted. "What instrument do you think she'd play?"

"Triangle," said Laura decisively.

"Or trombone," I suggested. "What d'you reckon Sporanti would make of her?"

"He'd go purple, and tell her to go wash-a the paint off-a her face," she said, in an exaggerated imitation of Signor Sporanti's Italian accent. "Listen, remind me to ask Mrs Nightingale tonight about the dorm, won't you?"

"Are you going to start boarding, then?" Emma asked me as we entered the classroom and sat down.

I told her about Daddy deciding to move back to Cornwall.

"*That's* where you come from," Emma sounded triumphant. "I've been wondering about your accent ever since you started here. It's ever such a long way, isn't it? How will you get home in the holidays?"

"I'll go by train, I expect!" I exclaimed. "We do have trains, you know – we're not total savages, just because we don't live in London!"

Emma went pink with embarrassment. "Oh, I know – I didn't mean that – it's just, well, I wondered if your new house was going to be out in the wilds or something . . ."

"In the middle of the Cornish jungle, you mean?" Laura snorted sarcastically. "You are dim sometimes, Mouse. Anyway," she turned to me again, "Simon will be pleased you're going to board."

Much to my annoyance, I could feel myself beginning to blush again. "Will he?" I couldn't resist asking. "Why?"

Laura looked hard at me. "Because you're my friend, of course, and so's he. Therefore you're *HIS* friend, too. I say, you're not falling for the famous Alexander charm, are you?"

But at that point the teacher entered the room and the lesson began, which saved me having to reply.

Laura and Simon Alexander have known each other for ages; they come from the same town and went to the same primary school. But Laura had come to Percy's after that, when she was eleven, and Simon, who's a year older than us, had only started at the beginning of that term, the same as me. In fact, he and I had been at the same audition. But whereas I hadn't known anybody when I started, Simon had seemed to know heaps of people; through Laura, I suppose. He had also had about five different girlfriends already, and he still always has heaps of girls hanging around him, hence Laura's comment about "the famous Alexander charm."

But I'm not interested in boys – not in that sense. Music takes up most of my time. That's what I tell myself, anyway. But I had recently noticed myself going red whenever I saw Simon, or someone mentioned his name, and I didn't know why. It made me feel uncomfortable – like when I'd bumped into Mr Hadleigh that morning.

And when I got home that evening. This is what I wrote in my diary.

I hope Mrs Nightingale says I can share Laura's dorm. She's a real laugh; it would be whizz. Emma's nice, too, but Laura's my best friend. I hope I get picked to go to France; Daddy says I can go if I am, and with any luck I should be – Sporanti's bound to need heaps of violinists. I hope the others get chosen too – Emma and Laura, and Simon. I've just thought – a whole week in France with Simon! Oh please, God, please let Simon be picked; I shall be good forever, I absolutely promise. Only let me and Simon go to France. After a week, he might start to notice me. Oh, and let Emma and Laura go too, of course.

3

My First Public Appearance

Signor Sporanti's notice was duly taken down two days later, and the following day another appeared in its place, complete with pink cardboard arrow.

FRENCH TRIP
Would all those who signed their names kindly meet in room
G3 at Break this morning (11 March)

Room G3 was already rather crowded when I arrived at eleven o'clock. I saw Laura and Simon sitting by the blackboard, so made my way over to them.

"Hi," I said. "I do hope we'll all be picked."

"So do I," Simon agreed. "What about Donald Duck, though?"

Laura clapped a hand to her mouth. "Oh crumbs!" she said through her fingers. "I'd forgotten all about that! What d'you suppose Sporanti will say?"

But it looked as though we were about to find out, because at that moment the door burst open and Signor Sporanti came bumbling in. There was a button missing from his shirt, showing an expanse of fat, vest-covered tummy, and his tie had biscuit crumbs and coffee stains down it. He read out all the names on the list. I held my breath – beside me, I could feel Laura and Simon doing the same. Perhaps we'd got away with it after all!

"OK!" Signor Sporanti pronounced. "Good! You're all here! Well, you all come here today so I can decide who is to go – we cannot have a chamber orchestra with five flutes and no violas, can we, heh?" We all laughed dutifully. I let my breath out slowly – perhaps he hadn't noticed. Or maybe he was just going to ignore it?

But I'd relaxed too soon, Signor Sporanti gazed down again at the list he still held in his hand.

"Allora!" he exclaimed. "We are not all here! There are some peoples missing! Where is – ah –" he glanced down his list. "Where is Donald Duck?" Everybody giggled. My wretched face started burning again. "Where is Mrs Thatcher? Where is my lady – Madonna?"

Everybody laughed loudly. I looked across the room to where Emma was sitting, and grinned at her. It proved my downfall.

"Leezie Oliver!" thundered Signor Sporanti. My heart did a fandango. "You know something about this, perhaps?"

Beside me I could feel Laura not daring to breathe. "Er – no, Signor," I lied. You could have fried an egg on my face.

"Then why you go blush?" he demanded. "Why you *look* guilty, heh?"

"I don't know, Signor," I mumbled. I forced myself to look him in the eye. "I didn't do it, Signor. Honestly." That, at least, was the truth.

"Hmmph," he grunted. "Then perhaps you tell me something, heh? Perhaps you tell me why the seely names and your name, and – er," he looked again at the notice in his hand, "and Emma Nash and Laura English – why they all are written *in the same pen!* Heh?"

I'd forgotten that we'd all borrowed Emma's pen to sign

up; Simon had used his own to write his name but had borrowed Emma's to add to the spoof names.

"I don't know, Signor," was all I could manage, lamely.

"Emma?" he demanded, turning to her.

"I didn't do it, Signor," she said truthfully.

"Mees English?" to Laura.

"No, Signor!" she replied, tossing her long blonde hair over her shoulders and sounding aggrieved. "I wouldn't do a thing like that! Your notices are – er – important." I could tell she was stifling a laugh. He turned to me again. "Hmmph," he grunted once more. "I think you know more than you say, Leezie Oliver. I shall be watching you," he said ominously.

I picked at the hem of my skirt. I didn't know what to say – I couldn't land Laura and Simon in it, although it did seem unfair that Simon hadn't even been suspected. So it seemed best to say nothing. I was just relieved that Signor Sporanti didn't seem too het-up about it; when he is in a real rage he is truly a sight to behold, and I had no wish to be on the receiving end of that.

Luckily, he appeared satisfied that he had made his point, and with a final "hmmph" in my direction, he got down to the serious business of sorting out who was to go to France. To my joy, all four of us – Emma, Laura, Simon, and I – were on the list of names he read out, although he gave me a long, hard look and another "hmmph" as he said my name.

"What a hoot!" laughed Laura as we walked down the corridor after the meeting. "Wasn't that a scream? Honestly, I never thought I'd keep a straight face. Thanks for not letting on – though I don't think he really thought it was you."

"He did," said Emma. "He did think it was you, Lizzie," she repeated calmly. "He'll be watching you too, like he said. He's like that. You'll have to be careful."

I saw Simon walking down the corridor towards us, and a strange feeling swept over me. I wanted to do something bold, say something provocative – something Laura might have done or said. I tossed my hair back, in unconscious imitation of my friend, although with less effect because my hair is dark mud-coloured and although I'm trying to grow it, it barely comes to my shoulders.

"I don't care," I said loudly. "Let him watch me! Just let him. I think he's a . . . " and I said quite a rude word.

Simon caught up with us. "Who is?" he said with a laugh. "Me?"

Believe it or not, I went red again. "No," I said. "Sporanti."

"That's all right then," he said. "Actually, I wanted to say thank you for not splitting on me."

"And me," Laura put in.

"No, not you," Simon told her. "You can do your own thanking." He turned to me again and looked me straight in the eyes. His were incredibly blue, and had very long lashes; I felt quite peculiar. "I thought you were really brave. Seriously; letting him go on like that and not saying it was Laura and me. Thanks Lizzie – you're a pal!" And to my enormous surprise he leant towards me and kissed my cheek before striding off away down the corridor.

"Ooh!" Laura crowed. "Never wash that face again! She that has been kissed by Simon Alexander is blessed indeed . . ."

"Shut up!" I said furiously, trying desperately to keep my blushes under control and obviously failing miserably. I scrubbed at the cheek where Simon had kissed me. "Just shut up, Laura!"

Laura shrugged, not put out at all. "Listen, I've got to dash," she said suddenly. "I'm supposed to be seeing gorgeous Mr Hadleigh about my history essay. See you in Maths," she yelled at me over her shoulder. I stood in the corridor feeling slightly dazed. I could still see Simon's blue eyes; I put my hand up to touch my cheek where he had kissed me.

"You want to be careful of those two," came Emma's voice.

She was still standing there, watching me. "I mean, I know they seem ever so nice and everything. But – well – they like leading people on."

"What on earth do you mean, Mouse?" I demanded, not at all dazed any more.

"Just don't let them," she said slowly. "Don't let them muck you about, that's all. I'll see you at the Workshop." And she turned on her heel, and was gone.

I pondered Emma's words as I ate my lunch – alone, that day, as Laura and Simon were off somewhere practising the duet they were to play at the Workshop later that lunch-break. I could think of no reason why she should say what she had done; Laura had been really friendly to me ever since I had arrived at Percy's. She had to be my best friend there; although part of me could hardly believe that she was. Laura was popular and clever and ever so pretty; she had been at Percy's for years, and by now was part of the scenery. Everybody knew Laura English. I was proud to count myself as one of her friends.

Emma, on the other hand, didn't seem to have many friends. I didn't really know her that well; she sat behind me for the Symphony Orchestra rehearsals, and a couple of times recently had loaned me a pencil or some rosin for my bow. I wondered if she was jealous of Laura; it seemed a bit mean to come to that sort of conclusion without really knowing her, but it was the only reason I could find for her words. Oh well, I thought, what does it matter? Laura and Simon are my friends. They don't muck me about – they wouldn't! But for an unknown reason, a shiver passed down my spine.

I picked up my dessert plate and stacked it neatly at the end of the table before leaving the dining hall.

"Lizzie!" a voice called. It was Laura; she had her oboe in her hand and a worried expression on her face. She came over to me in a flustered way that was most unlike her. "My reed has packed up – you couldn't rush up to my dorm and get another one, could you? I think there's an old one in a little leather box on my locker; it's a bit past it, but at least I've played it in."

Reeds are the bane of oboists' lives; they are two thin pieces of cane which vibrate together when air is forced down them, by blowing, thus producing the sound. Reeds are what make me glad I'm a violinist. I was just about to say yes, and go up to Laura's dorm to get her other reed, when I noticed the time. I was going to be late for my own run-through of the piece I was to play at the Workshop – but for some reason, I didn't say that immediately to Laura.

"What about Mrs Nightingale?" I said instead. "I thought she didn't let non-boarders into the dorms."

"Oh pooh," said Laura. "She won't even see you. Oh go on, Lizzie, be a pal."

"I can't." I looked at my watch. "I shall be late – Mr Owen's running through my piece with me. Sorry Laura."

She stared at me. "What piece?"

"For the Workshop," I explained.

"But you're not playing – you're not on the list."

"I am!" I protested.

"Well I didn't see your name. Oh go on, Lizzie – it won't take a sec."

"It won't take you a sec, either." I pointed out reasonably.

I was unprepared for Laura's reaction. "You are mean!" she exploded. "You're just scared of old Nightingale catching you. Well don't bother – I shall get it myself. Just don't expect me to ask her about you sharing with me after Easter, that's all." And she tossed her hair over her shoulders and swung up the stairs.

I was quite taken aback. I certainly hadn't expected Laura to take offence. And I thought she'd already asked Mrs

Nightingale about sharing . . . I dithered around at the foot of the stairs, wondering whether I ought to go after her, when someone called my name.

"There you are, Lizzie!" the voice said. It was Mr Owen, my violin teacher. "I thought you'd fallen off the face of the earth! We have a rehearsal – had you forgotten?" And he took me by the arm and bore me away, leaving Laura's huff to sort itself out.

As I played through my piece with Mr Owen accompanying me on the piano, I started to feel nervous. I never usually suffer from nerves when I'm playing, but this was a special occasion for me, a 'first'; the first time I was to play in public since starting at Percy's. Workshops are sort of concerts which happen every so often at lunch-times, a kind of opportunity for people to come and find out what we've been working on, and Daddy and Wendy said they would come and listen to me make my début.

I was playing part of a sonata by Mozart, not at all the sort of thing I'd played in public before; I usually play fast, almost show-offy sort of things, but this was very slow and smooth and sustained.

"Much more impressive," Mr Owen had said. "Shows off your technique much more than any flashy piece." I'd learnt a lot about music since starting violin lessons with him.

When we finished our play-through I joined the other performers in the 'wings' behind the stage in the main hall. My nerves increased as I peeped through a chink in the crimson velvet curtains. People had already started arriving – the hall was more than half full – and as I looked out at its Georgian splendour, the long many-paned windows and the crystal chandeliers, I saw Daddy and Wendy coming in through the big double doors at the back. Daddy was holding a programme and Wendy had a fast-asleep Flora in her arms, wrapped snugly in a yellow blanket.

Then all at once, so it seemed, the concert had begun. I was third to play, and I don't remember much about the two before me, or about making my way onto the stage. Mr Owen gave me an 'A' from the piano, and I carefully tuned my violin. Then he was playing the familiar introduction and I took a deep breath and launched into the music.

As soon as I started to play I knew it was going to be all right. I forgot about all the people in the hall listening to me – I even forgot about Daddy and Wendy – and all my nerves simply disappeared. All there was in the world was me and my violin and the glorious liquid emotion of the Mozart, the notes dropping one by one into the still air like jewels on to velvet.

When I finished playing there was a moment's utter silence before the applause began. Then the spell was destroyed, and I was back on the stage, in the hall, in what was only, after all, a school concert. But I felt numb and dazed; I had never felt like that before when I had played, although I had always enjoyed it. It had been wonderful. I wanted to feel it again; and I understood why Mr Owen had wanted me to play that piece, and why he had made me wait two months before playing it for an audience.

The rest of the concert went by; it over-ran a bit, and afterwards I didn't have the chance to speak to Daddy and Wendy before lessons started again for the afternoon. I waved to them from the back of the hall as they filed out with the rest of the audience in a buzz of chatter, Flora still sleeping soundly in Wendy's arms.

Backstage, the usual post-mortems were being conducted by the performers as we collected up our instruments and music.

"I got lost in the middle," said Jenny Worsley. "It was awful – Mrs Harvey will kill me."

She had played a Brahms piano rhapsody from memory.

Nobody had noticed she had got lost, but she had her hands to her mouth and looked pale and tearful.

Fancy getting in that state, I thought. Then I remembered how nervous I had felt before I had played, and how wonderful the feeling had been afterwards. "No she won't," I told her. "It was fine – honestly."

"Did you hear my reed buzzing?" Laura was asking Mr Owen. He patted her on the back. "Don't worry about it," he said kindly.

"I was so nervous," I told him. "I just wanted to run away before I went on."

"It doesn't get any easier," he told me. "Some of the world's most famous musicians are actually sick before they go and play."

"Golly," I said, horrified. "How awful. Why do they carry on?"

Mr Owen looked shrewdly at me. "Did your nerves go when you started to play?" he asked me. I nodded. "And how did you feel afterwards?"

I sighed dreamily. "Fabulous," I said. "It was just wonderful – it felt really ..." I noticed Laura looking curiously at me, and felt suddenly embarrassed. "It was good," I finished lamely.

Mr Owen looked me in the eye, and for a fleeting second I saw something wise and understanding and age-old there.

"You see?" he said softly, his Welsh accent very strong. "That's why. That's why." I felt a shiver run through me.

Then Jenny started bleating again about getting lost, and everything was back to normal as we all drifted off to our lessons.

Laura and I were talking about the Workshop as we waited outside the classroom for the teacher to arrive.

"Did you really not hear my reed quacking?" Laura

demanded. I had heard it, and quacking was a good description, but something made me not own up to having heard it. Something told me that I would have been blamed for it, because I hadn't fetched the other reed.

"No," I said instead. "It sounded OK, honestly. It was a really nice piece, too."

"*Nice*?" said Laura scornfully. "What a stupid word. Nice – it's so wishy-washy."

Our English teacher had said exactly the same thing about the word the previous week, so I wasn't as impressed with Laura's apparent command of the English language as I might otherwise have been.

"Don't be picky," I told her. "It's not my fault your reed was making a din."

"So you *did* hear it," Laura accused me.

I was suddenly exasperated with my friend. "Oh for heaven's sake," I told her. "Stop going on about your flipping reed. It's not the end of the world."

Laura looked taken aback, but only for a moment. "Simon wasn't pleased with the piece either," she said. He had been accompanying her – as well as playing the cello, he's a pretty good pianist. "He said your sister was putting him off."

I was puzzled. "Meg?" I asked, perplexed. "What do you mean?"

"I thought her name was Flora," said Laura. "Anyway, he said that babies shouldn't be allowed at concerts – they make too much racket."

"But she was asleep the whole time," I pointed out. "I don't think that's fair."

"I'm only telling you what Simon said. Although I agree with him, actually. What if she had woken up and started crying? It would have disturbed everyone." Laura looked closely at me.

"Well she didn't," I said huffily.

At that moment the teacher arrived, so the conversation ended. But I felt vaguely cross the whole afternoon. I had so enjoyed playing the Mozart and Laura's dig had somehow taken the edge off my pleasure. Just because of her stupid reed, I thought to myself. I didn't really believe that Simon had said that about Flora, but I couldn't be sure. Perhaps *he'll* be mad at me when I see him next, I thought, suddenly worried. But it's not my fault if Wendy decides to being the baby – it's not!

It was on my mind all afternoon. When I got home, I realized I had left behind the music I was supposed to be practising, which didn't improve my mood.

"Lizzie!" Daddy greeted me enthusiastically as I opened the back door. "Hello sweetie! You did do well this afternoon; well done!"

Fishpaste weaved around my ankles, miaowing hungrily. I nearly tripped over him. "Thanks," I said grudgingly. "Oh Fishpaste – get out of the way! Can't you feed him, Daddy?"

Daddy poured some milk into a saucer and started opening a tin of Whiskas. "We were really impressed," he went on. "I don't think I've ever heard you play as well as that – how long have you been working on that piece?"

"Dunno," I said, throwing down my bag. "What's for supper?"

"Well, it was really nice." Daddy put the cat's bowl down, and Fishpaste tucked into it greedily.

"Oh Daddy," I groaned. "What a stupid word – nice. It's so wishy-washy."

Daddy looked at me, hard. "You are in a sunny mood this evening," he remarked. "What's the matter?"

"Nothing," I muttered.

"Go and see Wendy," he told me. "She's in the sitting-room – she wanted to congratulate you on your performance, too."

I mooched into the sitting-room, kicking at the door frame

as I went. Wendy was sitting with her feet up on the sofa under the big bow window. She was feeding Flora – I could just see her little blonde head, half-hidden under Wendy's jersey, and could hear her greedy sucking noises. Laura's words came back to me, and for some reason the sight of Flora having her tea made me cross, and touched me at the same time. But I didn't want to be touched. I'd been feeling cross all afternoon, and somehow didn't feel able to stop.

"Well done, Lizzie!" Wendy said warmly. "We did enjoy your Mozart."

Daddy came into the room behind me. I don't know what made me say what I did.

"Why did you bring *her*?" I asked beligerently, gesturing to Flora. "What if she'd woken up and made a racket? It would have disturbed everyone."

There was a silence, except for Flora who carried on stolidly sucking.

"Then I would have taken her out," Wendy said calmly. But she looked hurt, and I knew I had upset her.

"Well, I think it's a bit much," I went on. My voice sounded very loud. "And I don't want you to bring her again!"

Daddy was outraged. "Lizzie!" he said.

"That's all right, Jamie," Wendy said, still calm. "But if Flora doesn't go to any more of your concerts, I won't be able to either. I'll have to stay here with her."

"Workshops!" I shouted. "They're Workshops, not concerts! And I don't care if you come or not! You can all stay away, for all I care!"

"How dare you speak to Wendy like that!" Daddy thundered. "Go to your room at once!"

"I'm not nine years old!" I yelled as I flung up the stairs. "Stop treating me like a baby!"

"Then stop behaving like one," I heard Daddy retort, as I threw myself on my bed in floods of sobbing.

"It's not fair," I muttered to myself. "It's not fair. It's all Laura's fault."

But I knew it wasn't all Laura's fault. I knew I had been rude and mean. And I didn't like what I'd discovered in myself, not one little bit.

4

Laura

By the next morning, things seemed to have quietened down on the home front. Wendy was busy with Flora, and Daddy was haring around getting various breakfasts - his own, Wendy's, Fishpaste's and Rufus'. Not mine though, I had to get my own. He was pretty sniffy when I spoke to him, too.

"Oh," I yawned, rubbing my eyes, "no waiter service for me, then?"

"You're quite able to get your own breakfast." Daddy rushed around with bags of dog biscuits and bottles of milk; he was practically a blur. "Look at the time; you're going to be late again."

"You've just put the cornflakes in the fridge," I pointed out. "It's all right - I don't have to be in until later this morning. There's a meeting for everyone who's going to France, so we don't have to go to prayers. Shall I take Wendy a cup of tea?"

Daddy looked marginally less harassed. "That would be kind."

Rufus accompanied me up the stairs, proudly bearing a baby vest in his mouth. He's not usually allowed upstairs but ever since Flora had arrived he had taken on the role of unofficial bodyguard to her. He loved her.

Wendy was in Flora's bedroom – 'the nursery' – and Flora was lying on her changing mat with nothing on.

"Hi," I said to Wendy. "Rufus has brought you Flora's clothes, and I've brought you some tea. Oh, isn't she lovely and squidgy?"

"Gorgeous," Wendy agreed, deftly putting a clean nappy on her baby daughter. She took the vest from Rufus' mouth, who relinquished it gently and trotted happily downstairs again, his mission accomplished. "So what's on the agenda today?"

I hesitated before answering. I still felt guilty about the way I'd spoken to Wendy the previous night, but was awkward about actually apologizing.

"A meeting about France," I said, fiddling with the top of the baby lotion and not meeting Wendy's eyes. "Then double Maths – yuck – Geography, violin lesson, lunch." I ticked them off on my fingers, "Piano practice after lunch. Some of the seniors are doing a concert I'll probably go to after that. Then Aural, and General Music. Then we've got break, choir practice, and home."

"Supper, practice, homework, bed," Wendy finished off. She wiped her hands on a tissue. "What a busy life. Don't you get tired?"

"Sometimes," I admitted. "But it's worth it. I really love it at Percy's – especially after Oaklands."

Wendy picked Flora up. "Little angel," she murmured into the baby's hair. "That's good to hear, Lizzie. And it's nice to see you looking happy again."

"Oh I am," I looked up at her suddenly. "Why don't you get Daddy to look after Flora some time? We could go and have a pizza or something."

Wendy smiled at me. Such a warm smile; all at once I thought I could see something of what had made Daddy want to marry her.

"Why Lizzie," she said. "That would be lovely. Much as I

love Flora, I must admit a bit of a break would be super. Babies are such jolly hard work."

I had a nice warm feeling inside as I got ready for school.

During morning break Laura and I were walking around the playground together. *Playground* is actually the wrong word for it – it's just a piece of concreted-over ground at the back of the ugliest bit of the building. Vast open spaces are a bit lacking in the middle of London; that's what I miss most about Cornwall. The playground in my old school in Penwithin, before Oaklands, looked out over the cliffs and sea. You could always hear the crash of waves on the rocks below and the mewling of the seagulls whirling above, and clumps of sea-campion grew between the cracks in the worn old paving. Here, at Percy's, all you could hear was the growl of traffic and the occasional rumble of the Underground, bearing the Piccadilly Line beneath our feet, and the only thing in the playground apart from people was litter, swirling desultorily around in the breeze.

But still, it was a lovely morning. The sky was blue as blue, and some early daffodils were growing in the square across the road. Laura and I were talking about the imminent trip to France, our tiff of the previous day forgotten in the excitement of what was to come.

"I'm dying to see Paris," Laura said. "I wonder how much time we'll have to go round by ourselves?"

I wasn't altogether sure I wanted to wander around Paris by myself – I was still getting used to London, the size and the noise and the bustle. But I didn't say that to Laura.

"It'll be great," I agreed. I suddenly spotted Simon on the other side of the playground, talking to a girl with very long auburn hair. I really wished mine would hurry and grow; it was at that awful, endy stage where it always looked a mess no matter what I did with it.

"Why don't we walk over there?" I suggested to Laura nonchalantly.

"What for? It's sunnier over here. Oh look, there's Simon." Laura looked at me, a funny little smile on her face. "He's talking to Olivia Seddon, look; he really fancies her. Shall we go over and talk to them?"

Olivia Seddon was sixteen, and in the year above Simon. I didn't know her, but I suddenly hated her. Why couldn't I be sixteen, with long hair like an Irish setter and a sophisticated name like Olivia, instead of me – plain old Lizzie Oliver? I trailed miserably across the playground after Laura. Even the sun went behind a cloud. When we were about half-way, Olivia put a hand on Simon's arm, laughed a silly tinkling laugh, and walked off towards the practice rooms.

"Stupid cow," I heard Simon mutter.

"Hi," Laura greeted him. "Been talking to Olivia?"

Simon turned to us and gave a smile so dazzling my stomach went cold and rumbly. "Hel-*lo*!" he said. "And how are you?"

"How's Olivia?" Laura persisted.

"She's all right until she opens her mouth," Simon said.

Laura looked puzzled. "I thought you liked her."

"She's all right I suppose." Simon shrugged. "Look, if you must know, I asked her out and she said no. She said she's practically old enough to be my mother. Silly cow. Just because she's going out with a twenty-one year old student at the Academy – how was I supposed to know?"

Suddenly the day seemed sunny again, and I realized how stupid my name would sound if it was Olivia. Olivia Oliver! Perhaps Lizzie's not so bad after all.

"Never mind," said Laura consolingly. "There's lots of other people you can ask out instead. Aren't there, Lizzie?" She emphasized my name peculiarly, and I felt the blood rush to my face.

"Er – I expect so," I mumbled. I looked at the ground. My feet seemed very big and clumsy, and I didn't know what to do with my hands. I made myself look up at Laura. "I've just remembered, I'm supposed to be seeing Mr Owen this break. See you later, " and I scuttled off across the playground.

I felt so stupid. I knew what Laura was doing; trying to get Simon to ask *me* out. I went into the girls' cloakroom and splashed my burning face with cold water.

The whole business of boyfriends baffled me, and in a strange way frightened me too. I didn't want a boyfriend, not yet; I wouldn't know what to do, what to talk about, how to behave. And anyway, Simon had all the girls in the Middle School after him; why should he be interested in me in that way? But I really did like him. He was so good-looking. I looked at myself in the mirror, at my messy growing-out hair and my unremarkable if not plain face, and sighed. Why should Simon look at me, I thought. I'm not even pretty.

A week or so later, on a Saturday, Daddy and Wendy took Flora to see Wendy's parents. They live in a big house in Richmond, not far from Barnes.

"We'll probably be quite late back, sweetie," Daddy said to me a couple of days beforehand. "We haven't seen Gordon and Constance for some time, and I know Wendy's got lots to tell them."

I wasn't going, as I had tons of homework and practice and stuff to do, but I could tell Daddy was a bit worried about leaving me on my own all day – heavens knows why.

Wendy noticed, too. "Don't you have a friend, Lizzie, you could ask to stay the night?"

"I don't need anybody to look after me," I said quickly. "I can look after myself – I'm fourteen now, remember."

"I know," Wendy said evenly. "It's up to you, of course. I just thought you might like some company, that's all."

"Well," I said, considering. "I could ask Laura. She might be able to come."

So I did, and she asked Mrs Nightingale, and slightly to my surprise she agreed that Laura could stay overnight.

When Laura arrived at Barnes on Saturday afternoon I went to meet her at the station. She was carrying a large squashy scarlet barrel bag.

"Good grief." I said as we went through the ticket barrier. "Are you coming for a month? What on earth have you got in there?"

"Oh, just a toothbrush and things," replied Laura airily.

It must be the largest toothbrush in the world, I thought, as I struggled with the bag across Barnes Common. Being the perfect hostess, I had offered to carry it for her, and being the perfect guest, she'd let me. I had brought Rufus with me – he's always on the lookout for any chance of a walk – and he was having a lovely time, rushing around encouraging Laura to throw sticks for him. He's supposed to be a retriever, but he always loses interest in them when he's brought them halfway back and drops them on the ground, and then you're expected to find another one for him.

"Why doesn't he bring them back?" Laura laughed.

"He's dim," I explained. "He only ever retrieves things he's not supposed to. Daddy says he's a mental defective."

"He's lovely," Laura sighed. "I wish we could have a dog. My mum says pets leave hair everywhere – she says she has enough cleaning up to do without all that. Though I s'pose she's got a point; we've got shag pile everywhere. The cleaning lady always says it's the devil's own job to keep it clean, and we've just got a new suite. It cost nearly two thousand pounds – you should see it!"

Laura sounded proud. Two thousand pounds seemed an awful lot of money to spend on a couple of chairs. And I didn't know what shag pile was, but if it meant no pets I didn't like the sound of it. I couldn't imagine life without pets. We'd always had them, as far back as I could remember.

"You can be Rufus' godmother if you like," I told her. "He'd like that."

As we turned in through the back gate, Fishpaste jumped down from his perch on top of the dustbin and yawned pinkly. It had started to drizzle finely, and he hates getting wet.

"Would you like a coffee?" I asked Laura when we got indoors. "Or a cup of tea?"

She was ferreting around in the scarlet bag. "I'd rather have some of this," and with a flourish she produced a bottle of wine.

I stared at her. "We can't drink that," I said, shocked.

She laughed. "I was only kidding. I brought it for your dad, to say thanks for having me. Honestly, your face! Haven't you ever drunk wine before?"

"I knew you were joking," I lied. "Of course I've drunk wine – and champagne." Somehow I didn't want her to know I'd taken her seriously.

Laura took her bag upstairs. I gave her a guided tour of the house, and then she inspected my bedroom; she looked at all the books on my shelves, the ornaments on the dressing table and the cuddly toys lined up on my pillow. Then she opened my wardrobe door. Two pairs of shoes fell out, and a blouse fell slitheringly off its hanger and on to the floor.

"You haven't got many clothes, have you?" said Laura. "Isn't your stepmother very modern – won't she buy you fashionable things?"

I'd never really thought about it. "I expect she would, if I asked her," I said. "There doesn't seem much point though, I mean, I wear school uniform all day."

"But what about when you go out?" Laura asked, holding an ancient dress up against her and pulling a face. "What do you wear then?"

"Oh – clothes," I said vaguely, taking the dress from her and sliding the wardrobe door shut with my foot. I made a mental note to get Wendy to take me shopping; I'd need some posh clothes for France. "Come on – let's go downstairs."

"In a minute," said Laura. She'd spotted my diary on my bedside table, where I always left it. "What's this – is it your diary?"

I crossed the room hastily. Laura had picked up the diary and was trying to open it; luckily, it's one of those five-year ones with a lock, so she wasn't having much success.

"Oh, it's locked. Can I read it, Lizzie?"

I thought about the last entry; it consisted mainly of how wonderful I thought Simon was. "I'd rather you didn't – you see, it's private," I explained.

"Oh, go on. I'll let you read mine – I've brought it with me." I have to admit I was tempted. There's something about other people's diaries.

"Maybe later," I said eventually. "Do let's go downstairs and have supper; I'm starving."

Wendy had left us chilli con carne for supper, so I heated it up and cooked some rice. Laura sat at the big pine kitchen table and picked bits out of the salad.

"This is a nice house," she said, crunching on a radish. "Lots of rooms. Nice."

"Don't you have many rooms in your house?" I asked.

"Of course we do. Tons. It's really big. And I've got my brother's old bedroom now he's gone – I re-decorated it myself."

"Where's your brother gone?" I said, dishing up the chilli. "Has he got married?" I had inherited my sister Meg's room when she married Charles, back in Penwithin.

"You must be joking," scoffed Laura. "Marcus doesn't know girls exist. He's up in Scotland studying medicine; he's supposed to be really brainy. Mum and Dad think he's the vicar's knickers. They never stop talking about him – it's always Marcus this and Marcus that. I get fed up hearing his name. Don't you think brothers and sisters are the pits?" I made a noise which could have meant either yes or no. I loved Meg, and Flora too, but didn't think Laura would have approved had I said so.

After supper, Laura went upstairs to the guest room to unpack her bag. I went with her and showed her where everything was.

"You can use this chest of drawers to put your things in," I said, "and Wendy's put a clean towel on the radiator for you. You've got your own shower room too – isn't it nice? – and I picked the daffodils from the garden this morning."

"It's all lovely," Laura turned round from the bed, and picked up something from the white candlewick bedspread. "Look," she said. "This is my diary. Do you want to read it now?"

My brain spun. If I read Laura's diary, I would have to show her mine in return. On the other hand, I had never read anyone else's diary, and the temptation of entering Laura's private world was huge.

"All right," I said.

She handed me the diary – it was really just an old exercise book, covered with wrapping paper in shades of pink and lilac. On the front it said LAURA'S DIARY – STRICTLY PRIVATE. MARCUS, THIS MEANS YOU.

"I thought you said your brother was at university?" I said.

"He is, but when he comes home he goes through my things."

He sounded horrible. I was suddenly glad I didn't have a brother. I opened Laura's diary at random, feeling peculiarly like a burglar, or as if I was cribbing during an exam. My eye was caught by Mr Hadleigh's name, half-way down a page.

Mr Hadleigh is so gorgeous I can hardly take my eyes off him when he's teaching us. He can only be about ten years older than me; wonder if he'd wait for me? I'll be sixteen in 18 months. I like it best when he wears those tight jeans . . .

Embarrassed, I turned back a few pages. The diary didn't seem to start on January the first, as Laura had already filled more than half the book. I turned back nearly to the beginning.

I'm getting fed-up with these holidays. Marcus is being a real pain, and even the weather is awful. I went round to see Simon this morning, but he was busy practising with Susy, so I came home again.

I wondered who Susy was, and a pang shot through me, like the one I'd had when I saw Simon talking to Olivia. All the same, this entry was boring. I turned on a few pages.

I'M IN LOVE!! Hugh is wonderful. He has the most beautiful brown eyes, just like a spaniel, and when he smiles; oh, my insides. He took me for a walk by the river this afternoon, because boring old Marcus was doing boring old studying. He told me he'd never have thought Marcus would have such a pretty sister! He held my hand all the way back. Older men are definitely better value. I wish I could be one of Hugh's patients when he qualifies. Bet he'll have a fantastic BED-SIDE manner, HA HA!!

I was fascinated, and turned over a couple of pages.
"Who's Hugh?" I asked Laura.
"He's a friend of my brother's at university. He came to stay last summer holidays; I had a huge crush on him. I was only a kid then," she told me. She held out a hand for her diary.

"Come on, Lizzie, give it back now. Let's read yours."

I was very reluctant, but knew it would be unfair to refuse. So we went into my bedroom, and I unlocked my diary and handed it to her. Laura flipped though it and read a bit, her face impassive. I felt the words I'd written the previous evening, all about Simon's amazingness, burning into my brain. Sure enough, Laura turned to the very last entry.

"D'you really think Simon's hair looks like silk?" she asked casually. "You should see it when it needs washing - looks more like straw then."

I gulped. "Does it?" was all I could think of to say.

Laura looked up at me. "Don't worry; I shan't tell him you write all about him in your diary. I always knew you fancied him, anyway."

"How?" I demanded.

Laura laughed. "Mainly because you go all red whenever you see him. Like you are now," she added. "But I don't suppose he's noticed; he thinks all girls fancy him, anyway."

Laura put my diary down and wandered out of the bedroom. After I had locked my diary up again I went to look for her, and found her in Daddy and Wendy's bedroom. She was looking in Wendy's wardrobe.

"Are these your stepmother's clothes?" She took out a pale blue silk evening gown and held it against herself. "Pretty. Can I try it on?"

"I don't think you should," I said anxiously.

"Why not? Don't you ever try her clothes on when she's out?"

Without waiting for an answer she put the dress down and moved over to the dressing table. She opened a drawer. "Oh goody - make-up! Let's do each other, shall we?"

"No," I said firmly. "It's Wendy's. She wouldn't like us touching her things without asking her."

"We can't ask her, can we?" Laura pointed out. "She's not

here. Oh go on, Lizzie – what harm can it do?"

"Well I'm not going to," I said. "But I suppose if you only take a little bit . . . "

Laura expertly applied foundation, powder, blusher and eyeshadow. She put mascara on her eyelashes, and finally pouted her lips and coated them with pearly pink lipstick. Then she regarded herself in the mirror.

"What do you think?" she asked me.

I stared at her – she looked about nineteen. "Wow," I said.

Laura giggled. "D'you think Toby would fancy me like this?"

"Who's Toby?"

"Mr Hadleigh to you, dear. Now let me find a dress . . ." As Laura spun around from the dressing table, her elbow caught a bottle of nail varnish and it fell on to the floor. The top couldn't have been screwed on properly, because a small pool of bright red goo started to ooze all over the pale cream carpet.

"Oh!" I wailed. "Now look what you've done!"

Laura started dabbing at it with a tissue, which only seemed to make the mess worse. "It'll be all right," she assured me. "Let me just . . ."

"I think you'd better leave it," I told her crossly. "I'll try and get it off with nail polish remover once it's dry. I think we'd better go downstairs – come on."

Once downstairs, Laura started prowling around. "I'm bored," she announced. "I know - let's go to the pub!"

I was shocked. "We can't!" I told her. "We're far too young – they'd never let us in, anyway."

"Oh pooh!" Laura pronounced. "I look at least eighteen with all this on." She touched her face.

"Well, I don't. Anyway, it's pouring with rain."

Laura shrugged. "OK, please yourself. Has your dad got anything to drink?"

"There's coke in the fridge," I told her. "And fruit juice and stuff. And I think there's some bitter lemon in the drinks cabinet."

"Not that sort of drink," Laura scoffed. "You are a baby, aren't you? Where's this drinks cabinet?"

That made me mad. "I'm not a baby," I flared. "I just think we're too young to drink, that's all."

"Actually, we're not," Laura informed me haughtily. "Legally, when you're fourteen you're allowed to drink beer or cider with a meal."

She wandered over to where Daddy kept the drinks and took out a bottle of sherry. "Just a little drinky?" she said in a wheedling voice, making pleading eyes at me, and despite myself I laughed.

"Just one, then," I said. I didn't suppose it would hurt, and after all, I was allowed to have the odd glass of wine, at Christmas and things. Martini too, sometimes.

Laura poured us both a small glass of sherry, and I switched on the television. There was a good film on; I became quite engrossed, and because of that, and the fact that the sherry was making me feel sleepy, I didn't notice what Laura was doing. When the film ended, I stood up and stretched.

"I'll just put Rufus out in the garden," I told Laura. When I went past her chair I noticed a different bottle, and a larger glass, beside her. I picked the bottle up – it was whisky.

"Laura," I said accusingly. "Have you been drinking Daddy's whisky?"

Then she looked at me. Her eyes seemed to be rolling backwards into her head, and her face was deathly pale under all the make-up. But when she spoke to me, her voice was quite steady.

"Lizzie," she said. "I must go to the bathroom. I think I'm going to be sick."

And she was. I stood outside the bathroom and listened,

and I'm ashamed to say I was so cross with her, so blazingly angry, that I didn't go in and comfort her and hold her head. Good, I thought instead; you deserve to be sick.

When she came out, she looked even worse. Mascara was streaked down her face, and she had eyeshadow up to her hairline.

"I feel awful," she groaned.

"I'm not surprised," I told her. "You look awful, too. We'd better get all that muck off your face and put you to bed."

So I scrubbed at her face, and somehow between us we got her clothes off and her nightdress on her, and she tumbled into bed with one last groan.

"You're going to have a dreadful hangover in the morning," I told her gleefully. I suppose it was a bit mean of me. But I don't think she even heard me.

Then I had to set to and clear up all the evidence. I was just dabbing vainly at the spilt nail varnish on Daddy's bedroom carpet when I heard the car draw up outside, and then Daddy's key in the lock. As I went downstairs I passed Wendy transporting Flora upstairs in her carrycot, and she smiled at me and put a finger to her lips, indicating the baby was asleep. I took a deep breath and went in to the sitting-room. Daddy was sniffing the air like Rufus does when he smells rabbits on the Common.

"Whatever's been going on?" he demanded. "It smells like a brewery in here."

"Oh," I said. "Um – I went in the drinks cabinet to get some glasses, and I knocked the whisky over. The top wasn't on properly. Sorry, Daddy. I wiped it all up though. It does pong a bit, doesn't it?" I was spared Daddy's reply because at that moment Wendy came through the door.

"What's happened to our bedroom carpet?" she asked me, "It looks like someone's been done foully to death on it."

"It does rather," I agreed. "It was Fishpaste – I don't mean he's been done foully to death, but Rufus was chasing him and he went in your bedroom and on the dressing table and knocked some nail varnish over."

"I suppose the top wasn't on that properly, either," Daddy said dryly.

"Mmm," I agreed vaguely.

"Where's Laura?" Daddy asked, looking around. "Not gone home after this catalogue of spillages?"

I just knew he suspected something. "No," I said, summoning up a weak laugh. "She was tired – she's gone to bed."

"And that's where you ought to be," Wendy came in again holding a cloth. She interrupted Daddy, who was about to say something. "Come on now Lizzie – up you go. It's late."

As I wearily got ready for bed I wondered what the morning would bring. I was furious with Laura, for playing around with Wendy's things and for drinking Daddy's whisky. But I was even angrier with myself, because I knew I should have stopped her.

5

Quarrels and Concerts

The next day dawned bright and fair – so, much to my surprise, did Laura. She came down to breakfast looking pink and scrubbed with not a hint of what had happened the night before.

I was feeling tired after such a late night, and didn't have much of an appetite for breakfast, but Laura tucked avidly into porridge, eggs, bacon and sausages, rounded off with three pieces of toast and several cups of coffee.

"Yum yum," she said, cramming a last piece of toast and marmalade into her pink mouth. She reminded me of Rufus when he bolts down his food in thirty seconds flat. "I s'pose I'd better pack my bag and go and catch my train – I told Mrs Nightingale I'd be back in time for chapel."

"I'll run you to the station," Daddy told her. They'd been talking about cricket over breakfast – Laura was chatting knowledgeably about it, and Daddy seemed quite charmed by her.

Laura turned her grey headlamp eyes on him. "Oh, Mr Oliver," she said "That would be really kind of you. I shan't be a sec," and she dashed off upstairs to fetch her bag.

After they had gone – Laura saying the most cursory of

goodbyes to me – I helped Wendy with the washing-up.

"She seems nice, your friend Laura," Wendy remarked.

I concentrated on drying a plate. "She's OK."

Wendy looked at me, hard. "What *did* go on last night?" she asked me. "Only you looked so guilty when we came in."

I put the cups away while I considered my answer. I was still cross with Laura; in a strange way, even more so because she was so bright and breezy that morning. I thought she deserved to be feeling ill and awful. On the other hand, she was still my friend, and I didn't want to betray her. And I dimly felt that it would somehow reflect on me, having a friend who behaved badly in my home.

"Nothing much," I said casually in answer to Wendy's question. "I fetched her from the station. We had supper – the chilli was great. We watched TV for a bit. Laura went to bed. Then you came back." I hung the tea-towel on the Aga to dry. "Is that the lot?"

Daddy was ages driving Laura to the station. When he eventually got back, it transpired that she'd misread the timetable, and missed the train she'd intended to catch.

"So I thought I'd better drive her back to school. She'd probably have got into trouble if she'd been late."

"No she wouldn't," I said. "Mrs Nightingale would have understood. She's nice."

"Well anyway," said Daddy brightly. "I enjoyed the drive. She's good company, that Laura. Smashing girl. Very bright, I shouldn't wonder."

"Very," I thought suddenly about Laura's diary, and how she was always going on about 'older men'. She couldn't! I thought. She couldn't fancy Daddy! Then I realised I was being ridiculous. I should be pleased, I thought. Pleased Daddy's obviously forgotten about last night. But somehow I couldn't shake off this weird uneasy feeling I had about Laura.

The feeling continued the next day at school. I went and sat with Emma during registration, and pointedly ignored Laura. She didn't even seem to notice; she was deep in conversation with Simon.

"What's the matter?" Emma asked me. "You look upset. And why are you ignoring Laura?"

I didn't think she was just being nosy. She sounded as if she really cared. So I told her about Laura's visit on Saturday night.

"Golly," Emma breathed when I'd finished. "I'm not surprised you're cross. Did you get into trouble?"

"No. Luckily Daddy seemed to have forgotten all about it the next day. He took a shine to Laura, too, which I suppose helped."

Emma looked across the room at Laura, who was still chatting animatedly to Simon. She sighed. "I know you'll think I'm being bitchy, I mean, I know Laura's your best friend. But she seems to – well – like making trouble. I know she's brainy and ever so pretty, and she's got lots of friends and everything. But she's very immature at times."

"She's not, Mouse," I replied heatedly. "She knows about things. She goes to pubs. And she knows how to put make-up on properly, and looks really grown-up in it, not like a bowl of fruit salad like I do. And you should see her diary! All about these older men."

Emma shrugged. "That doesn't make her grown-up. She just seems it, that's all."

"She's very sophisticated," I persisted. "She drinks whisky."

"And gets drunk," Emma pointed out. "Look, Lizzie, I know it's none of my business. And I'm not trying to – you know – turn you against her. I just think you should watch out, that's all." Emma frowned thoughtfully. "Listen, why don't you come to tea some time? I've just bought this whizz book of Haydn duets – my brother could play the piano for us."

"OK," I said. I half-imagined another Marcus. "I'd like that. Thanks."

Emma was nice. Friendly. But she wasn't like Laura. Emma had frizzy brown hair, which most of the time she wore scraped back off her face with anything that came to hand – a rubber band, a piece of string, once even a pipe cleaner. She wore thick, wire-framed spectacles which didn't suit her face, although her eyes behind them were startlingly beautiful – sort of topaz-coloured. Her face was inclined to be spotty; she invariably had ink on her hands, and her school uniform didn't seem to fit properly, with sagging hems and cuffs that were too long. I suppose she was a bit of a mess, really.

Laura, on the other hand, had glamour. From the top of the shining blonde head to the tips of her well-polished shoes, there was something about her that seemed to attract people; it wasn't just that she had lots of friends, either. All the teachers seemed to like her too. I suppose, if I'm to be honest, I thought that being her friend might make some of her glamour rub off on me. That, plus the fact that she's so palsy-walsy with Simon Alexander, a little voice inside me whispered. What nonsense, I told the voice crossly. That's got nothing to do with it. Go away.

Anyway the fact remained that, glamorous or not, Laura definitely was not in my good books. I was decidedly disgruntled; in fact, at that particular moment, I couldn't imagine ever feeling gruntled with her again. And the annoying thing was, she didn't even seem to have noticed. That's what I thought, at any rate. But at break she confronted me.

"Lizzie," she said. "What's the matter? Why are you ignoring me? Have I upset you? Do tell me what's wrong."

I couldn't believe she really didn't know. "You have to be joking," I told her. "You mean you always behave like that when you go to stay with people?"

"Like what?"

"Oh come on, Laura. You know jolly well like what. The make-up – and spilling the nail varnish. And drinking Daddy's whisky. And you read my diary," I finished, rather lamely.

"But you said I could." Laura sounded hurt. "And you didn't mind about the make-up, you said so. And I know I spilt that stuff on the carpet, but it *was* an accident. Anyway, I'm sorry. There! Can we be friends again now?"

"What about the whisky?" I demanded. "And the state you got in? You had no right taking Daddy's drink; what would have happened if they'd come home and seen you like that?"

Laura had the grace to look shame-faced. "I know. I'm sorry, Lizzie; I know I shouldn't have helped myself. But I only had a tiny bit, honestly; it wasn't the whisky that made me ill. I think it was something I ate at lunch-time – I was feeling a bit peculiar all afternoon. I wasn't drunk, Lizzie. Honestly. Don't tell anyone about it, will you?"

I thought about how I'd told Emma, and felt a bit mean. I believed Laura; anybody would have, she sounded so sincere. And I didn't think Emma would tell anybody.

"All right," I said grudgingly. "But I was really angry with you. I had to make all kinds of excuses to Daddy – he could smell it when he came in."

"Thanks for not splitting on me. Though I don't suppose your dad would have told me off; he's a sweetie, isn't he? Quite hunky, too."

"Oh do stop it, Laura," I told her crossly. "He's not Mr Hadleigh, you know. Sorry – I mean *TOBY!*"

"Don't be horrid," Laura pleaded. "I've said I'm sorry. Let's just forget about it, shall we?"

So we did. At least, I'm sure Laura forgot about it. But the memory lingered behind in my mind, like the way you can still taste garlic the day after you've eaten it. I did my best to push away the niggling feeling; she's your friend, I told myself firmly. She said she was sorry. And she sounded sorry. Just forget about it, OK? But somewhere, buried so deep I was barely aware of it, another little voice was talking to me. Hair like silk, it said; hair like silk. What if she tells him what you write in your diary? What then?

My sister Meg telephoned the following weekend, her usual fortnightly call. I was in the shower at the time. Daddy called upstairs to me.

"Lizzie! Meg wants a word."

I dripped downstairs with one towel round me and one around my hair.

"Sorry Lizzie," came Meg's voice across the wires from Cornwall. "Did I disturb you?"

"It's OK," I assured her. "I was just washing my hair. I'm going to the Festival Hall tonight with a gang from Percy's. It's lovely to speak to you, how are you all?"

"We're fine. Charles is busy, organizing things for Easter. You know what it's like this time of the year – sheer bedlam in the Trelawney household, I'm afraid," Meg laughed. Charles is the vicar of Penlorren, the next village along from Penwithin.

"Give him my love," I told her. "How's Katey, and Jacob? Did Katey have a nice birthday?"

"Smashing," Meg told me. "She had a party, in the church hall. All the village children of the appropriate age came. In fact she enjoyed it so much she asked me if she could have another birthday this weekend, but I told her she had to wait until she was three. And you wouldn't recognize Jacob; he's got two teeth, and he's crawling around on his tummy."

"I wish I could see him. I do miss you all."

"And we miss you, too." Meg's voice softened. "Listen, there's someone here who wants to talk to you. I'll just pass the phone over."

I was expecting the small baby-voice of Katey, and said "Hello sweetheart," as I usually did to my niece. When a deep, boy's voice answered, I nearly dropped the phone.

"Hello Lizzie," it said. I could hear the smile in the voice. "Or should I say, hello darling?"

"Ben!" I shrieked. "Ben! What are you doing there? What are you doing in *Cornwall*?"

Ben Polkerris is my very best friend. I've known him practically all my life. He goes to school in Devon, and since he started there we could only see each other in the holidays. When I moved to London, we saw even less of each other, and as we are both hopeless letter-writers, we don't keep in touch very regularly. But our friendship is the sort where you don't need that kind of thing. We understand each other, and when we do see each other, we just take up where we left off. I suppose Ben is the nearest thing to a brother – a dear brother, a kind brother – that I've got.

"Why are you at Meg's?" I demanded again.

"Exeat," Ben said economically. "Home for the weekend," he explained, remembering my understanding of his school's jargon wasn't up to much. "Mum wanted me to bring some eggs over to the vicarage, and Meg said she was due to give you a ring, so here I am. How are you – sweetheart?" he added. I could hear him grinning, all those miles away.

"Oh shut up, fatty," I retorted. "I thought you were Katey."

"Well yes, I can understand that. I mean, I'm a lot like her, really . . . " Ben hadn't changed, that was for sure. "Hey, what's all this about you coming back to Cornwall? Is it true?"

"Yes; Daddy and Wendy are fed-up with Barnes – Wendy says London's no good for Flora's health. I could've told them that this time last year. Anyway, Daddy's looking for another house in Penwithin; isn't it great?" I enthused.

"Ace!" Ben sounded pleased. "The Folly's been up for sale for a while – did you know?"

"No, I didn't," I told him. The Folly was our name for it – an old rambling red-brick house on the cliffs opposite the harbour in Penwithin. When we were small, Ben and I used to tell each other stories about how we would live there when we were married. We always assumed we would get married, when we were little; our stories to each other would always begin 'when we're grown-up and married'. I wondered if Ben remembered, and felt suddenly, inexplicably, embarrassed.

"Well," Ben said, musingly, "when I got home last night, the *For Sale* sign had a 'Sold' sticker over it."

"How exciting," I said sarcastically. "I expect that means it's been sold, then."

"I don't suppose you've bought it?" Ben asked me.

"No – the building society wouldn't give me a mortgage on two pounds a week, I don't know why."

Ben tutted. "I knew you were going to say that. You know what I mean. I say, d'you remember when we were little? We used to go to the Folly and look at it, and we used to say *we'd* live there when . . . "

"I remember," I said hastily. I couldn't understand why Ben remembering should make me feel hot and awkward, the way talking to Simon always made me feel. I changed the subject, and we finished our conversation, and presently Meg came back on the line to talk again to Wendy. I could hear them still discussing nappies and wind as I left the house twenty minutes later to walk to the station, calling goodbye as I did so. I was quite glad to go; the disgusting things women talk about. Yucksville. When I have a baby I hope they've invented one that comes with it's own nappy-changer.

The concert at the Festival Hall was given by a Danish youth orchestra with an unpronounceable name. They were on a tour similar to the one we were doing in France. "In only four weeks!" Emma whispered to me in that magic moment just before the conductor appears from the wings.

The orchestra was very good. They played a Rossini overture and one of Grieg's Peer Gynt suites, and then a very pretty girl in an emerald green taffeta dress came on to the stage. Her wheaten blonde hair was piled on top of her head in a neat squashy bun, and even from where we were sitting I could see that her eyeshadow exactly matched her dress. She was carrying an oboe; Laura leant forward on the edge of her chair with interest. I saw Simon lean forward too, but I doubted whether his interest was for the same reason as Laura's.

The Danish girl played an oboe concerto by the British composer Vaughan Williams. I'd never heard it before; it was gentle, and sounded like folk songs and the countryside. In a strange way it reminded me of Cornwall. She played it brilliantly. Then it was the interval. We all filed out of the hall and down to one of the bars. Mr Blenkinsop, the teacher who had taken us, said he'd buy us all a drink, and he nearly gave the barman a nervous breakdown by ordering twenty-one Cokes and a dry white wine. It was such a lovely evening we all took our Cokes out on to the balcony.

"What did you think of the Vaughan Williams?" I asked Laura.

She sighed dreamily. "Brilliant. I love that concerto."

"*She* wasn't bad, either," Simon observed. "Pretty tasty, I thought."

Some of the other boys murmured their agreement. I felt the familiar stab of – what? Jealousy, envy? How ridiculous to be jealous of someone you don't even know, I told myself.

"Well actually," said Emma, "I thought she looked a bit like Laura. Didn't you?"

Simon and the other boys burst into loud guffaws of laughter. "What, old Laura? You must be joking. That Danish bird was *pretty*." Laura flushed an angry red.

"Oh, I know she was," Emma agreed hastily, "but I still thought she looked a bit like Laura. Perhaps it was just the colour of her hair."

"Well, it couldn't have been anything else – Laura looks like the back end of a bus compared to the beautiful Helga," Simon pursed his lips and kissed the air, and the other boys laughed raucously.

"Thanks very much, Simon." Laura went even redder; she put a hand under my elbow and steered me away. "Come on, Lizzie. Let's go and have our drink somewhere more peaceful. Rotten so-and-so," she muttered.

Emma trotted along behind us, looking anxious. "Sorry Laura – I didn't mean to suggest – I mean, I *did* think she looked like you. Not just her hair, I mean."

Laura looked crossly at Emma. "Do stop wittering, Mouse. You're just making it worse."

"Well, I'm sorry," said Emma, bridling. "It's not my fault Simon doesn't think you're pretty."

I could see this turning into a full-scale argument. "Don't take any notice of Simon," I told Laura, soothingly. "You are pretty. And I know he likes you really."

Laura shrugged, "I couldn't care less about Simon. It was Tim Maynard; he was laughing too, didn't you see him? I really like him."

I couldn't keep up with Laura's men-of-the-moment.

"I'm doing that concerto at the moment. The Vaughan Williams," Laura deftly changed the subject and took a sip from her glass. "Mum and Dad are going to buy me a new oboe to play it on – my old one isn't really right for twentieth-century music."

"How nice – are you getting it for your birthday?" I hadn't known you needed different instruments to play different sorts of music on.

"No," Laura said casually. "My birthday's not until

November, anyway. They're just buying it for me; it's going to cost nearly three thousand pounds but Dad says it's a bargain. I can't wait to get it."

This seemed such an enormous sum to spend on an oboe that I was speechless. I glanced at Emma; she grinned, then stuck out her tongue at Laura and crossed her eyes, raising them heavenwards. Laura was looking out over the Thames and missed all this. Then she turned towards us again.

"Yes," she said. "I'll probably sell the old one – I should get at least fifteen hundred for it – and use the money . . ."

Emma put her glass down on the edge of the balcony, with a clatter. "I'm just going to the loo," she said loudly. "I think I might be sick," she added to me, with another grin.

I grinned back, but surreptitiously; I didn't want to hurt Laura's feelings.

"I'm hoping I might do it as the Concerto at the QEH this year," Laura went on, oblivious to Emma's faces and comments.

"The what?" I didn't have a clue what she was on about.

"The Vaughan Williams – at the QEH concert." Laura looked at me and realized that she may as well have been speaking Swahili for all the sense she was making to me. "Don't you know about it? Well, every year, at the end of the summer term, Percy's put on a public concert at the Queen Elizabeth Hall, just down there." She indicated to the right of where we were standing with her free, glass-less hand.

"The QEH," I said, the penny dropping.

Laura nodded. "That's right. One of the items is always a concerto; they don't let on who's doing it until a couple of weeks before. They say it's so we don't get nervous, but I reckon they just like to keep us guessing."

"And you think you might do the Vaughan Williams? How lovely," I told her.

"Mouse thinks she's in with a chance, but I don't think

she's good enough. Not that I'd tell her so, of course – she'd think I was just being nasty. Don't you think she's a bit of a wet?"

I conjured up Emma's face – her frizzy hair, and those glasses. And the way she had managed to take all the impressiveness out of Laura's new oboe with one silly face to me. "Maybe," I said neutrally. "I don't know her that well. She seems OK to me, though."

Laura drained her glass and set it down next to Emma's. "I must go to the loo, too. Are you coming?"

I told her I would stay behind, and looked out over the Thames as I sucked the rest of my Coke over the ice-cubes. It really was a lovely evening – the sun had just disappeared and I could see the lights on the other side of the river strung out along the Embankment, like fairies' necklaces. In the near distance the buildings of the City were lit up in the twilight; the dome of St Paul's looked age-old and magnificent and almost near enough to touch.

I suddenly realized I hadn't felt homesick for Cornwall for ages. I still missed it, yes, but not with the same dull ache like a squeezing hand around my heart. I like London, I thought with surprise. I really like it, the hustle and bustle, and the sense of everyone busily going somewhere, and Percy's of course, and over everything the sound of taxis' squealing brakes. I like it. And in four weeks' time we're going to France, and after that I shall be boarding. I hugged the happy thoughts to myself, and Simon's voice when it came made me jump.

"You are going to France, aren't you?" he said.

I was startled. "Do you mean me?" I said. "Yes, I am. Why?"

"Old Sporanti wants some people to do some chamber music, as well as the orchestra," Simon told me, "and I thought four of us could form a string quartet. I've just asked Mouse – you know, Emma Nash. Do you want to be in it, too?" too?"

His question was so casual I thought I'd misheard him at first. "What?" I said stupidly. "A string quartet?"

Simon sighed patiently. "Yes. You know, two violins, a viola and a cello. Are you interested, or not?"

"Yes," I said hurriedly. "Oh, yes. I am. Please. That is, if you think I'm . . ." I trailed off, feeling daft.

"Oh good. Second violin, OK? We'll rehearse after school on Monday." He started to move away. "Better hurry, Lizzie. The interval bell's gone."

I barely heard the second half of the concert, although it was one of my favourite Beethoven symphonies, the eighth. All I could think of was that I was to play in a string quartet with Simon. He asked me, I thought to myself as the Danish youth orchestra played their hearts out. At least I suppose they did. For all the attention I was paying, they might well have been standing on their heads and whistling 'God Save the Queen'. Simon Alexander has asked *ME*. Lizzie Oliver, me, who's not even pretty – to play in a string quartet with him. Yipperama! Hoorayville!

At the back of my mind I could hear the little voice I was beginning to recognize. Laura won't be playing in it, said the voice, because she plays the oboe and oboes don't play in string quartets. So you'll have Simon all to yourself; isn't that lovely? But I pushed the thought away. Why should I be pleased that Laura's being left out? She's my friend, I told the voice firmly. Laura's my best friend. Isn't she?

6

Simon's String Quartet

On Monday morning, Emma and I were discussing Simon's quartet; I could hardly wait for the rehearsal, at the end of lessons that day.

"I've never played in a quartet before," I confessed to Emma, excited. "I'm really looking forward to it, aren't you?"

Emma looked at me, an odd expression on her face. "I shouldn't get too worked up about it. It's only Simon, trying to be important; I expect it'll end in tears."

"What makes you say that?" I felt inexplicably cross that Emma had taken the edge off my excitement.

"He's always organizing these little groups; trouble is, it usually ends up with him yelling at everybody." She looked at my face, which must have looked as let down as I felt. "Sorry - I didn't mean to be a wet blanket. Perhaps this quartet will be all right."

"But why? Why does he yell at everyone?" I didn't like the thought of him yelling at me.

Emma pursed her lips thoughtfully. "I think he just likes the sound of his own voice. Plus he always wants everything his own way; it's OK if everybody else agrees with everything he says, but nobody ever does. I expect today will be just the same as usual. Of course," she went on, "if there's some really pretty girl playing in it, someone he wants to impress, it's quite different, but as it's just ugly boring old us . . ." she stopped abruptly, flushing. "Me, I mean. Ugly boring old me. I didn't mean you're ugly and boring."

I shrugged. "It's OK. Anyway, you're not ugly and boring, either," I added dutifully. But underneath I was wounded, without really understanding why. Don't be ridiculous, I told myself; you know very well Simon only asked you to play in this quartet because you happen to be a violinist who happens to be going to France, and who happened to be around at the time. You know jolly well he didn't ask you so he could impress you. Emma's right – you *are* ugly and boring. All the same, a tiny hopeful part of me still wanted to believe it was me as a person he wanted for his quartet, not just me as a violinist.

I was the first to arrive at the practice room where Simon had arranged for us to meet. For one horrible moment I thought I'd got the time or place wrong; then, for an even worse moment, I wondered whether there really was to be a string quartet at all. Perhaps Simon was just having Emma and me on?

Then the door opened with a burst, and a cello appeared around it followed by its owner clutching a bundle of music.

"Oh, hello," Simon said. He looked surprised to see me. "You're keen – it's not five o'clock yet."

I could feel the flush beginning to rise up my neck, and turned to get my violin out of its case in an attempt to hide it. I wanted to say something witty and clever but couldn't think of anything.

"Oh," I said instead. "My watch must be fast. Shall I help you put some stands up?"

Simon arranged four chairs in a horseshoe and put up three music stands while I fumbled with one for what seemed like about two hours. Trust me to pick the only stand at Percy's that wants to unfold backwards, I thought, as I wrestled with it and finally jammed my thumb in it. I yelped with pain, and Simon looked up.

"What on earth are you up to – haven't you done it yet?" He tutted impatiently. "Why can't girls ever put stands up properly? Better give it to me."

I gladly did so, ignoring the jibe about girls, and sucked my bruised thumb as Simon deftly unfolded the stand and stood it up in thirty seconds flat.

"How did you do that?" I asked him admiringly. "I thought it was broken."

"Skill," he told me modestly.

Just then the door opened again, and an Asian boy carrying a viola case came in. I knew him slightly; his name was Naresh Gourlay. I had seen him around school, and at the France meetings, and like me he played in the Symphony Orchestra which met at Percy's on Saturday mornings. He obviously recognized me because he greeted me first.

"Hi, Lizzie," he said, beaming at me. "How are you? I haven't had a chance to talk to you properly yet. How're you getting on at Percy's?"

I was quite bowled over by his friendliness, and couldn't help beaming back at him. "Fine, thanks," I told him. "Are you in this quartet too? I can't wait to go to France."

Simon interrupted. "Hello Naresh," he said drily. "Don't talk to me, then, will you?"

We all got our instruments out and tuned them up, and put rosin on our bows. Then we sat down; Simon on the right, then Naresh, then me. Simon had put some music on the stands – an early Haydn quartet.

"Is this what we're going to play in France?" I asked him.

"I don't think so – I thought we'd start with something easy, to get warmed up and get used to playing together."

I nodded. "Good idea. Shall we start, then?"

"Hardly." Simon indicated the empty chair next to me with his bow. "Mouse hasn't arrived yet. What on earth's keeping her?" he muttered, and looked at his watch. It was twenty past five.

We all jumped as the door was flung open, the draught sending the music on our stands fluttering to the ground. It was Emma.

"Whoops, sorry," she said. She looked red and hot and very dishevelled. "Am I late? Sorry, Simon, I was talking to Sally, and then I went to the wrong room."

Simon looked cross. "You mean you forgot. Charming."

Emma crossed her eyes and stuck out her tongue at Simon's back. "OK, OK, I've said I'm sorry. And I'm here now, so let's make a start." She plopped down on her chair, picked her music off the floor and put her violin under her chin.

The quartet looked really easy to play. It started off with Emma, the first violin, playing the tune, with the rest of the instruments joining in one by one; first the second violin (me), then the viola, and finally the cello. Then all the instruments played some twiddly bits in turn, but this time reversing the order of the first bit – in other words, starting with the cello and ending with the first violin.

It started off quite well. We all came in where we were supposed to, and I was quite surprised at what a nice sound we made together. Then I had six bars' rest before I came in with my twiddly bits. Simon was playing his bit; I looked across at him. He really was terribly good-looking. His face was stiff with concentration, and he reminded me of something I couldn't quite remember. Suddenly it came to me – a Roman emperor, one of the Caesars, whose picture was in my History book. I imagined Simon with a wreath of laurel round his neck, and smiled. Then he looked up at me and his eyes looking into mine made me feel quite funny. I half expected him to say something commanding and Caesar-like in Latin. But he didn't.

"Lizzie!" he shouted, making me jump. "Where were you?"

I nearly said 'in Rome', but managed to stop myself. "How d'you mean?" I asked instead. Then I realized I had stopped counting my six bars' rest, and hadn't come in at the right place. "Sorry," I muttered, "I got lost."

We went back a bit and tried again. This time I was so careful not to come in late that I played my twiddly bit too soon. Simon scrunched his bow across the cello's strings in exasperation. I smiled at him apologetically.

"Sorry," I told him. "I don't know what's the matter with me today. Can we go back to the same place?"

Simon sighed, "Do try and get it right this time. We haven't got much time left." He played his bit again – beautifully. His soft pale hair flopped across his eyes, and he was biting his lower lip with concentration. I felt quite hot with liking him, and made myself look at my music and count the bars as Naresh came in with his twiddles.

"Five, two, three, four, six, two, three, four," I whispered to myself, and came in bang on time, right note and everything. At least, I think it was the right note; it was difficult to tell, because my string broke with a loud "twaaang" noise, Naresh and Emma burst out laughing. My face did its famous impersonation of a beetroot. Simon threw his bow down in disgust, and said loudly, "I think this rehearsal is doomed!"

"Doomed!" repeated Naresh in a silly, ghost-story voice. "Doomed! We're all doomed!"

Emma laughed even louder, and I giggled nervously, "I'll just put another one on," I said, to no-one in particular. "Shan't be a tick." But when I looked in my violin case there were no spare strings. I wheeled round in dismay.

"Oh no," I said. "I was clearing all the junk out of my case just before my lesson today – I must have left the strings in Mr Owen's room."

"Oh for God's sake!" Simon exploded. "I think you left your brains there too. Are you always such a wally, or have you been saving it up for me?"

My face flamed even more. It felt as if you could have fried an egg on it. I looked down at my feet in an agony of embarrassment and awkwardness; part of me wanted to yell back at Simon, but the other part liked him too much. Besides, I thought he was at least partly right; I *hadn't* been paying attention, and it was daft of me to have forgotten the spare strings.

"Shut up, Simon," Naresh said mildly. "It's not her fault her string broke – leave the girl alone."

"You can borrow one of mine," Emma told me. She stood up and went over to her case. "Here you . . ."

Simon got to his feet. "Don't bother," he said crossly. He started to pack his cello away. "I'm not in the mood for it now. This rehearsal's been a farce. I just hope the next one is a bit better, that's all," he said, looking at me, "or else I might have to find another second violin. I don't want Sporanti thinking I can't get a string quartet together."

And with that, he slammed the door behind him and was gone. The rest of us were left looking at the music on our stands, and each other.

"What a wozzuck," said Naresh cheerfully. He sat down again and indicated the music. "Shall we have a go by ourselves? Who needs a cello, anyway."

I felt close to tears. "I don't really feel like it," I said. "Sorry." To my surprise, Emma put a friendly arm round my shoulders. "Don't worry," she told me. "It wasn't your fault. I told you Simon got nasty at times, didn't I? I shouldn't worry about it, honestly."

"Yeah," Naresh put in. "He's a good cellist, but boy, does he love himself. I can't understand what all you girls see in him. If you want my opinion he's not worth the bother." He started to whistle as he put his viola away.

29th March.

Dear Diary,

Ogodogodogodogod. I'm so upset I think I'm going to die. It was the first rehearsal of Simon's string quartet today, and I mucked everything up. I was so looking forward to it but everything went wrong. I don't think he's ever going to speak to me again, and I'm sure he won't want me in the quartet anymore. Oh, why do I have to like him so much? It wouldn't matter so much if I didn't. Does everyone feel like this about someone at this age? If so, there must be heaps of teenagers all walking around aching like I ache. I can't believe that's true. If it is, why does everybody else look so normal? I'm positive nobody else feels the way I do.

2nd April.

Dear Diary,

I still haven't seen Simon, and I'm sure he won't speak to me when I do. I just don't know what to do. Oh God, please tell me how I can get Simon to like me again; that is, if he ever did. I'm not even sure of that now. If he did like me, why was he so nasty to me? I know I was being dim, but I couldn't speak to anybody I liked, like he spoke to me. Why does liking a boy have to hurt so much? I can't believe Daddy and Wendy used to hurt this way about each other – or Meg and Charles. I read somewhere that when you fall in love for the first time it has to be painful or it doesn't mean anything. In that case, if this is being in love I'd rather be in hate.

5th April.

Dear Diary,

I felt miserable all weekend about Simon. Even Daddy

realized something was up, and he wouldn't usually notice someone was upset even if they did themselves in with misery under his nose. But I feel better now; correction, I feel heaps better, fantastic, ace, great, superb, in fact the total complete opposite of mizz. Laura told me today that Simon has been in the san. with some mystery illness since the day after that rehearsal; she went to visit him last night and he's coming back to school tomorrow, but he told her about the quartet rehearsal and gave her a note for me, apologizing for being nasty to me! Imagine! He said (in the note) that he's really sorry for being so mean but he was feeling ill and awful, and he hopes I'll forgive him. As if I wouldn't! I shall keep the note for ever. He has such lovely writing. I wonder why Laura only told me today that Simon's been ill?

There were only three more days before we broke up for Easter, but we managed to squeeze in several more rehearsals; lunch-times, breaks, and after school. This time the rehearsals went quite well. We were all pleased, because it was important that we played well when we went to France two weeks later. But I was the most pleased, because Simon was really nice to me. I mean, really, *really* nice.

The afternoon we broke up I was waiting outside the day-room for Laura to finish packing up her books and things, when Emma came along.

"Hi," she said to me. "Are you doing anything? Why don't you come home with me, for tea, if you don't have to get home."

"That would be lovely," I told her. "I'll just wait for Laura, and tell her where I'm going."

Just then, Laura emerged from the day-room. "Tell me what?" she said. "Oh, hello Mouse."

"Mouse has asked me to tea," I explained.

Laura smiled warmly. "How nice; can I come too?"

Emma looked slightly doubtful. "Aren't your parents coming to pick you up?"

"Not till six," said Laura. "I was wondering what I was going to do until then. Oh go on, Mouse – it'll be just like the old times. The Good Old Days!" she said, and laughed.

Emma said she didn't suppose her mother would mind either way, and so the three of us set off from Percy's to walk to Emma's house.

The Nashes lived in a huge flat in Rowan Place, a Georgian square off Marylebone Road. It was very quiet when Emma let us in with her key.

"Mum!" she yelled. "I'm home! Funny, she's usually home at this time." A scruffy grey dog of indeterminate breed came wagging up the hall to greet us. "Hello Deefer," said Emma, patting his head.

"What does your mother do?" I asked, picking up a funny-looking wood carving of a native head. The whole sitting-room was full of strange objects; drums on the walls, animal skins and lengths of brightly dyed fabric thrown on the floor and the furniture, and everywhere carvings and ornaments in dark polished wood and ivory, and what looked like bone.

"She pots," said Emma.

"Potters?" I asked. "So does Daddy, but usually when he's supposed to be writing something important."

Emma burst out laughing. "No, pots. Pots! she's a potter. She has a little studio in Camden Town, but she's normally home at this time. So's Teddie, come to think of it, and she's not here either."

"Who's Teddie?" I wanted to know.

But just then the front door opened, and in burst a girl dressed, like us, in the dark blue Percy's uniform. She was carrying a flute case and looked about ten. She also looked vaguely familiar.

"'Lo, Em," she said. "Where's Mum? Is there anything to eat, I'm starving."

"This is my sister, Edwina," said Emma, very formally.

The girl scowled. "Teddie," she said to me. "She knows I hate being called Edwina, it stinks. Who are you? Oh hello, smelly," she greeted Laura. She went over to the fruit bowl and picked a grape off the bunch. "Are you doing tea tonight, Em? Can I have cheese and marmalade sandwiches?"

Emma made egg and ham sandwiches and tea and took a plate of cream cakes out of the fridge. For someone who always looked so messy she made tea very neatly. Teddie hovered around, pinching bits of sandwich and getting in the way and addressing the odd comment to people.

"I do know you," she said to me. "You're new this term, aren't you? I s'pose if you're friends with Laura you know the blond bombshell."

I smiled at her, puzzled. "Who's that?"

"Simon Alexander." Teddie rolled her eyes heavenwards and made kissing noises with her lips. "Don't you think he's scrummy? All the girls in my class are just mad about him; my friend Clare, she's a real hoot, she's a boarder and every night she sneaks up outside the boys' dorm and kisses the door! One night she said he came down the corridor in his pyjamas, she nearly died. Did you know Em used to . . ."

"Here are your disgusting sandwiches," Emma told her firmly. "Why don't you buzz off to your room and give us some peace?"

Teddie flounced off, holding the plate in front of her like a tray. "I was going anyway," she announced. "Catch me hanging around listening to you lot talking about *boys*!" Her bedroom door slammed shut.

"I see your sister hasn't changed," Laura remarked as we all went into the sitting-room, Emma carrying the tea tray.

Tea was delicious. After we'd eaten, I went into the hall

and rang Daddy to tell him I'd be a bit late home. When I went back into the sitting-room Emma and Laura were deep in conversation about France; we talked about the places we were to visit, and Laura told us about the clothes she was going to take, and how much they'd cost, and then regaled us with stories of foreign holidays she'd had with her parents. Then we put some records on, and we didn't hear the front door shut over the music. I looked up to see a boy with Emma's frizzy brown hair and topaz eyes standing in the doorway. The hair and eyes looked better on him, and although he wasn't handsome he looked nice in a smiley sort of way.

Laura immediately stood up and went over to him. "Hello Theo," she said, and kissed him in continental fashion on both cheeks. "How are you? I haven't seen you for ages."

He looked at her slightly bemused. "I'm OK, thanks. Is there any tea left, Em?" and he went out into the kitchen. I realized he was Emma's brother, the one Emma had said would accompany us.

"Shouldn't you be getting back, Laura?" Emma collected up our tea plates and put them on the tray.

Laura looked at the carriage clock on the mantelpiece. She never wore a watch. "No, I've got heaps of time. It's only quarter past five."

"That clock's always slow. It's ..." Emma looked at her watch. "It's twenty to six. You'll be late if you don't hurry."

My watch said quarter past five, like the carriage clock, but I didn't say anything. After Laura had left, in a rush, Theo joined us in the sitting-room.

"Are you Lizzie?" he asked me. I nodded. "I thought so. You're the violinist, right?"

"Stop interrogating her," Emma told him mildly.

"Why did Laura kiss me like that?" Theo asked his sister. "Come to think of it, what was she doing here anyway? I thought you'd ..."

"She's OK," Emma interrupted. She shrugged. "She sort of invited herself. And I don't know why she kissed you. Probably fancies you."

Theo grimaced, "God forbid. Where's Mum?"

"Dunno. Got held up, I expect. Hey, Theo, d'you fancy playing the piano for us?"

"I would," Theo sighed, "but I've got tons of revision to do. A levels next term," he explained to me. "Nice to meet you, Lizzie. And watch out for The Lovely Laura," he added darkly, as he left the room. In the distance I could hear the tinny thump of pop music from Teddie's room.

"What did he mean, The Lovely Laura?" I asked Emma slowly. "And why did he pull that face when you said she probably fancies him?"

"Theo's not Laura's biggest fan," she said.

"Why not?" I persisted. "Why not, Mouse?"

She sighed. "We were friends when we were Teddie's age – best friends, even. I thought Laura was wonderful."

I was surprised. I'd never thought of Emma and Laura being particularly friendly. "So why aren't you now? What happened, Mouse?"

"Stop calling me Mouse!" Emma sounded suddenly cross. Then she pulled an apologetic face, "Sorry, I s'pose it's not your fault. Only nobody used to call me Mouse until Laura started, then everybody seemed to. Why do you think she calls me that?" she demanded.

"Well . . ." I didn't like to say, because you're mouse-like.

Emma read my mind. "Because I'm mouse-like, right? Laura started calling me Mouse because of what my family call me; Em. You know, Em for Mouse?"

"Like Deefer Dog," I said, remembering. The owner of the name who had been lying on the hearthrug throughout tea, thumped his tail in acknowledgement that yes, he was Deefer Dog.

"At least, that's what she said," Emma went on. "Laura's got this knack of saying nasty things in a nice way, or wriggling out of it, or somehow turning things round so that *you* thought of the nasty things in the first place, and she's totally innocent. I'm not mouse-like, not really, but because of Laura's nickname that's how everybody thinks of me."

She was silent for a moment, and I thought of Laura's visit that weekend. She'd certainly wriggled out of the whisky business all right.

"You know that French motto, *honi soit qui mal y pense?*" Emma asked me. "Evil be to him that evil thinks," she translated helpfully. "That's Laura. Nothing's ever her fault, it's always somebody else's nasty suspicious mind."

"But what happened?" I asked again. I was somehow desperate to know. "Why aren't you best friends any more?"

Emma looked at me for a long moment. "Nothing in particular," she said finally. "I just got fed up with her mucking me about. If you want to be friends with her, go ahead. Don't take any notice of me; you seem to give back as good as you get, anyway. I never could. Course, I was younger then."

Just then I heard the front door slamming, and a voice calling.

"Is that you, Mum?" Emma went to the sitting-room door. "You're late – are you OK?"

"Hello darling." A tall attractive woman came into the room. She had a strong brown face and what I was beginning to recognize as the Nash hair and eyes. On her the hair came to her shoulders in crimped waves, and the warm hazel eyes were outlined with black pencil. "Did you get some tea? – oh, good. Hello," she said to me. Her eyes crinkled. "Who's this? Another Percy's prodigy, I see. I'm Heather Nash."

"This is Lizzie," Emma introduced me.

Her mother shook my hand gravely. "Sorry I'm so late

darling," she said to Emma. "Are Theo and Teddie back? It's unusually quiet; it's normally like a madhouse in here this time of day," she explained to me.

"Why are you late?" Emma asked her again.

Mrs Nash sighed. "It's Grandpa. I had a phone call at the studio; he's back in hospital, I'm afraid. They don't think it's too serious though. My father," she told me, "is eighty-five, and insists on living on his own, even though he has a poorly heart and can hardly walk, poor darling. Aren't parents the pits?"

The word sounded so funny coming from her that I couldn't help laughing, and neither could Emma.

I left shortly after that, and Emma walked me to the Tube.

"Shall I give you a ring in the holidays?" she said. "You can come round again if you like."

"Yes," I said. "Great. Thanks for tea, Em."

She smiled, "You're welcome. You will come again, in the holidays, won't you?"

"I'd like to."

"Oh, and Lizzie, don't take any notice of what I said earlier. You know, about Laura. She's OK really. We've just got different ideas about things, that's all. That's the real reason we're not so friendly any more."

But I still had a feeling that Emma hadn't told me the whole truth.

7

The French Trip

I didn't get the chance to go and see Emma during the Easter holidays; things were just hectic in our house, what with Flora, and Easter, and Daddy and Wendy packing things up for the move back to Cornwall Daddy insisted was imminent (even though, as far as I was aware, he still hadn't bought a house there).

Then there was my packing to do; for France, and important things to take back to school with me. I was to start boarding as soon as we arrived back from France.

The day before the French trip I was just re-discovering some of my old exercise books from Oaklands days, and marvelling at how dim I was, when the telephone rang. And rang and rang.

"I'll get it, shall I?" I yelled in the direction of the kitchen where I could hear Wendy and Daddy cooing over Flora. "Don't worry about rushing to answer it. I'll just break my leg falling down the stairs trying to . . . Hello?" I said into the receiver.

"Is that you Lizzie?" It was Emma.

"Emma! Hi! How are you? I've been meaning to ring," I fibbed, "only I've been so . . ."

"It doesn't matter. I wasn't ringing because of that." She sounded upset. "Listen, I'm afraid I won't be going tomorrow."

"Tomorrow?" For a moment I wasn't sure what she meant. Then I realized. "You mean France? You're not going to France? But why not, Em? What's the matter?" She didn't answer straightaway, and then I thought of something else. "What about the string quartet? That means we won't be able to play!" I felt a chill of disappointment.

"I know. I'm sorry. I had to let someone know – I tried ringing Simon but there was no answer, and I don't know Sporanti's number, and I couldn't get through to Percy's either, and . . ." Emma's voice cracked in a sob.

I realized she still hadn't told me the reason. "What's up, Emma? Tell me what's wrong!"

"It's G-Grandpa. He died this morning in the hospital. He j-just died, and they found him in his bed when they brought his breakfast. They thought he was as-s-sleep." Emma was crying in earnest now. "Oh Lizzie, what's Mummy going to do?"

I was horrified. "You mean she doesn't know?"

"Yes, yes, she knows, but she's so upset, she's been crying like anything. Oh Lizzie I loved him so much . . ."

Emma's voice grew faint, and I heard the murmur of a lower voice, and then someone else came on the line.

"Lizzie? It's Heather Nash. Emma's rather distraught, I'm afraid." Emma's mother's voice was quiet but very calm.

Memories of my own mother's death swept over me in a sudden wave. I felt cold and wormy inside with remembering; the police on the doorstep, and Daddy's face stricken and unbelieving of the news they brought. He stood shaking his head and crying silently all the while they told him, and that frightened me more than anything before or since. I had never seen any man cry before, let alone Daddy, and I was sharply and horribly aware for the first time how *fragile* people were. Daddy could die too, I remember thinking. *I could die!* I was only ten.

"Mrs Nash," I gulped. "I'm really sorry. Really sorry," I repeated. I was gripping the telephone so tightly my knuckles were white.

"That's kind of you," Mrs Nash murmured. "Emma was very close to her grandfather. He was very proud of her – he's a musician too, you see, and she's his first granddaughter. Was, I should say. He's being buried on Tuesday; Emma's desperate to go to the funeral, so I'm afraid she won't be going to France. I do hope it's not going to mess up your plans too much?"

I assured her it wouldn't, and she told me she would ring the school again later, to let them know. After she had rung off, I was surprised at how much the news had upset me. Poor Emma, I thought. My poor friend.

We flew from Heathrow to Charles de Gaulle airport in Paris. I was really excited; for a start, I'd never been on an aeroplane before. Laura and Simon and I all sat together and chatted; I was a bit scared just before the plane took off – such a deafening noise, such an unbearable feeling of tension – and Simon laughed at me.

"The look on your face!" he teased me. "It's all right, nothing awful's going to happen! Do you want me to hold your hand?"

He did, too. I forgot all about what the plane was doing. When the stewardess brought round plastic cups of tea and coffee and little cellophane wrapped packets of biscuits, Simon and Laura and I exchanged biscuits with each other and chatted. In almost no time we had landed again.

A coach at the airport took us to the place where we were to stay for the week. Signor Sporanti and Miss Quentin, the other teacher with us, shepherded us on. They seemed in holiday mood too; even old Sporanti smiled a few times. He nearly cracked his face.

As we drove through the streets of Paris I was struck at how *foreign* everything seemed. I wished Emma was there to see it all; I had never realized that something as commonplace as a street – *boulevard* – could be so very different to the ones back in Britain. Even the people walking along looked different – more elegant, more put together; people were sitting outside cafés at little tables with spotless white cloths, drinking and eating interesting-looking things. Wine and croissants, I thought; that's what they have in France. Even the driving was different; faster, more impatient even than London, and of course on the other side of the road. And the horns too, people sounding their horns the whole time. I was a bit disappointed not to see any men on bicycles wearing striped jerseys and strings of onions round their necks.

We stopped in a side street outside a large white building with green shutters and window boxes blooming with red and yellow striped tulips.

"Auberge des Jeunes St Honoré," the coach driver announced, with a Gallic wave of his hand. Even the cigarette he lit smelt different to English ones; more pungent, cigar-like.

"Gauloises," whispered Laura as we passed him. "The type of cigarette," she explained, seeing my blank face. "Oh look, there's the Eiffel Tower! Isn't it big?" Fancy knowing the name of French cigarettes! I was very impressed.

The Auberge des Jeunes St Honoré was a kind of youth hostel cum arts centre. It was very posh, more like a hotel. Laura and I had a room together; twin beds, green and white striped wallpaper, and a bathroom which we were to share with the occupants of the room next door. It had two washbasins and an electric shower, "But no bath," said Laura. "Isn't it French?"

We didn't rehearse that day. The time was spent unpacking

and looking around; we went for a walk and bought some postcards, and then went back to the Auberge for my very first French meal. Laura was enchanted to discover that some German boys were staying too, and spent a fairly fruitless hour trying to chat them up. She's going to do GCSE German, but all she can say is things like 'where is the nearest railway station' and 'my younger brother is wearing a red shirt.' Not much use when you're trying to impress boys with your wit and sophistication.

I left her to it, and went to write a postcard.

Dear Daddy, Wendy and Flora,
It's brilliant here! We got here OK, the weather is nice. I can see the Eiffel Tower from my room. I'm sharing with Laura. We start rehearsing tomorrow. We had fish and chips for supper. I'm learning German. See you soon, lots of love,
LIZZIE XXXXX

The next day we started rehearsals. It was very hot; much warmer than the weather we had left in England. I had only packed one tee-shirt, an old faded one with Mickey Mouse on the front, but I wore it anyway. It was too hot for anything heavier.

Signor Sporanti had arranged for a group of French kids, pupils at the local Conservatoire, to swell the ranks of our chamber orchestra, and they were due to arrive after lunch. There were some juniors from Percy's too; a lot of the older ones hadn't been able to come as they were away on holiday that week. Teddie Nash was playing second flute; I wondered why she had come to France instead of going to her grandfather's funeral, like Emma, but didn't like to ask her directly.

"Is Emma OK now?" I asked her instead when we had a

break for lunch. "She seemed very upset when she rang me about your grandpa."

Teddie nodded, her mouth full of baguette. "I think so," she said through the crumbs. "She was his favourite. She wanted to go to the funeral. Must be mad – catch me going to a funeral."

"Why not?" asked Laura. "He'd probably have wanted you there."

Teddie spun round crossly. "No he wouldn't! Anyway, he's dead. He's not going to know who's there and who's not. And it's none of your business, either. Smelly pig," she added for good measure.

"Charming," Laura said, flushing. She walked away; I could tell by her shoulders that she was annoyed.

"Why did you say that?" I asked Teddie.

She shrugged. "Who cares. It's nothing to do with her. I didn't want to go, that's all." She looked down at her feet. "I didn't want to go. I was scared – I didn't want to see Grandpa being buried. It's horrible. D'you think he really would want me there?" She suddenly looked up at me, her eyes solemn and huge and frightened.

I thought once more of my mother, and her funeral. I had been Teddie's age, and scared, too.

"No," I told Teddie definitely. "Not if you'd be frightened. I'm sure he wouldn't want you to be scared, not if he loved you."

"Why do you bother with her?" Laura asked me afterwards, still cross from being called a smelly pig. "She's a real brat."

I shook my head. "No she's not. She was just upset, that's all."

"Funny way of showing it. Actually, I'm quite glad Mouse isn't here, aren't you? She doesn't seem to like me being friends with you."

"I'm friends with who I want to be," I told Laura. "I don't

take any notice of anybody else." But Laura was right, despite what Emma always said to the contrary. She clearly didn't like Laura and me being friends. And although I liked Emma very much, life with Laura did seem a lot simpler without her being around.

After lunch, the French contingent arrived. There were six of them, four boys and two girls, all looking terribly smart and clever. During the afternoon break I saw Simon talking to one of the girls. She was very slim, and had dark sparkling eyes and sleek black hair which curved to her jawbone in a shining bob. She waved her hands around a lot, in that way the French have, and her laugh was low and musical. Simon called me over.

"Lizzie!" he said. "This is Dominique. She's going to play in the string quartet instead of Emma – she knows the Dvořák, she's done it before. Isn't that lucky?"

"Isn't it," I said gloomily.

Dominique smiled and said hello to me. I felt extremely scruffy in my old jeans, which always make my legs look fat, and yesterday's Mickey Mouse tee-shirt. Dominique's baggy red sweatshirt looked really striking with her dark hair and eyes. Her thighs inside her jeans didn't have a spare ounce of flab. Her accent was very attractive. I hated her.

Over the next few days our time was almost all taken up with practising and doing concerts at local schools and colleges, which had already started their term. We did some sightseeing too; we saw Monmartre and Sacré Coeur and Notre Dame; and the Arc de Triomphe, looking like our own Marble Arch. Laura and I went everywhere together, ate all our meals together, and stayed awake at night in our room for ages, chatting and laughing. She was great fun, I thought to myself, not for the first time. It'll be whizz when we're boarding together.

But I wasn't having as good a time as I'd hoped. Mainly because of Dominique – she and Simon were always hanging around together. Her laugh and accent were beginning to get on my nerves. I knew it was only envy – mere jealousy, my little internal voice told me. But it didn't feel very mere; Simon had virtually ignored Laura and me since Dominique had arrived on the scene.

"I'm getting seriously fed up with that Dominique," Laura said to me one night after we'd gone to bed. We had done a concert earlier that evening in the concert hall at the Auberge, and the string quartet had played with Dominique taking Emma's place. She and Simon had gazed intently into each other's eyes all through it, and afterwards Sporanti had babbled away excitedly in Italian to Dominique. He was very impressed with her. Apparently her mother's Italian. Wouldn't you just know it.

"Me too," I agreed. "Did you see the way she and Simon were looking at each other?"

Laura giggled. "Oh darling, let me stare into your bootiful bootiful eyeses!" she said, in a silly voice. "And did you see the blouse she was wearing? You could see right through it. Old Sporanti's eyes nearly popped out of his head."

"D'you think Simon really likes her?"

"What do you think? I caught them snogging round by the dustbins during the interval – Simon said she had something in her eye, but I'd been watching them for five minutes. All I can say is, he never took anything out of *my* eye like that."

The familiar icy hand clutched my heart again. I suddenly thought about Simon kissing me instead of Dominique, and went hot.

"Are you still awake?" came Laura's voice.

"Yes," I said in a small voice.

"What's the matter?"

"I'm just tired." I wasn't really though. I lay there miserably for a moment, and thought. I had to tell someone how I felt about Simon or I thought I'd burst. And Laura was my friend, and Simon's too.

"Well actually," I said, "I quite like Simon too. Quite a lot, in fact. Well, lots really. I think I'm in love with him."

Laura was immediately interested. I could hear the rustle as she sat up in bed. "Golly, do you really? Oh, poor you; it must be mizz, seeing him with Dominique and everything."

She put the light on, and I squealed. "Oh, sorry," she apologized. "Listen, I don't really think you're in love with him. Not really and truly – I mean, you don't know him that well, do you?"

"Yes I do," I protested. "And I thought he quite liked me, too. Do you think I've got a chance, Laura? Any chance at all?"

Laura considered. "I don't know," she concluded finally. "The trouble is, I don't think of him in that way – as a boyfriend, I mean. I've known him practically all my life, and I suppose he's more like a brother."

Like Ben, I thought silently. I sighed. "It's awful," I told her. "Me liking him so much. He's always chatting up other girls, too. And he's hardly spoken to me since the French kids arrived."

"Did you know Dominique's seventeen?" Laura asked suddenly. "She thinks he's older, too. He hasn't told her his real age, in case she goes off him."

"Oh," I said. I didn't want to talk about Dominique. "I think I'll go to sleep now; I'm whacked."

Laura turned the light off again. "Night, then," she said. "And don't worry; I won't tell a soul you fancy Simon."

The next morning, we did a concert at a school just outside Paris, and Dominique lost her place when we were playing in the string quartet. Naresh and I looked at each other and carried on playing, and she eventually found her way back in again, but everybody must have noticed. On the way back she sat at the back of the coach and sulked, and Simon put his arm round her.

"I don't know why *you're* not playing first violin in that quartet," Laura said to me in a loud voice. "You're much better than her."

"Thanks," I said. On balance, I thought I would rather have been the one to get lost, and have Simon's arm around me as a consolation prize.

"In fact," Laura went on, even louder, "I don't know why *some people* bothered coming to play in this orchestra."

Dominique shouted something long and complicated in French, and all the French kids laughed. Simon laughed too, although I knew for a fact he didn't understand what she'd said.

"Ooh," said Teddie, who was sitting behind us, bouncing up and down on her seat. "Did you hear what she said? Did you hear what she called you?"

"What *did* she call me?" asked Laura, suspiciously.

"I don't know, but it sounded dead rude," Teddie bounced even more.

So Laura shouted something equally rude back, and the insults floated to and fro until Miss Quentin came down the coach to investigate. She nearly fell on top of Simon as the driver swerved to avoid something in the road.

"That's quite enough of that," she told us all. "Simon, sit up straight and put that girl down."

"You don't know where she's been," Laura whispered to me. I giggled, and Miss Quentin frowned at me as she swayed her way back to her seat.

It was hot and stuffy inside the coach. The stiff plush of the seat was prickling my bare legs. I looked miserably out of the window as we drove past the Seine, and felt slightly sick. What's the matter with you, I said crossly to myself. You're in

France. You've been looking forward to it for ages. For heaven's sake, forget about Simon and try and enjoy yourself.

"Cheer up," Laura passed me a toffee. "We're going to the Eiffel Tower this afternoon. That should be good for a laugh."

The Eiffel Tower did cheer me up, at least to start with. It was such a glorious, brilliant day, and the view from the top was stunning. I rested my elbows on the parapet and put my chin in my hands, and looked out over Paris. What a beautiful city, I thought. I imagined myself living there, studying music perhaps; and then later when I was quite old, say about thirty, striding through Paris with my violin, wearing swirling black clothes down to my ankles and growing my hair to my waist, and giving concerts that were always sold out. And then afterwards drinking wine in bars until three in the morning with my devoted male fans, all of whom bore a remarkable resemblance to Simon, and all of whom would beg me, simply beg me, to marry them.

"I cannot," I would say sadly, "for I am wedded to my art . . ."

"Penny for them," said a voice behind me, making me jump. It was Simon. I didn't think I ought to tell him about my devoted male fans, so I just smiled instead in what I hoped was a mysterious way.

"Where's Dominique?" Laura asked him.

"She's gone home. She wasn't feeling too well after that business in the coach."

"Aah, poor little thing," Laura said sarcastically.

Simon looked at her. "You weren't very nice to her. I don't know why you don't like her – she likes you, she told me."

"No she doesn't," I said. "She doesn't like any of us, apart from you. And herself," I added.

"The trouble with you two is you can't bear anyone else having all the attention," Simon said, and went crossly off to rejoin his friends.

Laura made a rude noise after him with her lips. "Good riddance!" she shouted. Then she saw my face. "Oh sorry, Lizzie, I forgot you fancied him."

"I do not fancy him!" I said, louder than I intended. Several people turned and stared at us and I felt my face going red. "I don't fancy him. I hate that word, it sounds so silly."

"Well, whatever it is you feel about him," Laura shrugged. "Personally, I'm getting a bit cheesed off with him ignoring us. We're good enough to be friends with at Percy's, but not here. Well as far as I'm concerned, he can just go and jump in the Seine!"

When we came down the Eiffel Tower, Miss Quentin divided us all up into groups and let us go and look around on our own.

"I want you all back here at the coach in an hour," she told us. Laura and I were in charge of Teddie and four other juniors, including Clare, Teddie's friend who always kissed the door of the boys' dormitory. They skipped along with us.

"You know Sexy Simon, don't you?" Clare said. She had a lisp, and it sounded like Theckthy Thimon.

"Yeth," Laura said gravely.

All the little girls giggled.

"Ithn't he thtunning? Have you ever kithed him?" Clare asked me. My face flamed again. "Certainly not," I said, with as much dignity as I could. "He's just a friend."

Laura flapped her hands at the girls. "Do leave us alone," she told them. "Lizzie and I want to look in the shop windows, not talk to you about boring Simon Alexander." They skipped off in front of us.

"Can I go in that shop?" Teddie asked us. It was a music shop; it looked dark and cool inside, and had musical instruments and sheet music displayed on a piece of burgundy velvet in the window.

"No," Laura said. "We want to go on down the street. We're not waiting for you in there."

We walked along, looking at all the fashions in the windows of the clothes shops and telling each other what we'd buy if we had the money.

"I wonder how Emma's Grandpa's funeral went?" I suddenly said.

Laura groaned. "Lizzie! Why on earth are you thinking about funerals?"

"I just remembered. It's a shame Emma couldn't come, isn't it? She'd have loved it in Paris."

"Well, *I* think it's been better without her. I mean, she's OK, but you're much more fun," Laura said.

I was pleased and flattered. "You used to be best friends, didn't you?" I said. "What happened, Laura? Why aren't you any more?"

Laura turned away from the window and looked at me surprised. "Is that what she told you? Poor Mouse." She sighed, and shook her head sadly. "We used to go round together a bit, ages ago, but we were never that friendly. We're too different. But Mouse has always wanted to be best friends with me, and I suppose pretending we used to be is nicer for her than accepting that we never will be."

"But why don't you go around together any more?" I persisted. I remembered how Laura had asked Emma if she could go to tea with us, saying it would be like The Good Old Days. "What happened?"

Laura sighed again, impatiently. "Nothing *happened*. I can't remember when we stopped; I think she took the huff over something and started to ignore me, it was so long ago I really can't remember. Hey, look at this shirt - wouldn't Mr Hadleigh look brilliant in it?" She turned back to the shop window.

I looked at my watch. "Golly, is that the time? We've got to be back at the coach in five minutes."

We hurried along the road to join the juniors, who were eating ice creams with great relish.

"Where's Teddie?" I asked them.

They looked at me, then at each other. "She'th with you," Clare said. "We haven't theen her - not thince we were talking about Thimon."

"But that was ages ago!" I cried. "Laura and I have been walking on our own and looking at the clothes - she *must* be with you!"

They shook their heads.

"Oh God," I said slowly, as the truth sank in. "She's lost. Teddie's lost. What on earth are we going to do?"

8

Boarding

Laura was keen to let Teddie find her own way back to the coach.

"She should have stayed with us, the little pain," she grumbled. "Why should *we* get into trouble for being late back?"

"We can't just leave her!" I said, horrified. "She's only little! Besides, we'll get into even more trouble if we go back without her – Miss Quentin put us in charge, remember?"

Laura grumbled some more, and Clare looked as if she was about to cry.

"Look, why don't you lot go back to the coach, and tell Miss Quentin what's happened?" I told Laura. "I'll go and see if I can find her." And I turned back down the street.

I ran along, trying to remember the direction we'd come. The pavement felt hot beneath the thin soles of my espadrilles, and my hair was getting in my eyes. None of the shops looked the least bit familiar. Oh Teddie, I moaned to myself, as my heart thumped painfully in my throat, where on earth are you? I stopped running and pushed a strand of wet hair from my forehead. There was the café where the juniors had bought their ice-creams – and over there was the shop where Laura had pointed out the shirt.

I went up the side street we'd come down, and suddenly I knew exactly where to look. I ran the final few hundred metres, and sure enough there was Teddie standing outside the music shop. She was clutching a brown paper bag, and peering around in a dejected way. She looked very little and defenceless in her yellow blouse and shorts. As I got closer I could see a scab on one of her knees, and a bit of her hair was sticking up at the front. I could also see that she had been crying.

I called her name, and as she turned round and saw me her face crumpled with relief. Then she stuck her chin out.

"I wasn't lost," she said defensively. "You lot just went on without me."

I stood close to her, out of breath. "Laura told you not to go in there, so why on earth did you? I was worried sick!" The relief at finding her had turned into anger.

Teddie scowled. "Bother Laura," she said, her lower lip stuck out. "I wanted some new music. I was only in there a couple of ticks."

I was so cross with her I wanted to shake her. "For heaven's sake!" I exploded. "We didn't have a clue where you were. You could have been lost. You could have been kidnapped, or - or abducted. You were in Paris all alone, and you could have been . . ." Suddenly the full horror of what could have happened to her dawned on me, and at the same time it dawned on Teddie, because to my dismay she burst into tears. All my anger evaporated as she struggled to find her hankie whilst not dropping her precious music. I put my arms round her and made soothing noises, and when she stopped I wiped her face with a tissue.

"There," I said. "That's better. Come on, let's go back to the coach."

Teddie sniffed. "You sounded just like my mother."

"Does she comfort you like that when you're upset?" I was touched.

"No. She nags too. Don't tell the others I cried, will you?" And she was off down the street, scuffing her sandals. Little tough Teddie.

As it happened, we were only a few minutes late getting back to the coach, so nobody noticed us sneaking on. Laura was deep in conversation with Tim Maynard, her latest fanciable, and Clare and Co. were lisping away at Simon.

"Gosh, Thimon," I heard Clare gush, "that'th really interethting!"

It was our last day in France, and that evening we had a disco at the Auberge. I had bought a new dress, with a little help from Laura, on one of the sightseeing trips; it was floating Indian cotton, black shot through with gold thread. I had got quite brown from the unseasonably hot weather, even though we hadn't been outside much, and with my tanned legs and hair freshly washed and looking quite decent for once, I felt rather dashing. Like a gypsy, almost.

"I'm looking forward to this disco," I said, twirling in front of the mirror and admiring the way my dress swung out.

Laura was fiddling with her thousands of little boxes and jars of make-up. "So'm I," she said, pouting her lips and applying half a hundredweight of cerise lip gloss. "That dress really suits you – bet he asks you to dance!"

"Who?" I asked, but I knew who she meant.

Laura caught my eye in the mirror, and winked. Then she tutted. "Come here and let me do something with your face," she told me. "You can't wear that dress without something on your eyes, at least."

I protested, but she ignored me. She plonked me down on the edge of the bed and made me stare over her shoulder while she did ticklish things to my cheeks and eyelashes. At one stage I thought she was going to stick a pencil in my eye.

"Now put your lips like this," she instructed me, but I'd had enough.

"No lipstick," I pleaded. "I can't talk properly with lipstick on - it feels all thick and horrible."

Laura laughed, and let me look in the mirror. I was astounded. The make-up was very light, you could barely notice it, but she had outlined my eyes with some sort of black pencil and they looked enormous. Enormous and shining.

"Golly," I said, impressed. "Aren't you clever!"

She laughed again. "He won't be able to resist you now - come on, let's go and knock 'em all dead!"

I hadn't been to many discos, and those I had been to I hadn't enjoyed very much, but this one was different. For a start, I was dressed up properly, and felt really good. Also, Simon was going to be at this one. Don't be stupid, I told myself fiercely. He won't ask you to dance. Why should he? But you still want him to, don't you? said my little inner voice. That's why you're all poshed up and looking forward to it. That's why . . . OK, OK, I told the voice. Just shut up, will you.

Laura got us both a drink.

"What is it?" I shouted, over the hubbub. Laura shook her head, and shrugged. I took a sip - I was certain it was wine. Then we went and had a dance. I looked casually around the room while we danced, looking for Simon. It was dead difficult to recognize anybody very much; coloured lights were sweeping around, and there was an occasional burst of pulsating blue-white light, a strobe, which gave everybody the jerky disconnected look of an old silent movie. I saw Sporanti jiggling around with Lisa, one of the clarinettists, and nudged Laura with a giggle. Sporanti's tummy was wobbling up and down in time with the music. Then I saw Simon. He was standing with a group of his friends, with one hand on his hip and the other propping him up on the wall, and his ankles crossed. My heart gave a lurch, and I looked quickly away in case he noticed me staring. I danced around frantically, willing him to notice me, but when I looked again he had gone.

"Good grief," said Laura suddenly. Dominique had just come in. "What *is* she wearing?"

She was dressed in a black leather mini-skirt, which looked more like a wide belt than a skirt, black fishnet tights, and a white blouse which she had tied in a knot above her smooth brown middle. All at once the music changed to a slow dance, and Simon was there beside her, leading her out on to the dance floor. He put his hands on her bare back and they both swayed gently in time with the music.

For the rest of the evening I tried to have a good time, but it was very difficult not to watch the two of them dancing together; Simon and Dominique wrapped around each other, Simon and Dominique boogying around, Simon and Dominique enjoying themselves. At one point Clare boldly asked Simon to dance and he obliged with a laugh. I could see Clare was in seventh heaven, even though she didn't even come up to his shoulder. Dominique didn't look too pleased though. Fancy being jealous of a ten-year-old, I thought scornfully.

"Look at old Domi-knickers," Teddie had materialized at my elbow. "She looks dead cheesed off, doesn't she?"

Laura had abandoned me in favour of Tim Maynard, but I danced on, with Teddie and various other girls. Then another slow dance was played. I heard a voice saying "Would you like to dance?" and turned round. To my utter astonishment, it was Simon; I just stared at him in disbelief.

"You mean me?" I finally managed to say.

"Well, I certainly don't mean Teddie." Simon put his arm around my waist and steered me through the dancers. As we stood facing each other I suddenly didn't know what to do with myself – I felt rooted to the spot. Then he put both his arms around me. I didn't quite know what to do, and rested my arms primly on his shoulders, as I had seen other girls doing when they danced slow dances. There was still about a foot of space between us. It wasn't exactly the most cosy of slow dances, but I didn't dare get any closer to him in case he heard my heart beating. It was practically deafening me.

Simon said something to me which I couldn't hear; then he raised his eyes expressively to the ceiling and pulled me closer. My heart beat even faster; I thought it was going to pound right through my chest. I felt terribly, horribly uncomfortable, hot and breathless, but at the same time curiously happy; light-headed with being so close to him and liking him so much. Simon's hands moved lightly on my back; his cotton shirt felt rough against my cheek, and he smelt of a light lemony scent. I thought it must be aftershave, and had a sudden sharp vision of his face totally covered in shaving foam, except for his eyes, and had an urgent desire to giggle.

"Dominique said I should ask you to dance," Simon yelled unromantically in my ear.

"Oh," I yelled back. I felt a sharp stab of disappointment; I had hoped he'd asked me to dance because *he* had wanted to.

"Yes," he went on. "She's got this weird idea you fancy me. Daft, isn't it? I told her you're just a friend of Laura's, but she insisted."

I laughed hollowly. "How stupid," I shouted.

"That's an interesting dress," he said, putting his hands on my shoulders and holding me at arm's length.

Oh goody, I thought; he thinks I look nice. "D'you like it?"

Simon considered. "It reminds me of the one my mum wore to my grandmother's funeral," he said.

I'd had enough of this dance. First I'm told it was Dominique's idea, then that my dress looks like funeral clothes.

"Really," I said loftily. "Thank you for the dance, I'm going to get a drink now."

I escaped into the Ladies, feeling a strange mixture of elation that I'd danced with him, and disappointment, and something else I couldn't identify. Dominique was standing in front of the mirror, admiring her hair and squirting great clouds of scent into her neck. She smiled at me, a little pussycat smile. I hated her more than ever. But the following day I was going back to England, with Simon, and she was staying here.

"Hello Dominique," I said chummily. "I like your skirt. Did you know Simon's only fifteen?"

She looked at me, puzzled, not sure she understood. "'Ow you mean?" she demanded.

"Fifteen," I repeated. "*Quinze. Il a quinze ans. Il est très, très jeune*," I added for good measure.

Dominique looked hard at me. I could tell she still didn't understand what I was getting at, and I nodded forcefully. "*Quinze*," I said again.

She suddenly twigged what I was saying. "*Quinze?*" Her right hand went up to her throat. "*Oh là là*," she said. I was thrilled. I never believed French people really said that. Somehow, the disco hadn't been a total disaster after all.

When we got back to England Percy's term had already begun, and I started boarding. It felt very strange for the first few nights; I missed Rufus and Fishpaste, and I even missed Flora crying for her feed at three in the morning. But most of all, of course, I missed Wendy and Daddy, even though I rang home every evening just to make sure they were all still there. On one of these phone calls home, Daddy told me that he'd finally found a house in Penwithin, and they would be moving in a few weeks' time.

"If all goes well," he told me. "But it's been empty for quite a while, so the owners are desperate to get a quick sale. It's a smasher, Lizzie – wait till you see it at half-term!"

"Can I bring Laura back at half-term?" I asked him.

"Of course you can, sweetie. She's more than welcome – such a nice girl. And there's plenty of room in the new house."

I was sharing a dorm with Laura, and three other girls, and it was almost like being back in France again, staying awake talking until really late. However, at school Emma seemed rather subdued; I thought she must still be upset about her grandfather dying, but Laura had other ideas.

"Have you noticed that Mouse is ignoring us?" she asked me one evening.

I was surprised. "No she's not – I was only talking to her this afternoon. Quite a long chat, as a matter of fact."

"Well, she's ignoring me – she hasn't said a word to me since we got back." Laura looked put out at the fact that Emma had been talking to me.

"I don't think she's ignoring you, Laura," I said placatingly. "She's just a bit quiet – I expect she's still upset about her grandpa."

"Oh pooh – it's got nothing to do with her precious grandpa," Laura said scathingly. "She's just jealous, that's all."

I couldn't think what of. "Why should she be jealous?" I asked her.

"Because we went to France and she didn't," she told me. "And because we're friends – sharing a dorm and everything. I think when you arrived she thought she'd take you under her wing. But I got in first, didn't I?"

I agreed that she had, but felt strangely uneasy about what Laura had said. However, one day I was telling Emma about France when Laura came wandering over.

"It was good," I told Emma. "But it seemed odd with you not there – especially the quartet, that was really weird."

Emma smiled. "Teddie's been going on about it non-stop since she's been back – we did this in France, and in France people do this. Mum says she's sick to the back teeth of France. But it does sound like you had fun."

"It was whizz," Laura put in. "Lizzie and I shared a room, and we had an ace time, didn't we Lizzie? We saw Notre Dame, and the Eiffel Tower, and all the French people really enjoyed the concerts, oh and you should have seen the French boys, they were something else. It was magic – you should have come Mouse."

Emma looked wistful. "I do wish I'd gone. But I couldn't miss Grandpa's funeral."

For the next few days, Laura gave Emma every last detail of the French trip. I began to feel quite sorry for her – you could see she really wished she'd gone.

"Poor Emma," I said one night. Laura and the others were getting ready for bed, and I was sitting up in bed writing my diary. "It was really mizz for her, having to stay here when we all went to France."

"Yes, it's a shame." Laura spat toothpaste into the basin. "Ooh, are you doing your diary? Can I have a look?"

Ever since I had started boarding I had been waiting for Laura to ask to read my diary, and had written it with that in mind. I didn't feel anxious about it; far from it. I was rather pleased with what I'd written, and to tell the truth would have been quite disappointed if she hadn't asked. But, oddly, it didn't feel like writing my diary any more. It was no longer private, so I didn't write my truest of true feelings any more.

I handed it over to Laura.

Poor Mouse really envies Laura and me. Laura has been great since I started boarding – she's a really good friend to have. I'm ever so pleased we're sharing a dorm.

I could see Laura smile, and she turned back a few pages. I craned my neck to see what she was reading.

Simon is so beautiful, I read. *When he danced with me that last night in France I thought I was going to melt. I am just madly in love with him. But what chance is there for me when girls like Dominique throw themselves at him? Oh, why do I have to suffer so much? Being in love is so painful, like a big purple bruise around my heart, a pall of suffering around my whole being.*

I was particularly pleased with that bit. It had taken me a lot of pen-top chewing to think of just the right words.

"Golly," said Laura, impressed. "That's really beautiful. It's like poetry. I bet Simon doesn't know you can write lovely stuff like that."

"You won't tell him, will you?" I was suddenly worried.

"Of course not." Laura gave me the diary back with a sympathetic smile. "Poor you. I do wish he'd ask you out. I think you'd make a nice couple, honestly."

I sighed soulfully. "So do I. Don't you think he's good-looking?"

"Oh, yes," Laura agreed. "If you like the blond sort. I go more for the dark chunky ones."

"Like Mr Hadleigh," I said.

Laura scoffed. "Oh him. I've gone off him since we went to France. He fancies himself too much." She threw herself on to her bunk and opened a pop magazine. "I wonder if my dad's bought a compact disc player yet?" I lay there and thought about Simon. If I was to be absolutely honest, I knew he fancied himself too, like Mr Hadleigh. Only that didn't make me like him any the less; more, if anything. He seemed to have this aura about him, this air of knowing he was attractive, that *made* him attractive. It was self-confidence, I supposed. Laura had it, too. And I would have given anything, at that time, to be like them.

After a few weeks, however, the excitement of sharing a dorm with Laura started wearing a bit thin. She seemed almost to have taken me over; we had all our meals together, and all our lessons, and all our free time as well. I was beginning to feel a bit stifled. And there was another thing. While it had been fun to stay awake for ages in France, chatting until eleven or midnight, I found I couldn't manage it at Percy's. I needed my sleep. The other three girls would fall asleep mid-conversation, and I would hear them snoring and long to join them, but Laura would get really stroppy if I did the same. As a consequence, my work was beginning to suffer because I felt permanently tired, and the teachers were starting to comment.

One Saturday afternoon I had arranged to go shopping with Emma. Laura wanted me to go for a walk with her in Regent's Park, but I wanted a break from her for a change.

"Sorry," I told her. "I'm meeting Emma – we're going shopping. Though I don't know where she's got to; she was supposed to be here half an hour ago."

"Oh go on, Lizzie," she wheedled. "Come with us; Tim's coming too, it'll be nice, it's such a lovely afternoon."

I muttered something about three being a crowd and tried to sidle off, but Laura wasn't letting me go that easily. "Emma's probably forgotten – you know what she's like," she said. "Oh, do come – Simon's coming too," she announced triumphantly. I was almost tempted but Laura had a strange gleam in her eye. I didn't like being set up.

"Sorry," I said quickly, "I've got tons to do." And I dashed off round the corner, straight into Emma.

"Hello," she said, beaming. "Where's Laura?"

"I don't know. Somewhere around, I s'pose." I was vaguely

irritated that Emma assumed Laura would be with me. "Why are you so late? I thought you'd forgotten."

"I couldn't find my purse," Emma told me, going into our classroom and opening her locker. "I've been looking everywhere for it – ah, here it is! Honestly, I'll leave my brain behind one of these days." I privately thought she already had, but it seemed unkind to say so.

"I'm fed up with looking scruffy," Emma went on. "I want to buy some new clothes, only I haven't got a clue what looks nice on me. Will you help me? You always look so nice."

I was flattered. Who wouldn't be? So we walked down Oxford Street in the bright May sunshine; Emma bought a new pink blouse, and we had a coke in a café in Regent Street. I suddenly felt very fond of her; she seemed so uncomplicated compared to Laura, and I was glad I had waited for her and not gone with the others.

I told her about the food in France, and Dominique and Simon.

"Teddie got lost, didn't she?" Emma said, sucking her coke up through the red and white straw. "She told me you went and found her. She thinks you're cool – her word, not mine."

I preened. "Does she? She's a laugh, your sister. She called Dominique Domi-knickers."

"Do you fancy Simon?" Emma asked me suddenly. I was so unprepared for the directness of Emma's question that I just sat there, like a lemon. But Emma went on. "You do, don't you. I can tell. I used to, as well. Fancy Simon I mean."

If Emma's question had surprised me, this piece of information flabbergasted me. Not Emma! Not scruffy, plain Emma, who everybody knew wasn't interested in boys!

"I know what you're thinking!" said Emma fiercely, reading my expression. "Emma Nash doesn't like *boys*. Well, I do, or at least, I did. Just because I'm not pretty doesn't mean I don't have *feelings* like everybody else." She banged her glass down on the table with a thump.

"I wasn't thinking that," I lied quickly. "I mean. I'm not exactly God's gift to the male species, am I?" I didn't want to hurt Emma's feelings by admitting that was exactly what I *was* thinking. Emma made a noise in her throat that could have meant anything. "I was just wondering," I went on, hoping she hadn't taken offence, "how you know Simon so well, when he only started at Percy's in January, like me."

"Through Laura," Emma explained. "They've known each other for years. He used to come to all Percy's concerts, and I saw him at Laura's house quite a bit, in the holidays. I've been to his house, too. I could tell you liked him; you look at him in exactly the same way I used to, and you're always talking about him."

"Yes, I do like him," I said defensively. "I think he's the best looking boy I've ever seen in my life. And he's such a good musician. And he's got a lovely smile."

I was half-expecting Emma to try and put me off him, like she had done with Laura. But she didn't. She sighed deeply, and looked up at me. Her brown eyes were very sad behind her glasses.

"I know," she said. "I know all that. People like Laura just don't know what it's like for people like us to fancy boys, do they?"

It wasn't until much later that I started to wonder how Emma had got to know Simon through Laura if, as Laura maintained, they had never been particularly close friends. Surely Emma wouldn't have seen that much of him – and surely she wouldn't have gone to Laura's house in the holidays if she hadn't known her that well? I was mystified; something, somewhere, didn't add up. I had a sneaking suspicion I knew who was telling the truth. And I didn't think it was Laura.

9

Marmite

I was beginning to feel very torn between my two friends. On the one hand, there was Laura. Pretty, sparky, streetwise Laura, who had done so much to help me when I had started at Percy's. Laura, with all her friends (particularly Simon . . .) and the larger-than-life personality.

And then there was Emma. I had thought Laura and I would become even closer friends when I started to board, but that didn't seem to be the case. Instead, it was Emma whose company I was seeking more. She was nothing like as *noticeable* – that's the only word – as Laura. She was quiet and scruffy and, well, mouse-like, I suppose. She would also get cross, quite often, at things people said. But after a while I began to realize what it was about Emma I liked. You knew where you were with her; she would tell you what was on her mind. She didn't like Laura – for that mysterious reason neither of them would tell me – and she was openly uneasy about me being friends with her, and Simon. But she also told me she wasn't trying to put me off them, and I believed her.

Laura, on the other hand, pretended she liked Emma; she was always really chatty to her. But I could tell it was an artificial friendliness. And, just lately, she always seemed to be telling me how dim Emma was, and how wet, and how no boy would ever fancy her, and how she didn't like us, Laura and me, being friends. In truth, it struck me as being the other way around; that Laura didn't like seeing Emma and me together. Why the three of us couldn't all be friends together was beyond me, but Emma and Laura clearly found the idea impossible.

Perhaps it sounds as if I was going off Laura. Well, I wasn't; she was great fun. Whoever I was with at the time was the one I liked the best. It was only when I was with both of them, or on my own, that I felt confused. And I couldn't really tell anyone how torn I felt; I wasn't living at home any more, with Daddy or Wendy to confide in, and I couldn't very well write it in my diary because I kept showing it to Laura. All in all, what with my feelings for Laura and Emma and, just to confuse things further, Simon, I was finding life and things pretty baffling.

However, I was still enjoying life at Percy's, despite my conflicting loyalties for my friends, I was studying a concerto by Mozart with Mr Owen, my violin teacher; he's a big fan of Mozart, he has a sticker on his violin case with 'I heart Wolfgang' (not the word heart, but a picture of a big red heart.)

One day in my lesson, Mr Owen took the music off my stand. "Try that movement from memory," he said. "Good practice."

I stared at him. "All of it? Without the music?"

"That's usually what 'from memory' means." Mr. Owen sat himself down at the piano, and smiled at me. "Just see how far you can get, love. And don't look so worried; that's certain death for the memory cells."

He started to play the introduction, the bit the orchestra would play if I had been playing with one, and to my great surprise I managed to remember the whole of the movement with only one odd moment, when I came in too early. But a couple of bars later I found my way in again.

"Wow!" I said afterwards, enormously impressed with myself. "That was brill! I've never been able to remember anything as long as that before."

Mr Owen came over to me. "Not bad," he said. "But you forgot all about your posture. You were throwing yourself all over the place – proper little *prima donna*, you looked."

"But moving around helps me feel the music," I protested. "Besides, all the big musical names do it."

"Feel the music by all means," said Mr Owen, mildly. "And when you're a big musical name you can do what you like. But for the moment, it's unnecessary. Don't sulk," he told me, as I put my violin away huffily. I had really enjoyed playing the Mozart, and Mr Owen had spoiled it for me by criticizing my moving around. Even though part of me, a little niggly part, knew he was right – it *had* been unnecessary.

"Good piece, isn't it?" Mr Owen went on, seemingly oblivious to having ruined my self-image for ever. Well, for a week or two, at any rate. "Mr Bishop's put that concerto on the programme for the QEH concert in July; it's one of my favourites."

Mr Bishop is the Musical Director of Percy's, otherwise known as God. It was only quite a bit later that I began to think about what Mr Owen had said. The *work* had been put on the programme, he had said, but he hadn't said anything about who was to play it. I remembered what Laura had said about the soloist not being chosen until just before the concert. I wonder, I thought; I wonder if there's any chance at all, just the teeniest weeniest of possibilities, that *I* might do it? The thought took my breath away. To play a solo, a proper concerto with a proper orchestra at a proper London concert! That would be mega-whizz.

The string quartet, with Emma reinstated, were rehearsing hard for another lunchtime Workshop. At our first rehearsal back in England, we wasted the whole time arguing about a name for ourselves. Simon wanted to call us the Alexander Quartet – "After all, it was my idea to start one" – but Naresh groaned.

"String quartets aren't supposed to be ego-trips," he said. "Besides, if they're called after anybody, it's usually the first violinist."

So we toyed with the idea of the Nash Quartet for a while, but Emma said she didn't want her name used in case anybody thought *she* was on an ego-trip, as Naresh had put it.

Then we tried making up words with our initials, but the best we could come up with was the Lens Quartet, which Naresh said sounded like two pairs of glasses, or the Snel Quartet, which was even worse. After that we all sat down with pencils and pieces of paper, and tried to make anagrams from the initials of our first *and* second names. It was a good game, but didn't produce anything except laughter. Naresh's best effort was Noelsang, which reminded me of a Christmas carol, and Simon was very pleased with his offering of El Sango until we told him it sounded like a Latin American dance.

"I'm not very good at anagrams," Emma told us. "But I did get Gelsano, Elnogsa, Snog Ale and Sona Leg." I snorted with laughter.

"Brilliant Mouse," said Simon sarcastically. "I can just hear it now: 'Welcome to the Central London School of Music, and here tonight to play for us at great expense we have THE SNOG ALE QUARTET!'"

We all collapsed into a hysterical heap, all apart from Emma who sat stoically looking at her piece of paper.

"I told you I wasn't any good at anagrams," she told us again. When we stopped laughing I told them mine – Glenosan.

"*Glen*osan?" queried Simon, starting to laugh again. "Sounds like Japanese whisky."

"Or medicine for fortifying the over-forties," said Naresh, which set us all off again.

"This is all very well," said Emma eventually, "but we still don't have a name."

"Oh bum," Naresh said. "Let's just call ourselves Opus Four, as there's four of us and we play opuses. Or is it opi?"

Nobody could tell him, but Opus Four we became. We were rehearsing a Beethoven quartet for the Workshop, and it was going quite well. We were all getting on well, too; Simon seemed to have forgotten all about Dominique, and he and Emma were actually being nice to each other for a change. The times we met to practice were the highlights of my week, which is why I couldn't understand how the others misjudged me so badly over what happened a couple of weeks into the term.

One afternoon we had arranged to practice at six o'clock (instead of our usual time of five) because Naresh had to see a teacher. As luck would have it I had an appointment at the dentist that afternoon, and I was rushing down the corridor, pushed for time as usual, when Emma came out of one of the practice rooms and I nearly cannoned into her.

"Whoops!" she said, stepping back. "Where are you off to?" I told her, and she pulled a sympathetic face. "Poor you. See you at Quartet, OK?"

"OK." I caught sight of the clock on the wall. "Help! I must dash, I'm supposed to be at the Torture Chamber at four! See you," I said, rushing off and flapping a farewell hand at her.

I had to have a filling, and as I didn't have to rush back to Percy's I bought myself a bar of chocolate to reward myself, and ate it strolling along Marylebone Road in the warm May sunshine. I stood outside the Royal Academy of Music and imagined myself going there. Then I caught the Tube to

Charing Cross and crossed the road to Trafalgar Square, where I bought a little bag of grain and fed the pigeons, like a tourist. To think I didn't want to live in London, I thought; I must have been mad. Cornwall is beautiful and wild and home, and I'm so looking forward to living there in the holidays again, but London is beautiful too, only in a different way. Beautiful and busy and exciting. I was very happy.

But it didn't last very long.

I got back to Percy's at ten to six, and by the time I'd told the duty teacher I was back and collected my violin, it was two minutes to. As I opened the door of our usual practice room, I could hear them playing, but it sounded different. The meanies, I thought: they've started without me. Then I walked into the room, and saw at once why it had sounded different. Emma was sitting in my place, and there on Emma's usual chair, the one on the end, sat Laura with her oboe. They stopped playing when they saw me.

"Well, well," Simon drawled. "How nice of you to turn up."

I looked at my watch. "It's only just six o'clock," I said.

"We've been here since five," Naresh said, but less sarcastically than Simon. "What on earth kept you? Have you had all your teeth out or something?"

I looked at each of them, perplexed. "But we weren't meeting until six today."

Simon tutted. "Lizzie, we've been playing since March, and we've always started at five. We got so fed up waiting for you I went and found Laura."

"But we changed it; don't you remember? Naresh had to see Miss Quentin, so we changed it to six o'clock."

Simon pulled a disbelieving face. "First I've heard of it."

I appealed to Naresh, "But you did change it. You told me we were meeting at six. Don't you remember?"

Naresh nodded. "That's right; but Miss Quentin managed to see me at break this afternoon, so we changed the time back to five, didn't we? That's why you didn't know, Si - there was no point, as we ended up back at the original time.

"But nobody told me!" I wailed. "*I* didn't know!"

Naresh looked perplexed. "I can't understand it," he said. "I was sure somebody had given you the message . . . " He trailed off and looked at Emma, who had gone bright red. "Emma!" he said, accusingly, "I might have known!"

Emma put her fist up to her mouth, overcome with remorse. "I'm ever so sorry," she said to me. "It's just - well - it totally slipped my mind. I was supposed to tell you, I remember now, only when I bumped into you in the corridor earlier, you were in such a hurry I forgot all about it."

"Well, why didn't you say you hadn't told Lizzie when we were whingeing about her being late?" Naresh demanded. Simon didn't say anything. He just looked like thunder.

"I didn't really think about it," Emma confessed. "I just sort of assumed she was late because of the dentist. Or something," she finished, lamely.

Emma's hopeless memory was justly famous. Even so, at that moment I could cheerfully have throttled her.

"Oh well," I said ungraciously. "If you lot have been moaning about me being late when it wasn't my fault, it looks like you owe me an apology, doesn't it?"

Simon puffed up like a pigeon in spring. "An apology?" he exclaimed. "You have to be joking! OK, it wasn't your fault this time, but how were we supposed to know that?"

I wondered what he meant by 'this time', but Emma spoke before I had chance to ask him.

"Oh don't, Simon," she said, uncomfortable. "It wasn't Lizzie's fault - it was mine. And I've said I'm sorry and everything. Can't we just forget it now? Naresh and I are supposed to be practising some duets for the Workshop, and we're ten minutes late already."

Simon looked furious. "We all know you'd forget your head

if it wasn't screwed on, Mouse," he said viciously to Emma, who went even pinker.

"Look," I said to the room in general. I was cross with Emma, but not as cross as Simon seemed to be. "There's no need to be nasty. Emma just forgot to tell me – it was just a misunderstanding, that's all. When shall we meet again?"

Simon and Laura exchanged glances. Then Simon sighed, and smiled at me. It wasn't a very nice smile though.

"Look," he said. "Is there really any point? I mean, it's not the first time you've been late. And when you do turn up on time, all you do is muck about."

I was stunned. "That's not true!" I burst out. "I've only ever been late once before, and that was because Mr Owen nobbled me about my scales!"

"You were late last week too," Laura put in.

I'd forgotten about that – I'd left my music up in the dorm, and couldn't find it when I went to fetch it. Laura had been up there, and had helped me look for it.

I glared at her. "Whose side are you on, anyway?"

Laura sniffed. "Sorry, I didn't realize it was a war."

I felt myself getting hot. "Anyway, I don't muck around. That's not fair."

"Oh, come on!" Simon said. "When we were trying to choose a name you were falling about."

"But we all were," I protested. "Remember the Snog Ale Quartet?"

"That's true," said Naresh. "We all thought that was pretty funny, Si. Look, I don't want to break up the happy party, but Emma and I are supposed to be rehearsing something else."

Simon shrugged. "All I know is, whenever there's hysterical laughter when we're supposed to be practising, it's usually Lizzie."

I felt really got at. "I don't think you're being fair," I muttered. If I did make jokes, it was only because I wanted to impress Simon with my rapier-like wit. But I could hardly tell him that. In fact, I didn't feel able to defend myself at all – I thought they were my friends, and you don't usually have to defend yourself against your friends.

Simon held his hands out, palms upwards. "Look," he said, in a reasonable way. "I think it's pretty obvious to everyone that this quartet isn't working."

I was even more amazed. "Well, I think it is," I protested. "I thought we were doing really well."

"Well we disagree," Simon went on. "In fact, we were discussing it before you arrived. And we all agree it's because you don't really take it seriously enough."

I stared at him. "You mean – you were talking about me? Behind my back? Charming. Even criminals have the right to defend themselves."

Simon smiled again. That smile really annoyed me, somehow. "Look Lizzie, don't get upset. It's not that we don't think you're any good, or anything. You're a good violinist, we all know that."

"Well, gee, thanks," I muttered sarcastically.

"It's just that – well – we don't think playing in a chamber group is the right thing for you, that's all."

I could feel myself going red to the roots of my hair, and tears were prickling in my nose and behind my eyes. "So now I know," I said, swallowing.

Emma had been hopping from foot to foot throughout all this, looking wretched. "Hang on a tick," she said, unhappily. "That's not fair, Simon. *We* never said that – *you* did."

"It doesn't really matter who said it, does it?" I said, in a loud voice; it had to be loud, or I knew I would cry. "I think I get the picture. You don't want me in your poxy quartet. Well that suits me – it suits me fine. It never sounded any good, anyway – Simon plays too loudly!" I finished, defiantly.

"Look," Naresh said quietly. "I don't think all this arguing is getting us anywhere. Why don't we just leave it for now, and see how things go when we meet again?" Emma and I looked at each other and nodded, and after a while Simon gave a bad-tempered shrug that could have meant anything. "Right," Naresh said firmly. "Now come on, Emma, or we won't have any time left." And they both left the practice room, but not before Emma threw me one last pathetically apologetic look. I felt horribly got-at, and Emma's obvious distress at having caused all the fuss just irritated me. I picked up my violin and flung out after them.

Laura had sat through all this drama without saying a word, apart from her comment about my lateness, and that upset me as much as anything. She might have stood up for me, I thought – she knows how much I like Simon, and how much I enjoy the quartet. It's not fair; it's just not fair! How could they be so nasty to me?

I went up to my dorm, even though it was almost supper time, and sat on the edge of my bed. I felt angry and upset and frustrated, and cross for not having stood up for myself more. How dare Simon say playing in a quartet wasn't right for me? How did *he* know what was right for me? But through all this anger came a clear thought; if the quartet breaks up, I shall hardly see anything of Simon. The fact was, I still liked him terribly, despite what he had said to me earlier.

I picked up a book from my locker and turned the pages idly. A piece of card fluttered to the floor, and I picked it up; it was a photograph, of Rufus and Fishpaste sitting together on the floor and looking up at the camera. They looked really sweet. In actual fact they were watching Wendy who had been cutting up some cold chicken, only you couldn't see her in the photo – that's the only time they sit quietly together, when they are united in their common bond of pigginess, but it was still a very sweet photograph.

As I looked at the photo, the tears welled up in my eyes

again. I really missed the animals. If I had been at home I would have taken Rufus for a long walk over Barnes Common. That would make me feel better. But I couldn't.

"Oh Rufus," I whispered. A tear rolled down my cheek. "Oh Fishie. Oh Simon," and I lay down on the bed and put my head down on my arms and had a good howl.

I felt a bit better after that. Not a lot better, but just a bit. I dried my eyes and had a sniff, then I went over to the washbasin in the corner of the dorm and washed my face in cold water. It was very quiet. The sun filtered in through the open window, and a gentle breeze played with the red gingham curtains that hung there. A blackbird chattered somewhere outside, and in the distance I could hear the rumble of the traffic on Tottenham Court Road.

Then I heard somebody coming up the stairs. Oh crumbs, I thought, I hope it's not Matron. She'll do her pieces – I'm not supposed to be up here at this time of day.

But it wasn't. It was Laura. She came into the dorm with an anxious look on her face and something wrapped in a paper napkin in her hand.

"Are you OK?" she asked. "I told them downstairs you had a headache and were having a lie-down, Matron's coming up to see you in a minute. Look, I've brought you some supper."

She handed me the napkin – it was a Cornish pastie, still warm. I wolfed it down. It had been a long time since that bar of chocolate outside the Academy.

When Matron came up she felt my forehead and gave me some tablets and a glass of lukewarm water to take them with.

"Go outside and get some fresh air," she told me. "That's the best medicine for you, I don't think you're dying, not this week."

So Laura and I went downstairs, and walked round by the back of the kitchens.

"Are you really all right?" Laura asked me. "I felt really sorry for you. I would have burst into tears, I know I would."

It crossed my mind to ask her why, if she had felt so sorry for me, she hadn't stuck up for me. But I didn't. I just told her I was fine.

"I told Simon he'd been a pig, after you'd gone," Laura said. "I said he shouldn't have gone on at you like that – anyone could see it was Mouse's fault, not yours."

I brightened. "Did you? What did he say."

"I think he felt quite guilty. He said he didn't mean to upset you – I was laying it on really thick, you see. I knew how upset you'd be if you couldn't see him any more."

"So what did he say?" I persisted. "Does he want to carry on with the quartet, or what?"

"I don't really know. But he does like you, you know, as a friend. He says you're ... " Laura stopped, and looked towards the kitchens. "What was that noise?"

I hadn't heard anything. I was dying to find out what Simon thought I was. "He says I'm what?" I prompted her.

But Laura was walking towards the bins. "There it is again – listen!"

I listened, and sure enough I could hear something. It sounded like a seagull, or a baby crying. Or, on second thoughts, a cat. We both poked around the bins, and just when I thought we'd both been imagining it, a small scrawny black kitten came bouncing out from inside a cardboard box. It was carrying its tail very high, and seemed extremely pleased to see us. It miaowed at me.

"Look, Laura!" I exclaimed. "It's a kitten!" I picked it up; it nuzzled into my neck, purring steadily and kneading my jersey with small sharp claws.

Laura started to stroke it, and it purred even louder. "Oh, isn't he sweet! I expect he's a stray – poor little thing, he must be starving. There must be something here ... " She took the lid off one of the dustbins and peered inside, gingerly. "Aha – I thought so!" She put her hand in, and took out a Cornish pastie with a single bite taken out of it, and two half-eaten sausages from breakfast.

I shuddered. "You can't give him that! It's all smelly from the bin."

"So what," said Laura. "I expect you'd eat it, too, if you were starving." As she laid out the feast on the ground the kitten, smelling it, let out a piteous miaow and struggled from my arms. Laura and I watched him tucking into it like fond parents.

"Why don't we adopt him?" Laura said to me. "We can go and buy cat food and a bowl and stuff, and sneak out every day to feed him."

I liked the idea tremendously. "Yes!" I beamed. "Let's! I know pets aren't allowed, but he found us, after all. What shall we call him?"

"Blackie," said Laura decisively.

I scoffed. "Wow, that's original."

"Well, you think of something, then." Laura was put out.

I considered. "Let me see – my other cat is called Fishpaste, and this one's black, so how about – Marmite?"

"Marmite?" It was Laura's turn to scoff.

"Yes," I said firmly. "I like it. Marmite. Now come on, we'd better be going back in, or they'll be sending out a search party for us."

But we'd reckoned without the cat species' ability to fall madly in love with anyone who feeds them. As we walked back to the main building, Marmite trotted along behind us, wailing.

"Come on," I said. "Run. Or he'll follow us in and give the game away."

But Laura stopped. "Oh, we can't!" she said, soppily. "Poor little sweetheart! He wants to come in with us – we can't leave him outside all night. It might snow."

"Laura," I said patiently. "It's the middle of May. I somehow don't think snow is very likely. He's got a full tummy, he'll be all right."

But Laura insisted, so we smuggled him up to the dorm. We swore the other three girls to secrecy and found two cardboard boxes; Laura snuck outside again and filled one with earth, for Marmite's necessaries, and we put a sweater in the other one. After being cuddled by each of us in turn, Marmite, to my surprise, climbed into his makeshift bed and fell fast asleep.

We pushed the boxes under one of the bunks when Mrs Nightingale came round to say goodnight, and prayed he wouldn't wake up, or miaow. He didn't. I was quite excited when I went to sleep. It was really nice to have a cat to look after, even though it was strictly against school rules.

10

The Pact of Silence

Laura wasn't so keen on having Marmite in the dorm at five o'clock the next morning. He woke up and had a prowl around, and then decided the curtains looked unfriendly, so he attacked them. That woke us all up; Laura was cross, and she was even crosser when she discovered the present Marmite had left by her bed. He had obviously decided the box full of earth really wasn't good enough for him.

"Why should *I* have to clear it up?" she moaned; in a whisper, so Mrs Nightingale wouldn't hear.

"Well I'm not going to," said Sophie, who had the bunk above Laura.

"You wanted him up here," I told Laura. "I knew it wasn't a very good idea."

In the end I had to put my coat over my nightie and smuggle Marmite back out to the dustbins, and run like mad so he wouldn't follow me in again.

"Pooh," I said when I got back indoors, wrinkling my nose. "It stinks in here."

So we had to open both windows wide to let the smell out, which made everyone so cold that none of us could get back to sleep.

"I think you're right," Laura said to me at break, yawning. We were walking around the playground with Emma. "It wasn't a good idea having him in the dorm last night. He'll have to stay outside in future."

Emma's eyes opened wide. "You mean – you had a *boy* in your dorm?"

"Don't be dim," I told her. I was still cross with her about the mix-up with the quartet. "Of course we didn't. It was a kitten."

"A *kitten*?" said Emma.

Laura sighed. "Yes," she said, in the sort of voice you would use to explain something to the village idiot. "A kitten. KITTEN. It's a sort of mini-cat – you know, small, furry, a leg in each corner."

"I know what a kitten is," Emma said, irritated. "I'm not that thick. I just wondered what you were doing with a kitten up in your dorm, that's all."

Laura and I looked at each other. "Well, you've already given the game away," I said to Laura. "We may as well tell her the rest."

So we did. Of course, that meant Emma wanted to see Marmite, so we all went round to the back of the kitchens to try and find him. When we got near the dustbins I could see somebody else there; it wasn't one of the kitchen staff, it was a boy, and he was holding Marmite.

"It's Simon!" I said. "What's he doing here?"

"I told him about Marmite this morning," Laura explained. "I didn't think he'd come looking for him, though. Hey, Simon." she yelled. "What're you doing?"

Simon turned round, and smiled when he saw us. He put Marmite down on the ground, and the kitten immediately ran towards us, miaowing, tail in the air.

"Hi," Simon said. "I think he's hungry. Isn't he cute?"

We dug around in the bins and found some kippers from

breakfast, which Marmite scoffed as if he hadn't seen food for months. Laura went into the kitchens, and came out again with a saucer of milk. Marmite made short work of that, too.

"How did you get that?" Emma asked her.

"My natural charm," said Laura, modestly.

Simon scoffed. "It's one of the chefs," he told us. "He fancies her."

Laura went red, and hit him in the chest. "No he doesn't. He's at least sixty."

"I thought you liked older men," I said. They all laughed.

Marmite had finished his breakfast and was playing with a leaf on the ground. He patted it and bit it, and then lay down and kicked it with his hind legs. A sudden breeze stirred up some more leaves and Marmite, startled and excited, scudded round the corner after them. I went after him, concerned that somebody might see him, and I picked him up and cuddled him to me. His purr started, like a motor being switched on. Simon came round the corner. "There you are," he said. "The bell's gone – the others have gone in." He stroked Marmite. "I think he likes you. Listen to him purring!"

I felt uncomfortable. I thought I had got over feeling like that whenever Simon spoke to me, but after the business with the quartet I didn't quite know how to act.

I put Marmite down. "I'd better go in." I said, not looking at Simon. "Mr Hadleigh goes mad if you're late for History."

"Just a sec," Simon said. He held my arm above the elbow and looked earnestly at me. "Laura said you were upset yesterday about, you know, what I said."

I looked at him. His eyes looked into mine, blue as blue, and I just couldn't seem to think of anything to say.

"I'm sorry," he said. "I didn't mean to upset you. Would you like to come out with me after school one afternoon? We could go and have a coffee, or something."

I couldn't believe he'd actually said it. I was rooted to the spot. My stomach and my throat both seemed to be in the same place, and my voice had disappeared. I stared at Simon; I could count every one of his eyelashes.

"Um," I said eventually. I cleared my throat. "Well. I'm a bit busy at the moment. Thanks anyway." And I turned and scurried off.

Afterwards, I wondered what on earth had made me say that. I had wanted Simon to ask me out for absolutely ages, and when he finally did ask me I turned him down. What's the matter with you, I asked myself furiously. You'll never get any boyfriend at that rate, let alone Simon. As usual, I tried to ignore what my little inner voice was telling me. You turned him down, the voice told me, because you don't want to go out with him. Not really. And the reason you don't want to go out with him is because he's not a very nice person. Yes he is, I told the voice hotly. He is a nice person. He is! All right, the voice said calmly. All right. But just tell me this, if he's such a nice person, why was he so horrible to you yesterday? You don't usually let people blow hot and cold with you. So why do you let him? You don't need boyfriends like that. For once, I realized the voice was right. But it gave me no comfort.

That evening, I telephoned home. I spoke to Daddy first, and told him all about Marmite – in a half-whisper, so nobody in the corridor by the telephone would overhear.

"Honestly Daddy, he's so sweet," I whispered. "Laura went out this afternoon and bought some Whiskas and a bowl, and he scoffed the lot. Not the bowl, just the food."

"He what?" Daddy queried. "Are you all right, sweetie? It sounds like you've got a sore throat. I should go and gargle if I were you."

"No," I said hoarsely. "I'm OK. I'm just telling you about Marmite."

"About your what?"

"Marmite – Marmite!" I gave up, and spoke properly. "Never mind, Daddy. When is it you're off to Penwithin, exactly? I keep forgetting."

"Ah, that's better!" Daddy exclaimed. "The line's just cleared. I can hear you now. We're moving this weekend, sweetie – it's been like a madhouse here this week, tea-chests everywhere, Wendy's been marvellous, what with coping with Flora and everything. Will we be able to see you before we go?"

I sighed. "I don't think so, Daddy. Sorry. I've got tons to do this week, and I'm going to Laura's on Friday evening – we've got weekend leave, and her mum and dad have invited me to some party they're having."

"Well have a lovely time, won't you?" Daddy said. His familiar voice sounded warm and loving; and for a moment I felt sad that they were going back to Cornwall, so far away, despite the fact that I loved being at Percy's so much. "Have a word with Wendy before you ring off." Wendy came on the line. Her voice, too, sounded its usual friendly self, and I suddenly ached to confide in somebody older and sympathetic about Simon.

"Wendy?" I said in a rush, mid-discussion about the arrangements for Rufus and Fishpaste during the move. "When you were at school, was there anybody you liked who wasn't very nice to you, but you still liked them and couldn't help it? A boy, I mean."

Wendy was quiet for a moment. "Yes," she said slowly, just as I thought she wasn't going to answer. "Yes, there was, Sebastian, his name was – Sebastian House. Gosh. I'd forgotten all about him."

"What was he like?" I pressed her. "Was he nice?"

"Oh, he was beautiful." Her voice went all soft and dreamy. "He had masses of auburn hair – not red, or ginger, but all shiny like a conker. And green eyes with goldy flecks, like a lion or something. And he was about six feet tall. He was the captain of the school's first eleven, and the summer I fell madly in love with him I had this thing about cricket, too. It was a really hot summer, I remember, and I would go home with my legs all red and rashy from sitting on the grass all afternoon, and dream about marrying him and knitting wonderful cricket sweaters for him."

I was fascinated. "Go on," I urged. "Tell me some more."

"Well," Wendy said. "He always had heaps of girlfriends. He was so good-looking, and the girls used to hang around him so much he just took his pick. Bees round a honey-pot - you know the sort I mean?"

"Yes." I said with a sigh, thinking about Simon. "Yes, I do. Did he ever ask you out?"

Wendy laughed shortly. "Not me. I wasn't in his league - far too unglamorous. But he did go out with a friend of mine, and I was so envious of her I couldn't speak to her for days. I was just eaten up with jealousy, it was awful."

"It's horrid, isn't it?" I said in a small voice. "Why does being in love have to be so ghastly?"

There was another silence, I felt close to tears. Then Wendy spoke again, and her voice down the wire was full of warmth and sympathy.

"I don't know, lovey," she said. "I really don't know. If you're sensitive, you have to suffer - it seems to be an unwritten rule. It makes you stronger and more loving in the long run, you know, but I know that's not much consolation when you're in the throes of unrequited love."

I was about to burst out that I wasn't in the throes of unrequited love, when something made me stop. The truth was, unrequited love was exactly what I *was* suffering from. Simon may have asked me out, but I couldn't kid myself that he felt the same for me as I did for him. I made a sort of agreeing noise down the phone instead.

"Anyway," Wendy went on. "Susy – my friend – only went out with him for a couple of weeks. She said he only had one topic of conversation – himself – and she couldn't stand it any longer. You see Lizzie people like that who are so good-looking they have people queuing up to go out with them, often have no personality to speak of. They're so used to relying on their looks to get girlfriends or boyfriends that they've never had to develop any sort of character."

I thought about it. "You mean, it's better to be plain and interesting than beautiful and boring?"

"Absolutely," Wendy agreed, chuckling. "I suppose it's best of all to be beautiful *and* interesting, but I guess you can't have everything in life. Anyway, Susy managed to put me off Sebastian for good; she pointed out that if I *did* marry him, my name would be Wendy House."

I laughed, and when I rang off I felt a bit more cheerful.

After supper, Laura and I were summoned to see Mrs Nightingale. She looked quite stern when she opened the door to the flat, and at first we couldn't think what we'd done. But she soon told us.

"It's come to my notice," she said, unsmiling, "that you two have been feeding a stray cat."

Laura's chin went up, "Yes, Mrs Nightingale," she said. "Is it against school rules?"

"Not in itself, I suppose, no," said our housemistress. "But having it up in your dorm is. And so is going round the back of the kitchens – you know jolly well that area is out of bounds. And so, now we come to mention it, is sneaking out of school to buy food." She looked sternly at Laura, and Laura went red.

"But what's going to happen to Marmite?" I said anxiously.

Mrs Nightingale looked at me, and her face softened. "Marmite? Oh, I see – the cat." A ghost of a smile hovered around her lips. "What a curious name. There's no need to worry. He'll go the to RSPCA, and they'll look after him."

"But that means we won't see him any more!" I felt like crying again. "He's so sweet. Oh, please don't give him to the RSPCA, miss – please don't!"

"I'm sorry, Lizzie," Mrs Nightingale looked sympathetic. "He is sweet, I agree. But living round by the dustbins is no life for a cat. Anyway, what would happen to him in the holidays? No, it's all arranged; someone's coming to collect him in the morning. And I don't want you two collecting any more illicit pets. Is that clear?"

We mumbled yes, and sidled out of the flat.

"Simon!" Laura burst out, when we got back to our dorm. "I bet it was him! I bet he split on us, the rotten so-and-so!"

"Do you think so?" I said, surprised. "Why should he do that?"

"Oh, I don't know – it's just the sort of thing he would do, that's all. He didn't find Marmite, we did, and he doesn't like being left out of things. Either that or he wants to get back at us for something. He really is the limit, sometimes."

I thought about how he'd asked me out, and how I'd turned him down, and wondered whether that could be the reason he'd sneaked on us. But why should it, I asked myself. Surely he didn't want to go out with me that much? I wanted to ask Laura what she thought, but somehow didn't want her to know the ins and outs.

When the other three girls came into the dorm Laura told them about Marmite's discovery and banishment. It was obvious from their reaction that none of them had let the cat out of the bag, so to speak – they were all quite upset.

"But who told Mrs Nightingale?" Sophie asked. "It was a bit mean, wasn't it?"

"Simon flipping Alexander, that's who." said Laura, grimly. "Honestly, I'm really getting fed-up with him. He used to be good fun when we were younger, but just now he seems to think he's God's gift to the female race. Remember how he ignored us in France, Lizzie, because of that tarty Dominique? I don't know what you see in him."

I went red, and muttered at Laura to shut up, but it was too late. The others looked at me with interest.

"Do you fancy him then, Lizzie?" Sophie asked me.

I went even redder. Even my redness blushed. "Yes, I do," I said defiantly, "So what? So does half Percy's. Well, half the girls, at any rate."

"I do, too," Sophie confessed. "Terrible, isn't it? You feel such a wally, knowing he's never going to ask you out when people like Olivia Seddon and Bethan Williams hang around him."

"Olivia Seddon's going out with someone from the Academy," I said. Then I remembered what Wendy had said. "Anyway, people like him are usually really boring, once you get to know them. They're so used to people wanting to go out with them because of how they look, they've never had to develop any personality."

Laura looked interested. "Yes," she nodded. "I think you're right. Simon's dead boring, really."

Sophie giggled, "Well, I wouldn't mind just going out with him for his body, and never mind his boring mind!"

Even Laura looked vaguely shocked.

Laura and I went for a walk before bedtime. We kept away from the kitchens, but even so, we couldn't help thinking about Marmite.

"Poor Marmite," I sighed. "I do wish Daddy and Wendy could take him back to Penwithin with them. But I don't think Fishpaste would like having another cat." Then I had a brilliant idea. "Hey," I said, stopping in my tracks. "D'you think Emma might have him?"

Laura stopped, too. "She might," she said thoughtfully. "It's an idea, isn't it? At least he wouldn't have to go to the RSPCA.

And we might be able to go and visit him. Tell you what, let's go and ring her up and ask her, then if she says yes we can tell Mrs Nightingale to stop the RSPCA coming."

As we walked back across the playground the sun went in, and we both shivered.

"Come on," said Laura. "Let's hurry up. Oh, blast Simon. I could kill him."

She sounded so vehement it almost frightened me. But in an odd sort of way, I was pleased she was cross with Simon; I suppose I thought I would have more of her friendship if Simon was out of favour. And the three-sided relationship we had confused me; I was sure Simon only saw me as a friend of Laura's, not a person in my own right, and if he and she stopped being friendly he might look at me differently.

All these thoughts were going through my head as I spoke. Not that that excuses me saying what I did next.

"Can you keep a secret?" I said to Laura.

Her eyes lit up. "Yes," she said immediately, in that way people who can't keep secrets always do. "What secret?"

"Well," I said slowly. "I'm not sure I ought to tell you."

Laura tutted, exasperated. "Oh, come on," she pleaded. "You can't not tell me, not now you've got me curious."

"If I do, you must swear never to tell anybody I told you."

"All right – I swear! I swear on the Bible! I swear on my mother's life! Will that do? Now come on, tell me; don't be mean."

I took a deep breath. "Simon failed the audition, but Percy's took him anyway," I told her.

Laura looked puzzled. "What do you mean? Simon did his audition the same time as you. Of course he passed! He came round in the Christmas holidays to tell me."

"No he didn't," I said calmly. "He failed. I know he did."

"Who told you that?" Laura scoffed. "Not Simon, I'll bet."

I smiled coolly. "Of course not. It was Mr Barnaby." Mr

Barnaby is my piano teacher, and Simon's too. "He was mad at Simon this morning about something – I don't think he's a fan of Simon's. He teaches him the lesson before me, you see, and it's not the first time he's been cross with him and made remarks to me about him."

"And he told you that? I don't believe it!"

I shrugged. "It's up to you, I was a bit surprised, too, I must say; and I think Mr Barnaby realized he shouldn't have told me, afterwards, because he went all quiet and didn't even tell me off for not practising the Rachmaninov."

"But you can't get in to Percy's if you fail the audition." Laura clearly wasn't convinced.

"Maybe. I only know what Mr Barnaby said. Something to do with Simon's uncle, or someone."

Laura's eyes widened. "Great-uncle. His great-uncle was at school with God." She meant Mr Bishop. "Golly. Perhaps it is true, then. So what exactly did Mr Barnaby say?"

"Just that," I said. "He reckons Simon's not that good, you see; he said he wouldn't be at all surprised if Simon failed the audition, and only got in because of his great-uncle. Having Connections, he called it – saying something about the Old Boy Network, whatever that means. D'you think we ought to tell the Press?"

Laura laughed in a stunned sort of way. Then she frowned slightly. "But he didn't say he knew Simon had actually failed – just that he wouldn't be surprised if he had?"

I shrugged. "Same thing really, isn't it? I mean he wouldn't actually say he had failed – not actually come right out and say it. Teachers have to be really careful what they say, don't they? But I could tell he knew. It was the way he said it."

I could also tell I had convinced Laura; I felt rather ashamed of myself for having exaggerated Mr Barnaby's remark to impress Laura, but at the same time elated at being able to tell Laura something about Simon that she hadn't known. Even if it wasn't actually accurate. Oh yes, said The Voice – you're terribly clever, aren't you? You should be proud of yourself. Really proud . . . Shut up and go away, I told it, angrily.

"Golly," Laura said again. She still sounded stunned. "What a little ratbag he is. He didn't even get in the hard way, like the rest of us had to. People like him always get things easy – it really makes me spit. Well, I've just about had enough of him. I feel like never speaking to him again, what with Marmite and now this. How about you?"

"Me too," I said, totally untruthfully. "Let's ignore him. Let's make a Pact of Silence – we're not going to talk to him, and we're not going to tell him why. That'll show him."

"A Pact of Silence! – what a brill idea. That'll show him." Laura repeated, with relish.

Neither of us was sure quite what it would show him, but as it turned out it wasn't Simon who was shown anything. It was me.

11

The English Family

Emma was out when Laura and I rang, but we spoke to her mum instead. Mrs Nash listened with interest to the tale of Marmite, and assured us that of course they would have him.

"I'd take him myself," I told her over the phone, "only Daddy and Wendy are moving at the weekend and they're flapping around like mad, and I think having Marmite to look after would be the last straw."

Mrs Nash said she quite understood and she would be flapping about if she were moving at the weekend, and she would make sure Emma came to school the next day with a basket to transport Marmite home.

"Of course," said Laura to me after the phone call, "I'd have loved to have him, only my mum won't have pets in the house – I told you, didn't I?"

I thought about the two-thousand-pound furniture, and how Mrs English didn't want it spoilt by animal fur. "Never mind," I said. "I'm pleased Emma can have him, aren't you?" Laura nodded.

Even Mrs Nightingale was pleased, despite having seemed so cross with us for having adopted Marmite.

"Oh good," she said. "I'm so glad he's going to a good home."

Only Emma seemed a bit odd, and I asked her before lessons started whether she really wanted Marmite.

Emma nodded vigorously. "Of course I do!" she said. "He's cute. I'm glad you thought of asking me. Was Mrs Nightingale really cross – I mean, really, *really* cross?"

Laura shrugged. "We survived," she said. "Didn't we, Lizzie? No thanks to Simon, though."

"Simon?" said Emma, mystified. "What about him?"

"He sneaked on us. Laura and I aren't talking to him any more – we've made a Pact of Silence," I told her. I was suddenly tempted to tell her about Mr Barnaby's revelation, but decided not to. Having made Laura promise not to tell anyone, I somehow didn't think it would be a very good idea to tell Emma in front of her. Emma, however, seemed strangely uncomfortable.

"Look," she said. "Don't ignore Simon. I think Pacts of Silence are silly. Ignoring people you don't like is really immature."

Laura stared at her. "Oh my, aren't we grown-up?" she said, in a hoity-toity voice. "I thought you didn't like Simon, anyway. Not that it's any business of yours what Lizzie and I do," she added.

Emma flushed vividly, and turned on her heel and walked off without saying another word.

"I think you've upset her," I told Laura. I didn't like the thought, somehow.

"Oh, who cares," said Laura off-handedly. "She's always interfering in other people's business - honestly, she's so moral it gets on my nerves. She's like an unmarried old aunt." And Laura screwed up her face in a witchy way and staggered around, holding a hand to imaginary rheumatism in her back and muttering, "I am not amused, my girl, I am not amused!" I had to laugh at her, although I felt vaguely guilty as I did so.

That morning, I had had a letter from Ben. This is such an unusual occurrence, Ben being a notoriously bad letter-writer (I mean he never writes them, not that he writes bad ones), that I had immediately torn it open to make sure there was no bad news. All seemed well on skimming through the letter, and I shoved it into my pocket to read properly when I got a chance.

The morning was so busy I didn't get a chance until after lunch, when I suddenly remembered it. I took the letter, rather crumpled, from my pocket.

"Who's that from?" Laura asked casually.

"A friend of mine," I told her, and started to read.

My first thought was that Ben had gone mad. My second thought, a moment later, was wonder at how I'd managed to miss what the letter was all about when I'd skimmed through it earlier. And my third was that he'd accidentally sent it to the wrong person.

But no – *Dearest, darling Lizzie*, it started. That wasn't all. It continued by telling me how much he thought of me, and how much he missed me, and things like that, and it ended *With all my love for all time, your very own Ben XXXXXXXXXXXXX*. There were other bits, too, that I don't think I can repeat.

As I read it I could feel my eyebrows getting higher and higher, until they felt as if they'd disappeared off the top of my head. When I finished, I glanced up. Laura was looking at me curiously.

"Are you all right?" she said. "You've gone all red. You look most peculiar."

"Oh yes," I said hastily. "I'm fine. Honestly." I tried to shove the letter back into my pocket but it fell on the floor, and to my horror Laura picked it up.

"What's in this?" she said, laughing. "What on earth does it say?"

I tried to grab it, but Laura held it out of my reach.

"Give it back, Laura," I said crossly. "It's private."

"Who's it from?" There was a teasing note in her voice. "I bet it's from a boy. I bet it's a love-letter!"

My face flamed even more. "I told you, it's from a friend. Now give it back."

Rather to my surprise, Laura did just that.

"Sorry," she said meekly.

Now I had the letter safely back in my hand I was oddly tempted to show it to Laura. I was sure she would laugh it off; but, of course, she didn't know Ben. She didn't know that we had been friends since we were tiny, and that me getting a letter like that from him was on a par with the Queen writing to me to ask me to pop round to the Palace for a cup of tea and a chat.

I handed Laura the letter. "Here you are, then," I said. "Seeing as you're so interested."

She took it eagerly. "Dearest, darling Lizzie," she read aloud. "Golly!" As she read on, her eyebrows imitated mine, and a surprised expression appeared on her face.

She read another bit out. "'Please, please send me a photograph so I can see your beautiful, angelic face first thing in the morning and last thing at night, and have wonderful dreams of when we shall be together again.'" I waited for her to say something sarcastic about my beautiful, angelic face, but she didn't. Instead, when she finished, she handed the letter back to me with a sigh.

"Golly," she said again. "What a stunning letter. I thought you said it was just from a friend."

"It is," I said. "It's from Ben. You see, we've known each other for years – I think he's gone . . . "

"Well," Laura interrupted me. "You are a dark horse! You've never told me about him – is he from Cornwall, like you?"

"Yes, but he's at school in Devon. He must be . . . "

Laura interrupted me again. "He sounds really nice. Well well, fancy you having a secret boyfriend.!"

"He's not a secret boyfriend!" I protested. "We're - well - just good friends," I finished.

Laura clearly didn't believe me. "Oh yes, and we all know what that means!" she said.

I protested a bit more, but rather half-heartedly; it was beginning to dawn on me that, far from treating the whole thing as a joke, Laura was immensely impressed by Ben's letter. I had obviously gone up in her estimation by several degrees, and I decided it would do no harm to let her go on thinking that Ben really *was* my 'secret boyfriend', as she put it. After all, I never told her that, I said to myself. It's what she assumed. I still wonder what on earth possessed Ben to write to me like that, though.

15th May

Dear Diary,

Off to Laura's this afternoon, for her parents' party - it's their wedding anniversary, twenty years Laura says. Just imagine being married to the same person for twenty years! What mega-boredom. Though I suppose if you really love the person it wouldn't be too bad; I just can't imagine it, that's all.

Laura invited Emma, as well, which surprised me a bit. I didn't think they liked each other, though Laura said she invited her as a way of saying 'thank you' for having Marmite. Emma accepted, too - perhaps we can all start being friends, at last.

Simon and his parents are going, of course. Groan (the Pact of Silence rules, OK!) I've been feeling quite strange about Simon for a few days, ever since he asked me out, I suppose (if asking for a coffee amounts to asking me out, that is.) The word AMBIVALENT came up in English the other day, and I looked it up in the dictionary. This is what it means: 'Feeling

*love and hate towards the same object, at the same time.'
That seems to describe my feelings for S. perfectly (although
HATE is perhaps too strong a word); I still fancy him, ever so
much, but I'm not terribly sure that he's such a nice person
after all. Can I be going off him?*

*Daddy rang Percy's this morning to tell me the move back
to Penwithin last night went OK. Can't wait till next weekend
(half-term) when I see them, and Penwithin again! D.
reminded me I'd asked if Laura could come for half-term –
she's thrilled ('Oh whizz, I can meet your Ben!')*

*I'm leaving you behind tonight, Diary – I suddenly got fed-
up of Laura insisting on reading everything I wrote, so I told
her I don't keep one any more, I just hope she doesn't
discover I'm lying . . .*

Laura and I caught the train from Paddington to the town in
Oxfordshire, where she lives. The taxicab from the station
took us along by the river, it was green and leafy, and couples
were strolling along hand-in-hand by the banks of the duck-
thick river, the girls in bright cotton summer dresses and the
boys eating ice-cream, all happy underneath the Saturday sun.

Laura wiped her lipstick off in the taxi. "Mum goes round
the bend if she sees me in make-up in the daytime," she
explained. "She's dead old-fashioned."

I looked out of the window. "It's really nice here," I
remarked. "Pretty, with the river and everything."

Laura groaned. "Deadly dull, you mean. There's nothing to
do here – give me London any time. Why the parents have
stuck it so long I really can't imagine."

Presently we pulled up outside a semi-detached house in
an unremarkable street. There were dazzling white net
curtains hanging in every window, and the front garden had
regimented flower borders with absolutely no weeds. It was a
perfectly nice house, just very ordinary, and I was quite taken

by surprise; Laura was always going on about her wonderful house, and all the things she had, and to be truthful I felt rather disappointed. I had expected something a little more impressive. We had to ring the doorbell, too, which also surprised me – if there's someone at home the door's always left unlocked, and if not, I use the hidden key. The lady who opened the door looked exactly like Laura will look in thirty years' time if she spends most of the intervening years locked in a deep-freeze. When she spoke, her lips moved, but nothing else did, and instead of looking at us she looked over our heads somewhere.

"Hello darling," she said to Laura. "And you've brought your little chum, how super." And she kissed the air on either side of Laura's face.

I was fascinated by her – she looked as if she'd be cold to the touch, like those effigies of old knights in cathedrals. She shook my hand, formally – it wasn't cold, but floppy and limp somehow, like a lettuce past its sell-by-date.

"You must be . . . um . . ." she said, looking over my left shoulder. "How nice to meet you. Do go up to Lalla's pad, make yourself at home. Tea will be at five." And she drifted off down the hall.

Laura heaved a huge sigh. "Nothing changes," she said gloomily. "Come on, um, bring your things up."

I heaved my overnight bag up the stairs. "*Lalla*?" I queried. "Did she say Lalla?"

"Don't you dare start calling me that!" Laura said fiercely. "I loathe it – they know I do, but it doesn't make them stop it."

I felt quite sorry for Laura – this was obviously to be the extent of her homecoming, after not seeing her parents for nearly half a term. She showed me in to her bedroom; a dark room at the back of the house, with the walls covered from floor to ceiling with pictures of motor bikes and Page Three girls.

"Good grief," I said weakly. "What interesting wallpaper." Laura strode over to the wall by the bed and ripped off a double handful of machinery and naked flesh, and grimaced.

"Disgusting, isn't it?" she said. "This used to be Marcus' room, but I got it when he went to university. I keep meaning to do something about it, but as I'm hardly ever here there doesn't seem to be much point."

"I thought you said you'd re-decorated it yourself?" I said. "When you came to my house that weekend. You said . . . "

"No I didn't," Laura said shortly. She indicated a campbed with a sleeping bag on it underneath the window. "Here, I'm feeling generous. I'll sleep on that, you can have the bed."

At five o'clock we went downstairs for tea. The table was laid, polished cutlery on a snowy white cloth, and at each of the five set places there was a plate of ham salad – one paper-thin slice of ham, three lettuce leaves, a quartered tomato and five slices of cucumber. Five sideplates, each with one slice of bread and butter, cut diagonally in half, completed this feast.

Mr English came in from the garden, where he'd apparently been watering his herbaceous border.

"Hello, Lalla," he greeted his daughter. He ignored me. "Well, I hope. Oh good, ham salad." He was a little watery wisp of a man, with receding hair, a small clipped moustache and a small clipped voice. It was difficult to know who Laura had inherited her colour and sparkle from. Mrs English came into the dining-room with an enormous brown teapot.

Have you washed your hands, Daddy?" she enquired of her husband.

"Naturally, naturally." He showed her how clean they were.

"When's The Boy due home?" He said it exactly like that, with capital letters.

Mrs English looked at the clock on the sideboard, and shook her head disapprovingly. "British Rail," she said. "I could swear they do it on purpose, sometimes. I could swear they knew his tea would be ready for him at five. I could swear it."

I couldn't imagine her doing anything so common as swearing. "Is Marcus coming home for your party?" I asked politely. It was the first thing I had said to either of them, and my voice seemed to echo uncouthly around the room.

They stared at me.

"Mummy!" said Mr English suddenly, making me jump. "Tea for our guest! - lest she faint through lack of nourishment." And he picked up his knife and fork and tucked avidly into his salad.

Mrs English wielded the teapot, we all started to eat, and to my relief Laura started to talk to me about Cornwall and the new house. After the salad there were shop jam tarts and fruit cake, and we were just brushing the crumbs off our laps (or at least, I was), when the front door slammed.

"Angel baby!" Mrs English cried, and ran into the hall. She came back with her arm around the waist of an extremely hairy young man in denim. He looked as though he smelt, although he didn't. Not so far as I could tell, at any rate.

"Look!" his mother cried shrilly. She looked alive for the first time since I'd met her, "Look, Daddy! Look, Lalla! It's Marky."

Marcus groaned, and removed her arm. "Do let go of me, Mother. I've brought you my washing - go and busy yourself doing that. I'm starving." And he slumped down at the table and began cramming food into his mouth, rather like Marmite used to.

Laura made a noise of disgust. "Oh God. That's all I need. I'm off - come on, Lizzie," and she practically dragged me out of my chair.

"Good riddance to bad rubbish!" Marcus shouted after us. "Who's your fat friend?"

"Isn't he just ghastly?" Laura said when we got upstairs,

collapsing on the bed. I had to admit, he was pretty revolting. And Laura had said he was studying medicine; the thought of him being a future doctor made me glad I was hardly ever ill. All in all, Laura's family were turning out not a bit how I'd imagined them to be.

Emma arrived on the dot of eight, and was greeted by Laura's parents with exactly the same lack of interest I had been shown.

"Hello Mrs English, hello Mr English," she said politely. She went through into the sitting-room where I was sitting gingerly on the new sofa, afraid I was going to spill something.

"Hi, Lizzie," she greeted me warmly. "Oh golly, I'm really glad you're here so I don't have to face the Ice Maiden on my own, honestly isn't she awful, and Mr English too – the Odd Couple my mum and dad always call them." She was oblivious to the frantic faces I was pulling, trying to warn her that Laura's parents had followed her into the room and had overheard every word. "I haven't been here for yonks," Emma went on. "Laura's been going on about some whizz new furniture they're getting; I expect they'll be glad when it arrives and they can get rid of this awful stuff, don't you? Yuck, what an awful pattern." Emma fingered the fabric with distaste, and glanced up to see Mrs English looking thunderously at her.

"I suppose it's too much to expect of an ill-kempt little girl like you that you should recognize quality when you see it," Laura's mother said icily, and swept off to talk to a man who had just arrived in the hopes that he would recognize quality when he saw it.

Emma went red. "Oh golly," she stammered. "I'm terribly sorry – how awful – I didn't mean – I expect it's quite a nice pattern, really, when you get used to it ... " She trailed off, covered in embarrassment.

"I shouldn't worry," I told her mildly. "She can't hear you, anyway - she's pushed off to be rude to someone else. She hasn't said a word to me since I got here; I think she deserves being told her precious new furniture is rubbish." Emma visibly cheered up, and we went and helped ourselves to the rum punch which was supposed to be for the grown-ups only.

By nine o'clock, I was beginning to enjoy myself. Quite a few people had turned up, Mrs English had brought piles of food in, and Laura had managed to replace Barry Manilow on the record player with something a bit less turgid, without anyone noticing. Just shows how much grown-ups listen to music at parties. The three of us were drinking cider in a corner of the sitting-room, giggling and throwing bits of pizza into Marcus' hair – he was deep in a book, and studiously ignoring everybody – when I suddenly looked up, and there was Simon, with two people I took to be his parents.

He was wearing faded jeans, white squash shoes and a white jacket with the sleeves pushed up to his elbows, and he looked stunning. My mouth went dry at the sight of him; so much for going off him, I thought. He saw us, and made his way over towards us, smiling.

"The Pact of Silence!" I hissed. "Remember the Pact!" and we pushed our way through all the people to escape him. At least, Laura and I did. When we got out of the sitting-room, we realized Emma wasn't with us, Laura went to find her, and came back looking cross.

"The traitor!" she exploded. "She's sitting there talking away to him, looking all pleased with herself. Wait here – I'm going to bring her back this time." And she disappeared again.

After about twenty minutes, I began to wonder what had happened to her. I went into the dining-room and got another drink, and picked idly at some chicken. Then I peeped cautiously into the sitting-room – Laura wasn't there, but Emma was, sitting on her own. She saw me and came over.

"Hi!" she said. "I wondered where you'd gone. I've got to go soon – my dad's coming to pick me up at half past."

"Where's Laura?" I asked her. "She was supposed to be looking for you. She was cross at you for talking to Simon after the Pact."

Emma pulled a face. "I never made any Pact. I told you I

wasn't going to. And Laura isn't sticking to it, either – she's out in the garden with Simon."

I was astounded. "Well! After everything she said about him! She said she was never going to talk to him again, after he split on us about Marmite."

Emma went red, and shuffled her feet. "Well actually, I've been meaning to tell you, but I didn't dare tell Laura, because I knew what she'd say to me. It wasn't Simon who told about Marmite. It was me."

I goggled at her. "You! But why, Em? I thought you liked Marmite."

"I did – I do." Emma looked upset. "I didn't mean to, Lizzie, honestly. But I was talking to Mrs Nightingale about Deefer – Mum used to bring him when she used to fetch Teddie from school, when she was little – and it just sort of slipped out. About Marmite, I mean. And I couldn't think of how to cover it up."

I was still not sure whether to believe her. "But we thought it was Simon! We were sure it was – Laura said . . . "

"I know," Emma said, miserably. "I know you did. I didn't know how to tell you, especially after that horrible business with the quartet the other day. I was sure you'd think I was being nasty to you, and that I told Mrs Nightingale on purpose. But I didn't – honestly, Lizzie. It was an accident. Honestly."

I looked at her – Emma, my friend. "I believe you," I said softly. "And I didn't think you were being nasty. You're not like that."

Emma smiled, relieved. Dimly, above the chatter of the party, I heard the doorbell go.

"That'll be my dad," she said. "I must go. You're staying the night, aren't you? Have a nice weekend, what's left of it. And Lizzie – thanks. Laura wouldn't have understood like you did." And she went.

Golly, I thought. Old Emma – I never thought it was her. I

suppose I'd better go and find Laura, and tell her it wasn't Simon after all.

I went out into the garden, gingerly, as it was dark and I didn't know where I was going. I heard voices, and made my way towards them. As my eyes grew accustomed to the darkness I could just about see that the voices belonged to Laura and Simon. But as I got closer, what I heard them say stopped me from calling out to them.

". . . thought I was proposing to her, or something," Simon's voice said. "I only asked her for a coffee – I thought I'd better, I mean the silly bag looked so put out about it all."

"She never told me," Laura's voice replied, aggrieved. "I wonder why not? I'd have thought she'd have been full of it, the way she goes on about you all the time."

I realized with a chill they were talking about me. They say an eavesdropper never hears good of herself, but I couldn't help it. I crept closer and listened.

Simon laughed. "I know she fancies me, if that's what you mean; and who can blame her?"

They both laughed, and there was a muffled thud as Laura thumped him. "Bighead!" she said. "So you asked Lizzie Oliver out and she turned you down, eh? Well, well!" Tell him about my secret boyfriend, I begged her silently. Tell him about Ben's letter – go on! But she didn't.

"I didn't ask her out!" Simon protested. "I told you – I just asked her for a coffee."

"She's too scared to go out with *boys*," said Laura, with a nasty emphasis on the word. "She wouldn't know what to do. Anyway, she thinks you're boring and uninteresting."

"Flaming cheek!" Simon sounded offended. "What does she know about me?"

Laura laughed again – a nasty little laugh. "But she said she wouldn't mind going out with you for your body, and never mind your . . . '

I'd heard enough "No I didn't!" I shouted moving forward so they could see me. "That's a lie, Laura English! I never said that, it was Sophie Pritchard, and you bloody well know it!"

They spun round, startled. "Lizzie!" said Laura. "I didn't see you. We were just . . . '

"I know what you were doing!" I yelled. I was practically choking with rage. "You were telling lies about me. I heard you."

Simon took a step towards me, and put a hand on my shoulder. "Take it easy," he said, soothingly.

I shook his hand off. "Get your hands off me!" I shouted at him. "You're just as b-bad. You did ask me out, you know damn well you did. And I turned you down – I wouldn't go out with you if you were the l-last man on the moon." I knew that didn't sound quite right, but was too worked up to care. "And what about the string quartet?" I turned to Laura again. "What about that? You w-wormed your way in . . . "

"I didn't!" Laura protested. "I didn't, Lizzie. I swear. Simon came to find me when you didn't turn up – he thought I might know why you were so late. When I didn't, he suggested I bring the Mozart oboe quartet along so the others could at least play something."

I looked at Simon accusingly, and he shrugged. "It's true," he said. "She didn't worm her way in. And as you've mentioned the quartet . . . '

"It's all right, Si," Laura said hastily. "I'll tell her."

"Tell me what?" I asked suspiciously. "And what happened to the Pact of Silence, now I come to think of it?"

"It wasn't Simon," Laura said. "He didn't know anything about Marmite being discovered, he told me."

"I know it wasn't Simon. I know who it was; I found out." But I wasn't going to tell Laura it was Emma – not now.

"There you are then – so your Pact was unfair, wasn't it?"

I wondered dimly why it was suddenly just my Pact, when

it was Laura who had originally said she was fed-up with Simon and felt like never speaking to him again. But I'd had enough of the Pact of Silence that never was. "What was it you were going to tell me?" I said again.

Simon and Laura exchanged glances.

"Look, Lizzie," Laura began. "I'm not being bitchy, but that quartet really didn't sound very good. It was much better that time you weren't there, honestly."

"When *you* were there, I suppose you mean," I said bitterly.

"No it wasn't," Simon said quickly. "It was never any good. It wasn't you, Lizzie; I just don't think it worked. The three of you can carry on if you like; find another cellist, I won't mind. But I don't want to do it anymore."

"Simon and I are forming a duo instead," Laura informed me. There was a note of triumph in her voice. "Oboe and piano. We're calling ourselves 'Opus Two'."

It was the final straw. I turned and rushed off without a word, in tears, and pushed my way through the party and up the stairs to Laura's cheerless bedroom. I flung myself on to her bed, weeping under the fixed glassy smiles of her ghastly brother's ghastly pin-ups, and felt utterly betrayed.

12

Seven Rowan Place

"Lizzie!" A voice was hissing in my ear, and a hand shaking me. "Lizzie, wake up! I've brought you some tea."
I shook off the last remnants of sleep and sat up, stretching.

"What time is it?" I yawned. The sun was streaming through the curtains, the birds were singing their joyful hearts out, and it was going to be a glorious day.

Then the events of the previous evening came back to me, with a jolt, and I lay back down again, feeling slightly sick.

"It's seven o'clock," said Laura. She was standing over me with a mug of tea in her hand. "I've been awake for ages – I just couldn't sleep. So I made you some tea; I didn't really want to wake you up, you looked so peaceful lying there, but I really need to talk to you . . . "

I took the tea, and sipped at it. "Seven o'clock!" I exclaimed, yawning again. "For heaven's sake! It's still the middle of the night."

"You're not cross with me, are you?" Laura looked anxious.

"Oh well," I said, "I suppose if you couldn't sleep . . . You might have left me, though."

Laura sat on the edge of the bed. "Not because of the tea," she said. "About last night."

I sighed deeply, and didn't answer her immediately. The truth was, I had never felt so let down in my life – not even when Daddy had told me he was marrying Wendy, or that she was going to have a baby, or that we were moving to London. Upset and upside-down, yes, but not betrayed like this. Laura had let me down over the Pact of Silence, but it was worse than that, much worse. To stand there like that and talk about me to Simon in the way she had; little snippets of their conversation came back to me, like wearing a walkman I couldn't switch off. Laura saying I'm always going on about Simon; Simon saying "I know she fancies me" in that horrible snidey way. But most of all, the tone of Laura's voice when she told Simon that I'm too scared to go out with *boys* (that hurt because I recognized the truth in it), and when she told me they were forming a duo; "We're calling ourselves Opus Two," she had sounded smug and self-satisfied, and totally unlike the Laura I knew.

Or at least, the Laura I thought I knew. Because the horrible truth was beginning to dawn on me that I didn't really know Laura at all. I had thought she was a good friend; a bit impetuous, maybe, but fun, exciting and talented. I had confided my most secret secrets in her – shown her my diary, even. I had trusted her completely, and she had let me down. I *liked* her – she was my friend. And the knowledge that she had worn our friendship so lightly hurt with a hurt I had never in my life felt before.

I sighed again. "No," I said resignedly. "I'm not cross with you." What use was being cross? The damage was done.

But Laura jumped up from the bed, beaming. "Oh, whizz! I knew I could count on you, Lizzie. I told Simon you wouldn't mind about the quartet. Now, why don't you get up and we can have breakfast? Then we can go for a walk by the river – it's brilliant this time of the morning, when there's no one about, then if you feel like it we can take a picnic lunch down there and take a skiff out, and perhaps even go for a swim if it's . . . "

"I'm going back to Percy's," I said shortly, getting out of bed and picking up my sponge bag. "Can I use your phone to call a taxi?"

Laura's face fell. "Liz-zie!" she wailed. "Don't be such a spoilsport! It's going to be a lovely day, and we don't have to be back until this evening."

"Sorry," I said firmly. "But I want to go back now."

"But why?" I could tell from the look on Laura's face she genuinely couldn't understand why I didn't want to stay at her house. Then another look crossed her face. "Simon said he might pop round later," she said, with a wheedling note in her voice. "We could all go out together – shall I ring him up and tell him to come round now?"

"Of course not!" I was amazed she should even suggest it. "I don't want to see Simon – he's the last person on earth I want to see right now, as anyone with an ounce of common sense would know without having to be told!"

Laura looked petulant. "I don't see why," she said. "You said you weren't cross with me, and if that's true I don't see how you can be cross with Simon. I mean, he didn't do anything, did he? It was me who broke that stupid Pact."

"Look," I said, throwing things into my overnight bag. "I'm not cross with Simon, and I'm not cross with you, all right? I just don't want to stay here any longer."

"Charming," Laura muttered. "My parents will be flattered, I must say." It was on the tip of my tongue to ask Laura if she was sure they'd even notice I had gone, but I stopped myself. "What *is* the matter with you then," she went on, "if you're not cross?"

I looked at her. Her lower lip was stuck out, and her eyes were narrowed in a way which made them look unattractive and piggy. I realized how thoroughly spoilt she looked, something I'd never noticed before, and I sighed again.

"If you don't know," I said slowly, shaking my head, "I'm certainly not going to tell you. And I'll tell you something else, Laura – I feel really sorry for you."

"Not half as sorry as I feel for you," she yelled after me as I went into the bathroom.

I locked the door and ran a hot bath, and sat in it for a long time, wondering if I'd ever be able to trust anyone again. On the whole, I thought not.

That feeling didn't last very long, though. The taxi dropped me off at the station, and I bought some coffee and a doughnut from the station buffet and went down to the river to eat them. Having some food in my stomach cheered me up a bit. Then I began to think how rude it was of me to have rushed off like that without thanking Laura's parents for having me.

I bought a postcard from the paper shop next to the station, and after much pen-chewing and debating what to write 'thank you very much for a lovely party' didn't seem quite truthful, somehow) I managed to come up with *Dear Mr & Mrs English. Thank you very much for inviting me to your party, and letting me stay the night. It was very kind of you to ask me and I hope you enjoyed your party and have many more happy anniversaries. With best wishes, LIZZIE OLIVER.*

I was quite pleased with that; it thanked them for the party whilst managing to avoid telling them what sort of a time I had had. I found a crumpled stamp in the bottom of my purse, and put the card in the post box. Then I went through the ticket barrier and got on the train.

When the train pulled in to Paddington, I wondered what on earth I was going to do with myself for the rest of the day. It wasn't even nine o'clock yet; on a leave weekend, Percy's was barely up and stirring at that time. I supposed I would have to go back, nonetheless, even though they weren't expecting me, almost everybody else was away for the weekend, and I'd have nothing to do. Oh well, I thought, sighing; I suppose I ought to do some revision for the end-of-term exams, and there's always practice to be done. The thought didn't thrill me at all, and I was suddenly swept with homesickness. I missed Daddy and Wendy, and the animals, dreadfully; boarding was all very well, but there's nothing like home for a bit of comfort when life kicks you in the teeth. For two pins I would have thrown myself down on the station concourse and had a good howl, but I gritted my teeth instead and swung my bag over my shoulder. I'll go and see Emma, and Marmite, I said to myself. She did say I could go and see him any time.

It didn't occur to me that normal people aren't up and about at nine o'clock on a Sunday morning. Mrs Nash eventually opened the door, with her hair on end and her eyes full of sleep, and a red silk kimono wrapped about her.

"Lizzie!" she said, yawning. "How lovely. How – early!"

I was embarrassed. "I'm dreadfully sorry," I stammered. "I forgot the time, I didn't mean to wake you up. I'll come back some other time, shall I . . . ?"

But Emma's mother had clearly seen something in my face, because she drew me into the black-and-white tiled entrance hall and closed the front door.

"Don't be silly," she said gently. "I've been up for ages. I was just reading the papers – I always look like this in the mornings. The entryphone's on the blink, that's why I came down – it takes ages from up there. Come on up, I'll make you some coffee and you can see how we've been looking after Marmite for you."

I didn't believe that I hadn't woken her up, but when we got up to the Nash's flat and into the kitchen I could see an enormous half-drunk cup of coffee on the breakfast table, and the debris of the *Sunday Times* strewn about the floor. There was some wilting honeysuckle in a jam-jar on the table, a delicious smell of coffee in the air, and Marmite was curled up fast asleep between the front paws of Deefer, who thumped his tail when he saw me. The whole picture looked incredibly homely and cosy, and tears pricked my eyelids.

Mrs Nash followed my gaze towards the jam-jar. "Teddie," she said, with a grin. "She spent yesterday with a friend, and they went out to 'the countryside.' Hampstead Heath I think it was, bless her." Something – the tenderness in her voice, the thought of Teddie bringing honeysuckle home for her mum – undid the knot that had formed inside me the previous evening, the knot I hadn't even realized was there, and to my horror I dissolved in tears.

Mrs Nash didn't seem at all nonplussed. She put a cool hand on the back of my neck, and when the worst of the sobs were over she handed me a large wodge of Kleenex.

"That's better," she said, softly. "Now then, you tidy yourself up, and I'll make that coffee, and then if you feel like it you can tell me what's upset you so much."

Along with the coffee, fragrant and sweet and milky and served in a huge bowl that reminded me of France, came a thick doorstep of brown toast dripping with butter and honey. Mrs Nash watched me while I ate.

"I'm sorry to be such a nuisance," I said when I'd finished.

She snorted. "You're not a nuisance, my dear. With two daughters and three sons and all their assorted problems and heartaches, nothing much fazes me any more."

"Three sons?" I was puzzled. "I thought you only had Theo."

"Theo, and the twins – Thomas and Jeremy. Thomas is being a missionary in Africa, and Jeremy . . . " Mrs Nash's face darkened with pain. "Jeremy died two years ago. He'd been very ill; he had leukemia." She finished her own coffee, and pushed the cup away.

I didn't know what to say. "I'm sorry," I muttered into my coffee. "I didn't know . . ."

"Of course you didn't know – how could you? Emma certainly wouldn't have told you; she never speaks about it to anyone. She was hit harder than any of us by Jess's illness. She adored him; she was absolutely devastated when he died." Mrs Nash smiled suddenly at me, and her clear hazel eyes looked sad but resigned. "He would have been thirty this year; Thomas still will be, of course. Poor Tom. He did tend to get rather forgotten amidst all our misery."

Thirty! I was astounded. That would make her at least . . .

She read my face again, and laughed. "Yes, I am old, my child. Older than you think. Older, I hope, than I look."

"Oh no," I lied hastily. "I mean, you don't look old. But I wasn't thinking that."

She laughed again, throwing back her head. "Lizzie Oliver, you have such a charming transparent face. I wish I painted instead of being a potter. Is it Laura English?" The suddenness of the question threw me, and I blushed. "It's all right," Mrs Nash said, shaking her head, "you don't have to answer me. I'm just an interfering old woman. Ignore me."

"But it was," I said, wonderingly. "It was Laura. How did you know?"

"It didn't take much working out; I knew you were at the party last night, Emma told me, and then you turn up on our doorstep this morning at the crack of dawn, in floods of tears. Besides," she added darkly, "I recognized the signs."

I didn't know what she meant. "What signs?"

But she didn't answer me. Instead, she took my hands across the table, and looked into my eyes.

"Laura," she said, slowly, as if searching for words. "Laura is an – unhappy girl." I was about to interrupt, to say she seemed perfectly happy to me, but Mrs Nash held up a hand to stop me. "Oh yes, I know how she seems; blithe and bonny, to use an old-fashioned phrase, and full of the great I am. But she isn't really, not underneath. She's desperately insecure and unsure of herself, as most bullies are."

"Bullies?" I burst out, amazed. "But she's not a bully!" I thought of Amber Delaney. "At Oaklands, that's my old school, there was this girl, Amber, who terrorized me. At least, she tried to; she made fun of the way I spoke, and kept picking on me, and once she broke my violin bow."

Mrs Nash nodded, and let go of my hands. "Yes," she said, "I know the type. But there's more than one sort of bully, and personally I prefer the sort like your Amber – at least you know where you are with them. The other kind, like Laura, are infinitely more difficult to spot. They make friends with you and get you to like them, and then they play fast and loose with your feelings. And all the while *you* feel guilty, you think *you've* done something wrong, because after all, she's your friend."

"How do you know Laura so well?" I asked Mrs Nash. I wasn't sure I agreed with her, but didn't like to say so.

But again, she didn't answer my question. "You mustn't blame Laura," she said instead. "Her parents are – difficult. Not very supportive. She's lived her life in the shadow of her brother. The brilliant Marcus," she said bitterly. "Loathsome creature. No, don't blame Laura. Just try to distance yourself from her and her little psychological games, and you'll find she loses her power to hurt you. Like she hurt my Emma." I hadn't understood everything she'd said, but the last sentence was plain enough.

"What *did* she do to Emma?" I asked. "Nobody will tell me. They were friends, weren't they? Only Laura reckons they were never that friendly, just that Emma wanted them to be."

Mrs Nash got up from the table and smiled at me. "Not true, I'm afraid – just wishful thinking on Laura's part. Oh yes, they were friends all right. They were inseparable when they were Teddie's age, them and Simon Alexander. But as to what happened, you'll have to ask Em. I'll go and give her a call; it's time she was up. I'm off to have a shower – do make yourself at home until my slothful daughter appears, won't you?"

As it happened, I didn't have long to wait; Emma came into the kitchen five minutes later, washed and dressed.

"Hi!" she said. "I thought I heard your voice when I woke up. Mum says Laura's been mucking you about; what on earth's been happening? Was it that stupid Pact of Silence?"

For the second time that morning I recounted the events of the previous evening, and Emma listened with a sympathetic look on her face.

"Golly," she said when I had finished. "What a bag Laura is. How mizz for you."

I smiled ruefully. "Well, you did try and warn me about her," I said. "Only I wouldn't listen."

"If it's any comfort," Emma said, not looking me in the eye. "She did the same sort of thing to me." And at last she told me what had happened between them.

They had been friends, Emma told me, since they both started at Percy's at the age of eleven. Laura had boarded straight away, and had missed home; so she went to Emma's house a lot, for tea and for overnight leave, and even for half-term several times. Emma had stayed at Laura's too, in the holidays, and had got to know Simon. "We were best friends," she said simply. "Laura and me."

Then as they got a bit older, Laura started to tease Emma, "Mostly about how I looked. She got pretty, and I didn't, and she called me Ugly Mug. Then I had to wear a brace for a year, and she started calling me Tin Grin. That was Marcus' name for me; he was gross, even then. I pretended I didn't mind, but it really hurt."

Then Laura started other things; whispering about Emma to other girls, befriending new girls who came to Percy's and temporarily dropping Emma, lifting up Emma's skirt in the playground so all the boys could see her knickers - "But that was when we were still quite young." All the time, Emma was loyal to Laura. Not being her friend any more didn't occur to her "because I thought it was me. I thought it was my fault. I didn't have any friends except for Laura, and Laura had tons - it was magical, almost, being her friend. Because she wasn't nasty all the time, and when she was nice she was just lovely. She would give me presents and tell me I was her best friend ever, and I just sort of assumed that when she was rotten to me it was because of something I'd done."

When they went from the Junior School to the Middle School, Emma started to make other friends. Ones who treated her in the same way all the time, and didn't suddenly turn round and call her names, or ignore her. And Laura didn't like it.

"I knew she had hatched something," Emma said. "I didn't know how, I just did. But I could tell she didn't like me having any friends except for her." Then, in the Christmas of that year, it happened. There had been an outbreak of stealing at Percy's, Emma told me; little things at first, then quite large sums of money, radios from dorms, and once, a valuable violin that its owner had left in a practice room.

"I think it was the violin that gave Laura the idea," said Emma. "She went to Mr Bishop and told him that she knew who the thief was."

I stared at her; I couldn't believe she meant what I thought she did. "You mean - you? She said it was you?" Emma nodded. "But - but surely he didn't believe her? I mean, it was only her word against yours - surely he . . . "

"He did believe her," Emma had gone white. "Apparently Laura burst into tears and got all worked up, and said she didn't want to sneak on her best friend. She made up some tale about how she'd been worried about me for ages, and she thought I was only doing it to get attention." Emma gulped, and for a moment I thought *she* was going to burst into tears, but she didn't.

After a moment, she went on. "Even after the missing violin turned up again, in a cupboard in another practice room, they thought it had been me. They just wouldn't believe me – it was awful, Lizzie, they were talking to me in kind voices with kind looks on their faces, but they were accusing me of stealing and I just couldn't make them believe that I hadn't done it. And the worst thing was that Laura *knew* they wouldn't believe me; she just *knew* they would think it was me, because of how I'd been ever since Jess . . . " she gave a sob, took off her glasses with an angry movement, and dashed away two tears with the back of her wrist. "It was just so unfair," she said, bitterly. And then, embarrassed, "Sorry."

"It's all right," I said softly. When the tears had gone, and the glasses were back in place, I prompted her. "So they thought it was you because you'd been so upset since your brother died? It seems very strange – why should being upset make you steal things?"

Emma sighed heavily. "You don't understand," she said. She didn't seem to find it odd that I knew about her brother. "I wasn't just upset about Jess. It was more than that. It was as if I couldn't feel any more – as if . . . " she stopped, floundering for words. "As if I wasn't me any more. My body was still doing things – getting up, going to school – but my mind wasn't there at all. When people spoke to me it sounded like I was at the bottom of the sea, and they were talking through all that water. And I couldn't concentrate on anything; I kept getting lost. Once I got lost coming home, and Theo eventually found me wandering round Regent's Park." Emma shuddered. "I was frightened; I didn't know what was happening to me. Mum and Dad were worried about me too,

I knew they were, but I couldn't seem to do anything about it. I've never told anybody about this before." She gave me a quick look.

"But you got better?" It sounded dreadful; poor Emma. "I mean, you're not like that now, are you?"

Emma grimaced. "Oh yes – I got better. I was just starting to feel like myself again when all this stealing business happened."

I was beginning to understand. "I see; they believed Laura when she said it was you because you'd been – well – not yourself."

"Barmy, you mean." Emma stopped my protests. "It's all right; I know what people thought about me. I expect you've been told all about it; mad Emma Nash, who went round the bend just because her brother died."

"No!" I was horrified. "Nobody's ever said anything like that about you; I only knew about your brother because your mum told me just now, before you got up. I don't expect people thought that at all; they understand if you feel awful because somebody dies. Truly they do. My mother died," I told her. "Four years ago. And everybody realized why my sister and my father and I were a bit odd for a while."

Our eyes met, and the hard challenging look went out of Emma's. "Well, anyway. The fact is, Mr Bishop believed Laura, and Mum and Dad were dragged up to Percy's protesting my innocence – at first, that is. After a while even *they* seemed to think I'd done it; Mum would sit around at home, looking broken, saying things like *Of course we believe you darling*, when I could tell they didn't know what to believe. I couldn't think what to do to prove I was telling the truth; it was like being stuck in the worst kind of nightmare." Emma took a deep breath.

"Eventually I had to see an educational psychologist, and then I began to think perhaps I had stolen those things after all. I remember asking him – the psychologist – if people could do things without knowing it, and he said sometimes, and I thought *This is it.* I'm a thief. And I shall go through the rest of my life doing awful criminal things and not even knowing it, and I shall end up in prison, or a lunatic asylum. I thought I was going mad. I thought I *was* mad; first Jess dying, and then this." Emma shuddered again.

I couldn't take in the awfulness of it, how alone and helpless Emma must have felt. And I couldn't believe the enormity of what Laura had done; the wheels she had set in motion. "But they did believe you eventually?" I said.

"Oh yes – eventually. The psychologist told them he didn't think it could have been me after all. Everyone was very nice about it; they said they were sorry and everything, but they had been so concerned about me." Emma laughed, a mirthless noise at the back of her throat. "If that was showing concern, I'd have rather they hadn't bothered."

"What happened to Laura after they believed it wasn't you?"

Emma shrugged. "Nothing. I think they'd forgotten who'd told them in the first place. Mum and Dad hadn't forgotten though; Mum said Laura must have known what she was doing, saying it was me. She said she must have known that people would have thought it was out of character for me to steal, but as I had been behaving out of character they would be more ready to believe Laura. Mum kept apologizing to me, for believing Laura rather than me. My dad says she's evil – Laura, I mean."

"But didn't you remind them – Mr Bishop, and everyone? Why didn't *she* have to see an educational psychologist, after telling all those lies about you?" It seemed so dreadfully unfair, even though I didn't know what an educational psychologist was.

"There didn't seem much point," said Emma. I could tell

from her face that the whole thing still hurt awfully. "They wouldn't have thought she was telling lies; they'd have thought *she* was being concerned as well. And to be honest, I didn't want it all raked up again."

"So you didn't talk to Laura again. I'm not surprised," I said.

"Not exactly," Emma said. She gave a wry little laugh. "My mum persuaded me that people like Laura were to be pitied, not hated. She said that rising above things like that made people like me much bigger than people like Laura. So I decided not to ignore her, and she was full of apologies of course. She said she hadn't told Mr Bishop she knew it was me; only that she thought it might be, because of how strange I'd been lately. She said she knew people under stress sometimes did odd things, and that she only told him so that I could get help. But I knew she was lying; I knew getting help for me was the last thing she intended. She just wanted to cause trouble. Although I must say I don't think she realized, when she did it, just how much trouble there was going to be. Anyway, Laura and I had a sort of truce, I suppose. Then I went and started fancying Simon," she said bitterly.

It had been the previous summer, the summer after the stealing business, and Simon and Laura and Emma were all at an orchestral course at a school in Berkshire during the holidays.

"I hadn't seen Simon for ages, and he suddenly looked different. Grown-up, and handsome," she said. "And he was the first boy who had taken any notice of me; he was really nice to me. We went round together quite a lot, and of course Laura tagged along too because she knew both of us. It was great; for two weeks I felt like a *girl*, if you know what I mean. Equal to Laura. Then one evening Laura and I were sitting out on the grass by the tennis courts, and we started scribbling on a piece of paper; Laura had bought this new italic pen, and she was showing me how to use it. We both wrote our names, and then she said something about my name sounding nice with Simon's surname, so I wrote 'Emma Alexander' a few times. The next thing I knew, she was off with the piece of paper, yelling to Simon that I wanted to marry him, and I was already practising my new signature." She looked at me solemnly. "I know it sounds stupid, and childish," she said. "But it was so embarrassing. I knew Simon would never look at me again, after that."

I could imagine only too well how embarrassed Emma must have felt, and suddenly everything became clear. Why she had warned me off Laura and Simon; why she had told me not to let them muck me about. She could have told me all this months ago, to put me off them, but she hadn't; she was still loyal to them, even after having been treated so badly. And now I had found out for myself what they were like.

"Poor you," I said slowly. "Poor, poor you."

Emma jumped up suddenly and smiled faintly. "Never mind," she said. "It's in the past now. What shall we do today? – you will stay for the rest of the day, won't you?"

We had a lovely day, Emma dug out her old violin and let me play her good one, and we played lots of duets, with Theo accompanying us. He's pretty good, and the sort of older brother I would want. Much nicer than Marcus.

Then Mrs Nash cooked Sunday lunch, and we all helped, only it wasn't the usual sort of Sunday lunch; it was pieces of pork cooked with apple and cider and cream, in the pressure cooker, with egg noodles and courgettes and leeks, and heaps of salad. There was a wonderful ice-cream gâteau for pudding, and we were all allowed to have wine, even Teddie.

After lunch Emma and I went up to the roof garden – I didn't know there really were such things – and sunbathed amongst the pots of petunias and nasturtiums. There was one strange moment, when Emma told me the piece she was currently studying with Miss Quentin, her violin teacher.

"It's a Mozart concerto," she said. "In D – K218, I think. D'you know it? It's fabbo." And she rolled over to tan her back.

I did know it, for that was the very concerto I was working on. The one Mr Owen had said was to be the solo work at the QEH concert.

Finally, it was time to go back to Percy's.

"It's been a lovely day," I said to Mrs Nash, as she and Emma stood on the doorstep to see me off. "Thanks ever so much for having me. Sorry I was such a misery when I got here."

To my surprise she kissed my cheek. "Don't worry about it," she told me. "And you're welcome to come any time."

When I got back to Percy's, the other girls looked at me oddly.

"Mrs Nightingale's about to ring the police," one of them said.

"The police?" I said, puzzled. "What about?"

But Mrs Nightingale's voice came from behind me. "Lizzie Oliver!" she said, in tones of fury mixed with relief. "Where on earth have you been? I've been worried sick."

And as I turned round, the first thing I saw was Laura's white and anxious face.

13

Seadrift

Dear Diary,

What a peculiar, uncomfortable weekend it's been. First Laura's parents' party and all that horrible business with her and Simon. Then that lovely day yesterday with Emma and the Nashes, and finally discovering what the big mystery with E and L is. Finding that out really knocked me for six; I thought Laura had been nasty enough to me, but compared to how she has treated Emma I think I've got off lightly. Why does Emma still speak to her? – I don't think I would. She must be mad.

That wasn't the end of the weekend, though, because when I got back to Percy's Mrs Nightingale was doing her pieces because she didn't know where I was. It didn't even occur to me to tell anyone I was at Emma's, not Laura's, where everyone thought I was; I wasn't late back, but of course DARLING LALLA decided she'd get back half-way through the afternoon and started shrieking that I must have done something awful to myself, because I'd left her house at eight o'clock that morning and nobody had seen me since. They might have thought to check Emma's; honestly, what

171

idiots they are, Laura's beginning to be a real pain in the bum.

Which leaves me in a bit of a quandary, because she's supposed to be coming home with me for half-term on Saturday. I suppose I can't really wriggle out of it this late. Besides, her parents are apparently off somewhere exotic for that week, and she'd be all on her own. So it looks like I'm stuck with her. Wow. What a fun-filled week it's going to be. I'm sure.

I barely spoke to Laura when I got back to Percy's. I was so overcome with pity for Emma that I felt quite protective towards her; at break on Monday morning, she and I were wandering around the playground.

"I've been thinking about what you told me," I said to her. "About Laura. I can't get it out of my mind."

Emma grimaced. "Don't," she said, looking down. "It was a long time ago. It was pretty ghastly, dragging it all up again yesterday; I think I'd rather just forget about it now."

"Of course," I said. "I understand." But I wanted to tell Emma something in return; something equally awful and mind-boggling. So I told her what Mr Barnaby had told me, about how he reckoned Simon had failed his entrance exam but had got in to Percy's anyway.

Only I told her that Simon had definitely failed, and when I had finished I had this nasty niggling feeling that I shouldn't have told her. But the goggle-eyed look on her face make me perversely glad I had.

"Good grief!" she said. "How did you find that out?"

"Mr Barnaby," I told her, neglecting to mention that it was only speculation. "So it must be true; he wouldn't make something like that up, would he?" Emma agreed that he wouldn't.

Later that morning Laura asked me why I was ignoring her; she looked really upset, and begged me not to stop being friends with her.

"I know I've been really horrible to you," she said, "and I'm sorry, Lizzie – truly."

So I told her I knew about what she'd done to Emma, and I told her I thought it was the meanest, most disgusting thing I'd ever heard.

"Only I suppose you've got some excuse," I said, in a hard voice. "I suppose you'll wriggle out of it somehow."

To my surprise, Laura didn't make excuses. She shook her head. "No," she said. "I'm not going to wriggle out of it. Only you don't know why I did it; I wasn't just being spiteful. But I don't suppose you believe that, and I can't say I blame you. But just think about this for a moment. If it really wasn't Emma who stole those things," her eyes looked into mine absolutely steadily. "how come nothing else went missing after she was caught? I don't suppose she told you that, did she?"

Laura's question really bothered me. But I didn't like to ask Emma if Laura was right, and the stealing *had* stopped; she might think I believed she had been the thief after all. It was at the back of my mind the whole time, gnawing away.

Added to this was Laura's almost pathetic gratitude when she realized I wasn't going to stop her coming to Cornwall after all. She kept thanking me, and apologizing for being so horrid to me, and she looked so craven and humble and dog-like that I wondered if I could have misjudged her after all. She seemed so sincere. All in all, I felt horribly uneasy and confused about my friendship with them both. Why can't we all just be friends together, I wondered, not for the first time. Why do things have to be so *complicated*? I couldn't remember having these problems when I was younger. Ah, said my inner voice, this is what happens when you grow up. If you thought life got easier when you were a grown-up, you were wrong. It gets more difficult; much more difficult. I was filled with gloom at the prospect.

Saturday arrived, all too soon it seemed, and with it came half-term. I was looking forward immensely to seeing Daddy and Wendy again, and Flora, and Meg and Charles and the children, and Ben, and the new house; but the anticipation was spoilt by not really wanting Laura to be there, and I resented Laura for spoiling it.

But I soon realized it would be a pretty miserable half-term if I carried on feeling this way. We were sitting on the train, about an hour after leaving Paddington, and Laura was telling me yet again how kind it was of me to let her come.

"I really do appreciate it," she gushed. "After all, you could easily have said . . . "

"Laura," I interrupted her. "Do stop going on about it, I'm willing to try and forget what's happened if you are. Only it won't be much of a holiday if I keep ignoring you, and you keep thanking me."

So we agreed on a truce, and I was surprised at how easy it seemed to slip back into the old friendship with her. Looking back, that should have warned me; I should have remembered how she had wormed her way back in to Emma's life, only to hurt her yet again. But at the time I was just glad to be friends with her again – amazing really, considering all she had done and all I had learnt about her.

Daddy met us at the station, and when I saw him I started to cry, like an idiot.

"I've missed you," I choked, my arms around his neck, trying to wipe my tears away on his jacket so nobody would see what a wally I was being. But if he or Laura did see, they didn't comment.

"I've missed you too, sweetie," he said, and it's a funny thing but his voice sounded choked too.

Then he drove us the twenty or so miles to Penwithin. As soon as I saw the sea again my heart began to leap – home! I was home again!

For all that I loved Percy's, the music and the atmosphere, and even London itself, Cornwall was where my heart belonged.

Laura scrambled around the back of the car, trying to see out of both windows at once. "Isn't it beautiful?" she kept saying. "You are lucky, living here. Oh, just look at those seagulls – aren't they huge?"

Daddy drove right through Penwithin, and I was dying to see where the new house was.

"Is it in Fore Street?" I kept saying. "Is it in Rose Lane?"

But Daddy just smiled, and wouldn't answer.

He drove up the track which eventually leads to the top of the cliffs. There are only four things up there; the non-conformist chapel, two tiny cottages, and the Folly. He pulled up outside the Folly.

"Here we are," he said. "Home sweet home."

I thought he was joking. "But this is the Folly," I said, frowning. "It's empty. Ben says it's been up for sale for . . . " I trailed off, and looked at the red-brick house. It had a new roof – shining grey slate. The white shutters at the windows looked freshly painted, and there was a new front door, with a large brass door knocker. There were curtains hanging at all the windows, and in the large window of the sitting-room I could see a small table with a blue Delft vase full of early roses.

From all the evidence, the Folly was very much lived-in. Then the penny dropped. I turned to Daddy.

"You've bought the Folly?" I said, beaming. "This is the new house – we're actually going to live in it?" I could hardly believe it. But just then the front door opened, and there stood Wendy with Flora in her arms, and out bounded Rufus, wagging a welcome from the neck down in his usual excessive way, and I had to believe it.

"Wow!" I kept saying, grinning like a lunatic. "The Folly! Whizz! Ace! Wait till Ben finds out!"

Daddy put his arm round me, and gave me a hug. "I'm glad you approve," he said. "But why do you keep calling it the Folly? The house's name is Seadrift."

I woke up the next morning at five o'clock. It was already light, and I lay there for ages, listening to the seagulls and hugging to myself the thought that I was actually back in Cornwall. It had been a lovely evening. It was so warm we had supper out on the patio, and we stayed out there for ages, chatting and looking out over the tangled garden while Daddy and Wendy drank Pimm's from tall frosted glasses. Then Laura and I had a guided tour of the house – the decorators had been in for weeks and had only finished the previous day, so everything looked fresh and new. It was still light when Laura and I went to bed; Fishpaste had somehow worked out which was my room, and was waiting there on my bed, purring his own special 'welcome home'.

I lay there thinking about it all; it was no good, I couldn't get back to sleep again. I slipped out of bed, pulled on jeans and a jersey and espadrilles and crept down the stairs, trying not to make them creak. When I went into the kitchen, Rufus opened one eye; when he saw it was me rather than burglars he got up and stretched and yawned, wagging good morning to me. I opened the fridge and poured myself a glass of milk.

"It must be your birthday," I told Rufus. "I'm going to take you for a nice walkies on the cliffs." As soon as I uttered the magic word 'walkies' he started prancing round on stiff legs, making excited little woofs, and wouldn't shut up until I let him out. I thought he was going to wake the whole house up.

We went out of the garden gate and up the cliff path. *My* cliff path – I had been coming up here practically since I learned to walk. I breathed in the clean sea air appreciatively; it was as different to the muck in London as lemonade is to champagne, and I could almost hear my lungs sigh with relief. When I got to the top of the cliffs I sat down, out of breath.

I lay on my back with my hands behind my head, watching the gulls and listening to the swish and shoosh of the sea against the rocks, far below me. It was going to be a glorious day; the sky was that pale hazy blue which promises high temperatures later.

"Boo!" said a voice. I nearly jumped out of my skin, and sat up with a start. When I saw who it was I leapt to my feet, beaming.

"Ben!" I exclaimed. "It's you! Oh, it's so good to see you!" And without thinking I threw my arms around him and hugged him, hard. It felt so natural to hug him, and he hugged me back, too. I suddenly thought of Simon - there was no way I'd have greeted him like that. But the thought of Simon got in the way, and I drew back, embarrassed.

"Hi," I said, in a more normal way. "What are you doing up so early?"

"I couldn't sleep," Ben explained, sitting down, "so I thought I'd come for a walk. Then I saw this familiar dog bouncing along the top of the cliffs, and decided you must be up here somewhere too. Didn't expect such a warm welcome, though, I must say!" He grinned at me.

I looked sideways at him, still faintly embarrassed. "Well," I said, picking at my shoe. "I was pleased to see you. It's been such ages since I was home; I'm really glad to be back." I suddenly remembered Seadrift. "Hey," I said, "you'll never guess where we're living now! Go on - take a guess!"

Ben wrinkled his forehead. "Let me see now - um - the Folly?" I felt vaguely disappointed, but Ben grinned at me. "I cheated. The rumour that it was your dad who bought it has been going round the village for weeks, and then of course your folks turned up a fortnight or so back. Is it as good inside as we always imagined?"

"Come back with me for breakfast," I invited him. "You can see for yourself. There's someone there who's dying to meet you!" I told him that Laura was convinced he was my "secret boyfriend". "It was because of the bizarre letter you sent me," I said. "What on earth was it all about? I thought you'd finally flipped."

To my huge surprise, Ben went bright red. "Oh that," he muttered, and got up. "What about this breakfast, then?"

But I pulled his arm. "Not until you tell me what made you put all that slushy stuff," I said firmly. "After all, I did send you that photo you asked for."

Ben sighed, and sat down again, "OK, fair play," he said. "It's just – well – one of the lads at school gets a really sizzling letter from his girlfriend every week, absolutely covered in perfume – you should read it! Actually, I reckon he sends it to himself, but of course he denies it."

"But what's that got to do with me?" I persisted.

"Hang on, will you? I'm just about to tell you. One evening Patrick – the one who gets the letter, he's in my dorm – he starts talking about this cousin of his who goes to this music school in London, and I just mentioned that a friend of mine goes to a school like that, her name's Lizzie and she plays the fiddle, and isn't that a coincidence? Anyway, all the other lads start going 'Lizzie, eh!' and 'Woooo!' and assorted other noises, and well, I sort of – told them you were my girlfriend. I didn't think you'd mind."

"I don't, I suppose," I conceded. "But what about the letter?"

"Well, Patrick starts thinking, you can practically hear the ticking as the cogs go round, and eventually he says 'if this bird's your girlfriend, how come you never write to her? And why haven't you got a photo?'"

"Charming!" I said, bristling at being called a bird. It made me sound like a sparrow. "He sounds a right cretin. You should have asked to see a photo of *his* girlfriend."

"Oh, he's OK, old Patrick," Ben said. "Anyway, I concocted this letter, and just sort of casually left it lying around the dorm where I knew he and the others would be bound to see it, and hoped that would convince them. Then when you sent the picture, that really did the trick! I didn't think you would. It's in a frame beside my bedside," he added.

"I still can't understand why you said I was your girlfriend in the first place," I said. The very idea was ridiculous.

Ben scratched his ear. "Don't go on about it," he said, going red again. "I told you. Besides, all the others seem to have girlfriends at home they write to, and I didn't want them to think me odd for not having anyone. Honestly, you've no idea how difficult it is to meet girls at a boys' school."

We walked back down the cliff path, Rufus busily rummaging around behind us, and chatted about school and Penwithin, and what we would do that week. It was good to be home.

I was just cooking scrambled eggs when Laura appeared in the kitchen doorway, yawning. She was in her dressing-gown and had bare feet and tangled hair, but she still looked fresh and pretty. I suddenly wondered what Ben would make of her – whether he would go ga-ga over her like most boys seemed to.

Laura didn't notice him immediately. "It's the crack of dawn!" she exclaimed, yawning again. "Why are you cooking at this hour?"

"It's half-past eight," I told her airily, putting toast under the grill. "I've been up since six; I took Rufus for a walk, and we met Ben on the cliffs. He's come back for breakfast – aren't you going to say hello?"

Laura took another step into the kitchen and saw Ben sitting on the kitchen table. She smiled that Laura smile, and put her hand out.

"Hello!" she said. "So you're Ben. Lizzie's told me so much about you – it's really good to meet you at last!"

Ben unravelled his legs and stood up; he was much taller

than Laura. He shook her hand gravely, and to my amazement he blushed again. I wondered when he had started going red like that; I thought I had the monopoly on technicolour faces.

"Hello," said Ben solemnly. "It's nice to meet you, too."

When the eggs were cooked, Daddy emerged from his study, and Wendy brought Flora downstairs, and we all sat round the kitchen table to eat. It was a nice meal, but as far as Laura was concerned there may as well have been nobody else in the room apart from Ben; she talked to him the whole time, sparkling away like she usually does with Tim Maynard.

Afterwards, when Ben had gone home and Laura had at last got dressed, we went for a walk down to the Strand at Penlorren, the next village along.

"He's really fanciable, your Ben," Laura said. "Only I thought you said he was your boyfriend? He told me about that Patrick, and why he wrote to you like that – I said I'd write to him, if he wanted."

Irritation stirred inside me. He certainly hadn't wasted any time in setting Laura straight. "I never said he was my boyfriend," I said crossly. "You did. I told you we were just friends."

"Well anyway," Laura said dismissively. "I think he's very attractive. D'you think he fancies me?" she asked, turning to me and opening her eyes wide.

I skimmed a pebble across the sea, the irritation rising now like milk coming to the boil. But I swallowed it.

"I've no idea," I said. "Probably. Boys usually do fancy you, don't they?"

To tell the truth, I was expecting Ben to fall for Laura, and memories of my friend Maudie came flooding back. She and Ben had spent one entire summer holiday going around together, and I had been consumed with jealousy that they should prefer each other's company to mine. It was the summer after I had moved to London, and I was convinced that they didn't want me any more; it had been the most miserable summer of my life. Maudie was living in Scotland now.

But although Laura tried her hardest, Ben didn't seem to notice. He remained polite and slightly distant to her for the rest of the week, despite her eyelash-fluttering and frequent displays of long brown leg. I was quite amused by it all, although Laura wasn't.

"What's the matter with him?" she asked me crossly one night. "Why doesn't he like me?"

"Of course he likes you," I told her. "He's perfectly friendly to you, isn't he?" But I knew what she meant, although I pretended I didn't.

I could see why she found him attractive, although I had never thought of him like that before. He was just Ben, the friend I had known for years. But he was tall for his age, and the rowing he did at school in Devon had filled him out and made him very brown, and his eyes were warm and friendly. He was like my brother, but I could see he was good-looking.

"He seems older than he is," said Laura. "Compared to someone like Simon. Simon's all blond and skinny and weedy, but Ben looks about eighteen." She mentioned Simon to have a dig at me, but oddly I didn't care.

One afternoon Laura fell asleep sun-bathing in the garden, so I sneaked off to the Polkerris' shop. Ben's mum gave me a bar of Fruit & Nut – I'm sure she still thinks I'm about ten.

"Ben's watching the cricket on the television," she told me, beaming. "Go on up, my dear." I went up the stairs to their flat.

"Do you like Laura?" I asked him, without preamble.

"She's all right," he said, still watching the cricket. "Oh, shot!"

"But do you fancy her?" I persisted.

Ben sighed, and tore his eyes reluctantly from the set. "Not really, no," he said. "She's not my type." He gave Somerset his full attention again.

"Well, what is your type?" I stood in front of the TV.

"Lizzie! I'm trying to watch this!" He sighed again, but it wasn't an impatient sigh. "What is all this? I don't know what my type is, really, but it certainly isn't Laura."

"Why not?" I suddenly really needed to know. "What's wrong with her?"

Ben thought for a moment, biting his lower lip. "She's too – keen. She tries too hard – all that silly giggling, and waving her eyelids around. It might impress some boys, but not me. I mean, she's pretty and everything, but that's not all that matters; you can't just look at a girl the whole time, can you? You need to talk, as well."

It was almost what Wendy had said when I was upset about Simon. "You mean she's boring?"

Ben shook his head. "I don't know. She's your friend, isn't she? I don't want you to think I think your friends are boring. But there's something else." He stopped, biting his lip again. "There's something else about her I don't really like. She reminds me of a kid at primary school who used to pull the wings off flies, just to watch them wriggle. Something – not kind. Spiteful. I can see it in her face. You want to watch her, Lizzie."

When I got back to Seadrift Laura was sitting up on the sunbed, rubbing suntan cream dispiritedly into her arms.

"There you are," she said crossly. "Where on earth have you been? I woke up five minutes ago and you'd disappeared. I nearly burnt."

"Sorry," I said off-handedly. "I went for a walk. I got bored watching you sleeping."

Laura creamed her legs, and lay down again on her tummy. "I'm bored too," she announced. "There's nothing to do here.

You never told me Cornwall was so boring."

You wouldn't find it boring if Ben was paying you more attention, I thought, but didn't say it. I was getting seriously fed-up with Laura. There was silence for a moment. I watched Fishpaste winding himself round inside a clump of catmint and lying down; he closed his eyes blissfully and turned his face up to the sun. Then Laura sat up, abruptly.

"Lizzie," she said. There was an odd note in her voice. "I've got something to tell you. I promised I wouldn't, but you're my friend, and I think you've a right to know."

"To know what?" I said, baffled.

"You know what Mr Barnaby told you about Simon?" Laura said. I nodded. "Did you tell Emma?"

"Yes," I said, with a twinge of guilt. "But it's all right. She won't tell anybody."

Laura gave a little laugh. "Not much she won't. She can't keep her mouth closed. She's only gone and told Simon."

I went cold, as though someone had put an ice-cube down my back. "Oh my God. What – what did he say?" I vaguely thought I could always deny the rumour had started with me if Simon challenged me about it, but it was worse than that. Much worse.

"He was furious," Laura said. "He told his parents you've been spreading lies about him, and they're hopping mad. Apparently he told them other things too; the bother with the string quartet, and things like that. They think you're deliberately causing trouble for him, and affecting his work at Percy's; they're writing to your dad about it."

I felt ill. All I could think about was what I should say to Daddy when he got the letter; of all the things he hated, gossip and tale-telling were what he despised most. And how could I ever face Mr Barnaby again? The truth of the matter was that he had said something to me in anger about Simon, something that was probably nothing more than a rumour, and I had latched on to it and spread it around and told people it was true. Not just Laura and Emma, either; I had told Sophie, and the others in the dorm too. Perhaps it was indiscreet of Mr Barnaby, perhaps he shouldn't have said it to me, but I certainly shouldn't have passed it on to other people as though it were gospel. I couldn't blame Mr Barnaby for the mess I was in. It was my own fault.

I looked at Laura, and she looked at me. I was close to tears. The horrid thing was, she didn't look concerned, or even particularly sympathetic. There was a little smile on her face, and it was a smile of triumph.

14

Simon Takes a Swim

For a whole day, the thought of the letter Simon's parents were to write hung over me, like the sword of Damocles. Laura's smug look gave way to one of concern, so quickly that I began to wonder if I had imagined it.

"Honestly, it's typical of Emma," she kept saying. "She can't keep secrets for toffee. Remember how she told Mrs Nightingale about Marmite? Simon always says she's got foot-in-mouth disease. I shouldn't worry too much – his parents will forget all about it in a week or two."

"It's all right for you," I said, miserably. "It's not your father they're writing to. Daddy's going to kill me; he thinks passing on gossip is the Eighth Deadly Sin."

The truth was, I felt guilty. I knew that I had exaggerated what Mr Barnaby had said, made it out to be a cast-iron fact when there was probably little or no truth in it at all. And I had used Mr Barnaby's comment to make me seem important; passing on something scandalous about Simon that no one else knew had made me feel part of the crowd. But realizing that it served me right didn't help at all; it just made me feel worse, and added to that I felt dreadfully sorry for myself. They're supposed to be my friends, I kept saying to myself; why do they keep mucking me around?

The following day, we all went to lunch at the vicarage with Meg and Charles. The delight at seeing them all again made me temporarily forget about the mess I was in. The children had grown so much – Katey had been two in March, and Jacob was ten months old, crawling around and babbling and constantly grinning, showing off two pearly white teeth. To my surprise, Laura fell instantly in love with the children, particularly Jacob – she carried him around and showed him things, and she even changed his nappy.

"I love babies," she said, planting a kiss on his blond head. "I wish I had a little brother. They smell gorgeous, babies, don't they?"

But after lunch, when Katey and Jacob and Flora were upstairs having a nap, I started worrying again. Charles took the others off to the church to show them the new community centre that had been built, but I stayed behind to help Meg with the dishes.

"Laura's very good with the children," Meg remarked, rinsing the glasses under the tap. "Shame she doesn't live nearer – she'd be a brilliant babysitter!"

"She's hardly looked at Flora since she's been here," I said. "I think Wendy was quite surprised when she offered to change Jacob."

Meg started on the plates. "Small babies are a bit daunting if you're not used to them," she said. "Jacob's almost a toddler, compared to Flora – she's not three months old yet, is she?"

I was silent. I didn't want Meg to defend Laura; she hardly knew her.

"Is anything the matter?" Meg asked me. "You've been really quiet since lunch-time."

"I don't always go round making a noise, you know," I said huffily. I picked up a glass and dried it roughly.

Meg looked at me. "Lizzie," she said mildly. "This is me –

Meg. Your sister. You don't have to pretend with me. And mind my best glasses; I'd quite like to use them another day."

I heaved a sigh. I could never hide anything from Meg. She always knew when something was up. With some relief, I told her the saga of Mr Barnaby and Simon, and when I had finished she clicked her tongue and shook her head.

"What a pickle," she said. "That's the trouble with being told secrets – it's always such a terrible temptation to pass them on."

"But I don't, usually," I said. "What am I going to do?"

Meg considered. "I should tell Daddy, if I were you. Get in first."

I was horrified. "I can't do that! You know how he feels about telling tales – he'll go round the bend."

"Very possibly," said Meg. "But at least he'll hear your side of it first. It's got to be better that way round than getting a letter like that out of the blue."

It preyed on my mind for the rest of the day, but deep down I knew Meg was right. So that evening, when we got back and Laura had gone to bed, I screwed up my courage and told Daddy and Wendy what had happened.

"I know I shouldn't have told the others," I said. "But I honestly didn't think it would get back to Simon. And now he's told his parents." I told Daddy they might be getting in touch, but didn't mention the letter; I thought I would cross that bridge when I came to it.

Daddy looked at me gravely. "That's what happens with gossip," he said. "You're told in confidence, then you tell someone else in confidence, and before you know where you are, the whole world knows. All in confidence, of course."

I looked at my feet. "I know," I said, shamefaced.

"And when you embroider what you've been told," he went on, sternly, "that's when the big trouble starts. It sounds to me as though your Mr Barnaby has a private theory about this

Simon character which is based on nothing more than disliking the lad. Although he should have kept his mouth shut, of course; that kind of theorizing is best kept within the walls of the staff room."

"But what if Simon's parents go and see Mr Barnaby?" This worried me more than them thinking I had deliberately been making trouble for Simon. "He could get the sack!"

Daddy shook his head. "I doubt it; it's only their word against his, isn't? Besides, it sounds as if it's you they're gunning for, not Mr Barnaby." He looked me straight in the eye. "Why did you make out to the others it was true, Lizzie? That's what I can't understand. The last thing I heard, you were pretty keen on Simon."

I flushed; I hadn't realized I'd been that obvious. "I don't know," I mumbled. "I didn't even mean to tell anybody; Mr Barnaby told me not to."

But then Daddy surprised me. "Oh, cheer up," he said. "It's not the end of the world. You're not the first person ever to have embroidered the truth and passed on gossip to impress people and be in with the in-crowd. I guess we've all been guilty of it at some time. Although that doesn't excuse it," he went on sternly. "And I hope it's taught you a lesson about tittle-tattle."

"Oh, yes," I said. "But I'm sure Mr Barnaby didn't intend to tell me; I think it just slipped out. It was all my fault. I shouldn't have told anyone." I was so relieved that Daddy wasn't furious with me that I was willing to take the whole blame.

"Don't overdo the sackcloth and ashes bit," said Daddy, but he didn't sound stern any more. He looked at Wendy, and she smiled.

"Don't worry, Lizzie," she said. "If the Alexanders speak to us about it, we'll be on your side. Although you're right; you shouldn't have told anyone. But I don't think much of a fifteen-year-old boy who runs to his parents every time someone's nasty to him. How's he going to learn to fight his own battles, for heaven's sake? No, we'll just tell them we encourage you to sort out your own problems with your friends, and suggest they do the same."

29th May

Dear Diary,
THE LETTER arrived this morning. I was in the hall when the postman arrived, and there was this envelope with an Oxfordshire postmark and writing I didn't know. I was so panicked I just picked it up and put it in my pocket; I don't know what came over me.

Anyway, in for a penny in for a pound – I locked myself in the loo and read it. It was the most disgusting rubbish – 'Simon is very upset at the way your daughter is treating him. He is a sensitive boy, and your daughter's antagonism is having a detrimental effect on his playing and concentration.' Blah blah. Not a word about Mr Barnaby, thank God, although I was dead glad I said my piece to Daddy first. Anyway, I know I shouldn't have done it, but I ripped the whole thing up and flushed it away. It'll be feeding the fishes in the Atlantic by now.

I'm beginning to wonder about Simon. Wendy's right – what kind of person rushes to his parents every time somebody says something nasty? If I did that I'd never be off the phone. I'm definitely going off him; but I still think he's really good-looking – at least, I think I do. When I was reading his stinking parents' stinking letter I couldn't remember what he looks like. I couldn't conjure up his face at all. Weird. Back to Percy's tomorrow. When I come back in the summer I shall be on my own – I'm not inviting Laura back here again. I'm fed-up with being mucked around by my so-called friends.

Back at school, I resolved to be very cool to the three of them – Laura and Simon, because I was fed up with them blowing hot and cold with me, and Emma, because I felt I could no longer trust her not to tell people things she shouldn't. If I don't have much to do with any of them I won't get hurt, I reasoned. The trouble was, it wasn't as easy as that. Deciding to ignore people was simple in Cornwall, at home, surrounded by my family and people who loved me. At Percy's, it was a different matter – I couldn't totally avoid them, we were in classes together, and besides, what was I to do when they spoke to me?

So we carried on with a watered-down friendship, and I cursed myself for being weak. So far as Laura and Simon were concerned, I couldn't seem to help myself. It was easier with Emma; she tried to talk to me a few times, but when she got a lukewarm response from me she gave up, looked exasperated, and spoke to other people instead. I used this as a further reason for not being friends with her any more; she didn't try very hard to find out what was wrong, I kept telling myself fiercely. She's obviously not bothered about being friends with me; she's more interested in other people. I hadn't really noticed before, but she did seem to have lots of other friends, whereas Laura and Simon and I seemed to be locked into this odd, three-sided relationship with no room for anybody else. A month or two ago, this was what I had wanted; now, I was beginning to feel stifled. I missed Emma's friendship more than I cared to admit, even to myself, and it hurt that she hadn't tried harder to find out the reason for my coolness.

Two weeks after half-term, there was another lunch-time Workshop. End-of-term exams had begun, and I was starting to feel rather stretched; I wanted to do well in the exams, but it was difficult to revise and do lots of practice as well. There didn't seem to be enough hours in the day.

The upshot of all this was that I didn't play in the Workshop.

"Save yourself," Mr Owen told me, with a grin, but he didn't say what for. I had my hopes, though.

Laura played a movement from the Vaughan Williams oboe concerto, the one the Danish girl had played at the Festival Hall, and Simon accompanied her on the piano. They played brilliantly together. They looked so good too, the two blond heads bowed over their instruments. The old feeling for Simon came flooding back, and a poisonous slimy worm of jealousy wriggled inside me. Why didn't he want to accompany me? Why does he prefer Laura to me?

Afterwards I joined them backstage. Simon, pleased with his performance, seemed to have forgotten about his parents' letter and the 'detrimental effect' I was supposed to be having on him; he chatted away to me, and I wished it could always be like that. As the three of us walked back through the concert hall, I saw Emma talking to a lady in a violet headscarf. She broke off what she was saying, and looked at each of us in turn – when she looked at me there was such a strange look in her eyes. The look of a dog abandoned on the motorway – betrayal. Tough, I thought. Some friend you are; you tell me all those awful things about Laura and Simon, after hinting for months about some deep dark mystery, and then you land me in it by passing on my secrets. I don't need friends like that. I looked away, and walked past.

But the lady with the headscarf seemed to know Laura, and was calling her name.

"Yoo-hoo!" she called, waving a hand. "Laura! Over here!"

But Laura walked on without seeming to notice her.

"Look," I said, catching her arm and pointing. "That lady's waving to you. D'you know her?"

Laura stopped and turned to me. "Oh God," she said,

raising her eyes in disgust. "I'm trying to ignore her. Quick, let's get out!"

"I'm sorry," she called back across the hall, "but we've got to go, haven't we, Lizzie?" She made frantic faces at me.

"Do we?" I started to say, but Laura bore me off.

Outside, she pulled a face. "God," she said. "What a narrow escape. She usually stands nattering for hours."

"What was that all about, and why were you so rude?" I asked. "That lady was only trying to be friendly."

Laura was cross. "She's a dreadful woman," she muttered, scowling.

I was bemused. "Is she?" I said. "She seemed perfectly nice to me."

To my surprise, Laura rounded on me. "Well she's not," she said angrily. "She's a - a common old woman. Emma keeps on inviting her to Percy's; she's an aunt of hers, and she always buttonholes me, and my mother, too, when she's here. My mum doesn't speak to her, but she never takes the hint. She still blathers away about nothing. She's awful."

I still didn't see why. "But what's wrong with her?" I asked Laura.

"You wouldn't understand," Laura replied, still cross. "She's just not our sort, that's all. She's always yelling at people across the street; she wears awful clothes, and she's fat, and she smokes, and she works a till at Sainsbury's in the evenings. She's - she's common, that's all. Common as muck," she ended, wrinkling her nose and looking exactly like her mother. To Laura, being common seemed to be the worst sin imaginable. I was hit by the realization that Laura was a snob.

When all the exams were over, a group of us went off to Hyde Park to celebrate. It was a beautiful Saturday afternoon, hot and sunny without a hint of a breeze; the sky was that artificial sort of blue you see on postcards with not a cloud to spoil it. People were lying on the grass in bikinis and swimsuits, trying to brown their office-pale bodies before work again on Monday.

We bought ice-creams and watched the riders on Rotten Row, and then someone suggested we take a boat out on the Serpentine.

"What, eight in one boat?" said Tim Maynard. He put his arm around Laura, and she looked like the cat with the cream. "We'd sink it!"

So we hired two boats; I was in one with Laura and Tim, and Naresh. I was disappointed; I wanted to go with Simon, but he jumped in with Beth Williams and I was left standing there like a lemon.

"Come on Lizzie," Naresh said, and started to sing. "I am sailing, I am sailing . . . "

"Rowing actually," I said in a posh voice, and they laughed. It made me feel good. I looked at Simon; he was trying to impress Beth Williams, and he kept splashing the oars on top of the water and sending the boat round in circles. The other two in his boat, Adam and Helen, were laughing at him, and I could see he was getting cross. I thought suddenly of Ben; we both learnt to row and sail when we were small, like many children who live by the sea, and Ben now rowed for his school. He wouldn't have any trouble impressing a girl with his rowing, I thought, with a sudden feeling of scorn for Simon's rather pathetic efforts.

"Let me have a go," I said to Naresh, and I put the oars straight in the rowlocks and pulled us firmly into the middle of the Serpentine.

"Look at Lizzie!" I heard Adam yell. "She can do it, Si – why can't you?"

"I can do it!" Simon puffed angrily. "It's these stupid oars – they keep slipping out."

There was a fresh burst of laughter, and Laura looked over

her shoulder and started to giggle.

"I don't believe it!" she said. "He's dropped one, and he can't reach it! Should we go and help, d'you think?"

I turned the boat round and started back to the others. Tim Maynard looked at me with admiration. "You're really good," he said. "Where did you learn to do that?"

"At home," I told him. "In Cornwall. All the kids there can row; I'm not that good. You should see my friend Ben, he's whizz."

Laura scowled. "I'm not surprised they learn to row," she said sulkily. "There's nothing else to do there." She leant against Tim, but he was watching me and didn't take any notice of her.

When we reached the others, Adam was leaning out over the side of the boat, trying to reach the oar which was floating maddeningly just out of reach. Beth and Helen were laughing and clutching at each other, and Beth grabbed the back of Adam's shirt.

"Don't fall in!" she shrieked. "I'll save you, Adam!"

Simon looked furious, and stood up, making the boat rock alarmingly. The two girls shrieked again, and held on to the sides.

"Get out of the way," he said impatiently to Adam. "I'll get it – move out the way," and he took two lumbering steps down the boat, which made it lurch about even more. Half a gallon of the Serpentine slopped in over the sides, and Beth and Helen cackled like two laughing hyenas.

"Sit down!" I yelled. "Simon, sit down! You'll tip everybody over!" I hate seeing people messing around in boats – the lifeboat crew at Penlorren are kept busy all summer by visitors doing just what Simon was doing, and then falling overboard.

But Simon muttered something I couldn't hear and took another step towards Adam, who had stopped leaning over the edge and was holding on to the sides like the girls.

"Stop it, Si," he said anxiously. "It's not safe."

"We'll get the oar," Naresh shouted. "Lizzie will row us over."

"Good for Lizzie," said Laura sarcastically. "Leave him alone – he's not doing any harm. Go on Simon!" she bellowed. "You can do it!"

He reached the middle of the boat, and Adam scrambled past him to the other side. Simon knelt on the seat and reached out at an impossible angle; what happened next seemed to be in slow motion, like an action replay of a good bit on the television. The boat tilted alarmingly, and Simon slid gracefully down the seat and into the water with hardly a splash. Beth and Helen burst into fresh shrieks of laughter, and Tim Maynard guffawed loudly. We all laughed, actually – we couldn't help it, it looked so funny.

But Simon wasn't laughing when his head broke the surface. His mouth was open, and his eyes filled with panic.

"Help!" he gasped. "Help! I can't swim!" His arms thrashed around, and then his head disappeared under the water again.

I pulled my shoes off to jump in after him, but Naresh beat me to it; he dived in over the side and reached Simon in seconds. He grabbed him by the hair and hauled him to the surface. Simon's face was deathly white, and there was pondweed stuck to his left cheek. His eyes were closed. Oh God, I prayed silently, please let him be all right. Please, please, please. The air buzzed with the drama of it, and I could dimly see Beth with her hand clapped to her mouth, her eyes round O's of horror. But Simon opened his eyes almost immediately and coughed and spluttered, and started thrashing around again.

"Stand up," Naresh was urging him. "You'll be all right – just stand up."

"I can't swim," Simon kept saying. "I can't swim!"

"You don't need to," Naresh told him. "The water's not that deep. Look!" and he pulled Simon up by the hair again. Sure enough, the water barely reached his shoulders. "For heaven's sake, Si, STAND UP!" Simon eventually got the message. His feet found the bottom and he stood up, rubbing the water from his eyes and spluttering.

"Let go of my flaming hair!" he shouted at Naresh, "What are you trying to do, scalp me or something?"

Naresh let go. "Sorry," he said. "Only it was the first thing I got hold of. You'll be all right now."

"Of course I'm all right!" Simon yelled. "I was only mucking around – what the hell did *you* want to jump in for?"

"It didn't look like you were mucking around to me," Naresh said calmly. "Don't you think we ought to get out of the water? I don't know about you, but I'm up to my ankles in yuck down here."

But Simon carried on yelling. If he had been white before, he was red now; red with rage.

"You just like making people look ridiculous, don't you?" he shouted. "You just wanted to be a hero and impress the others. Stupid idiot! Bloody *Paki*!" he flung at him. Then he started to swear; dreadful, ugly words. I was shocked, and frightened too; Simon looked almost mad with temper. People in other boats and on the bank turned and stared at us.

But Naresh ignored him, and waded impassively through the water to our boat, where Tim Maynard hauled him back in. When we took the boats back Laura announced she was going back to Percy's with Simon.

She glared at me. "If you hadn't been flirting with Tim," she said, "and had got there a bit quicker, this wouldn't have happened!" And the two of them flounced off.

I was speechless. "I never!" I said eventually. "I never flirted with him!"

Naresh sat on the grass and wrung the water from his

socks. "Of course you didn't," he said evenly. "Only they've got to blame someone, haven't they - think of Simon's poor hurt pride. Of course it's not your fault the great pranny fell in, everybody knows that."

"Those awful things he said to you," I said slowly, remembering.

Naresh shrugged his shoulders. "Doesn't bother me; I was born in Birmingham, anyway." He looked at my face. "Look, Lizzie, don't take so much notice of them; they're just a couple of idiots. What does it matter what they say, or do? You're better off without them. Come on, I'll buy you another ice-cream."

I knew Naresh was right, but I felt really peculiar inside. I realized that Simon, with his horrible remarks to Naresh, had finally killed off whatever feelings I had had for him. They had drowned in the Serpentine, along with his wounded pride. But instead of feeling relief I just felt terribly sad. Why couldn't Simon be the wonderful person I wanted him to be, I kept asking myself, miserably. What a dreadful judge of character I must be; not only did I get Simon totally wrong, but I've also managed to lose the friendship of both Laura and Emma. Perhaps I am better off without them; but who's left? Who'll be friends with me now?

15

The Mozart Concerto

For a while, I was irresistibly reminded of my time at my old school, Oaklands. Plenty of people spoke to me, but I didn't seem to have any real friends any more. Emma looked as if she'd like to talk to me once or twice, but then she'd turn away with an odd look on her face. Laura asked Mrs Nightingale if she could change dorms; when Mrs Nightingale said no, she started telling Sophie and the others in the dorm nasty things about me, and hiding my things. At least, I never actually caught her at it, but I'm pretty sure it was her; I mean, toothbrushes and nighties don't just grow legs and commit suicide by throwing themselves out of windows, do they? But I tried to ignore it; she's just childish, I kept telling myself, gritting my teeth.

Then one evening I went up to the dorm and they were talking about me. I couldn't hear exactly what they were saying, but I caught the words 'Simon' and 'diary' and 'slushy rubbish', and then Laura's voice quite distinctly saying " . . . wouldn't touch her with a barge pole", and then a burst of unpleasant tinkling laughter, like ice-cubes in a glass. When I walked in the laughter stopped abruptly, and Sophie went red and started talking very quickly about something else. I ignored them all, pointedly. Let them laugh, I thought furiously to myself. What do I care? I don't need them as friends. I don't need *anybody*.

Two weeks before the end of term I had a message that Mr Owen wanted to see me. When I walked into his room, I was surprised to find Miss Quentin and Emma there too.

"Come in and sit down for a moment," said Mr Owen. "Miss Quentin has something to tell you both."

My heart leapt – Miss Quentin is the Head of Strings at Percy's, so I knew it was something important. She stood up, and smiled at us.

"Emma, Lizzie," she said. "You know about the concert on the seventeenth at the QEH. And I think you both know that the solo concerto this year is to be the Mozart K218." We both nodded, not looking at each other. "Now then, Mr Bishop particularly wanted somebody from the Middle School to play the concerto this year to show what goes on at the lower age range at Percy's, and about six violinists have been studying that concerto so we – Mr Owen and I – could get a better idea of who to pick."

She stopped for a moment. I held my breath; I knew what was coming, had known ever since I found out that the solo concerto was to be the one I was learning, and that Emma was studying it too. It was to be between her and me. And she was bound to get it; she had been at Percy's for years and years, whereas I was just a new girl.

Miss Quentin looked serious. "It was very hard," she said, "to make a final decision. Mr Owen and I have been discussing it for days. But eventually, this is what we decided." She turned to Emma, and my heart sank. "Emma, my dear," she said gently. "We are enormously impressed with your playing. You have a fine technique, and a very musical style. But after a lot of thought, we would like you to understudy Lizzie."

I couldn't believe I had heard correctly. "To understudy me?" I gasped. "Then – you want *me* to play the concerto?"

Miss Quentin laughed. "Yes, you!" she said. "Don't look so flabbergasted! Well done. I know you two are friends," she went on, "and I'm sorry if this causes any bad feeling between you both. But I'm afraid it's a hard fact about life in the music business; it's all about competition, and winning and losing." She smiled at us both, sympathetically.

Emma lifted her chin. "It's all right, Miss Quentin," she said steadily. 'Lizzie and I aren't friends, so there won't be any hard feelings. Thank you for considering me, anyway."

I was on cloud nine all afternoon. I'm going to play in the QEH, I kept saying to myself; I'm going to do the concerto! I'm going to be famous! The only slight disappointment was that I couldn't confide my delight in anyone; you just don't go around at Percy's telling everybody what you've achieved, mainly because people there are always doing brilliant things. Telling anyone other than your closest friends is considered boasting – which left me with a problem, because I was burning to tell someone, but I didn't seem to have any close friends left.

Then, quite by accident, I discovered a way of becoming popular with my classmates. We were in an English lesson with Miss Carter, a student teacher. It was the beginning of July, and very hot, almost thundery; nobody was paying much attention to the lesson, it was too soon after lunch, and too near the end of term. I sat by the window and looked out at the shimmering silver sky and thought about the amount of roast beef and stewed apple and custard I'd had for lunch, and wondered if Miss Carter would notice if I had a little snooze. On the whole, I thought not. As teachers went, she was about the drippiest I'd come across. She was quiet and mousy and timid-looking, and always had problems controlling classes. I turned what little attention I had to her.

We had been reading *Tess of the d'Urbervilles* with our usual teacher, and Miss Carter picked the book up enthusiastically. She was obviously a fan of Thomas Hardy. None of us were, though; we were dead bored.

"Now then, class," said Miss Carter, beaming away behind her little round granny specs. "Can anybody tell me something about Angel Clare – where Tess first met him, for example?"

I put my hand up straight away; I thought the lesson could do with being livened up.

"Yes?" Miss Carter said. "I'm afraid I don't know your name."

"Lizzie," I said, helpfully. "Please miss, why has he got such a spazzy name? I mean, Angel Clare – it's a girl's name, isn't it? Tess must have been mental to fancy a man with a name like that."

A couple of people snorted, but Miss Carter didn't hear them. "Perhaps," she said, seriously. "But Hardy often gave his characters names that sound strange to our ears. He often drew from the Bible – Bathsheba Everdene, for example, in *Far From the Madding Crowd.*"

"Oh," I said. She had obviously taken my question seriously. Then I thought. "Please miss, did he call any of his characters Herod? Or Pontius? Or – or Nebuchadnezzar?" A ripple of laughter went round the class, and a slight frown crossed Miss Carter's face.

"No," she said, turning away from me dismissively. "I don't think so. Now, can anyone tell me . . . "

I put my hand up again and bounced up and down in my seat. "Please miss!" I said.

Miss Carter pinned on a patient expression. "Yes, Lizzie?" she said. "What is it now?"

"Miss, d'you think Mr and Mrs Clare wanted a girl and they were going to call it Angela, but when he was born he was a boy so they called him Angel instead?" This time the whole class laughed, loudly. Robert Wells raised his hand. He's usually a pain in lessons, always messing around, but today I was glad he was joining in.

"Perhaps Clare's his middle name," he suggested. "I reckon his surname is something dead silly, like Snodgrass, or Pratt or . . ."

"Higginbottom," I put in, helpfully. "Shufflebum."

The rest of the class joined in, trying to outdo each other with silly surnames, and pretty soon Miss Carter's gentle little voice couldn't be heard above the general racket. Eventually she wrote on the blackboard 'Read Chapter 6 QUIETLY', and sat down at her desk with her hands over her ears. After a few minutes the teacher in the classroom next door came in to find out what all the chaos was about, which made us all sit hastily at our desks with our books open in front of us. I had to stuff my fist in my mouth to stop myself giggling, and when the teacher had gone back to his class I realized I had *Tess* upside-down.

After the lesson, several people crowded round me in the corridor.

"That was ace," said Robert Wells, grinning. "How did you keep a straight face when you said Nebuchadnezzar?"

I looked modest. "Easy, really," I told him.

"Honestly, old Carter didn't know whether you were serious or not," someone else said. "She's so easy to wind up."

"I haven't enjoyed English so much for ages," said another girl. "That was whizz, Lizzie!"

Emma was just about the only one who didn't look amused by it all. In fact, she looked very disapproving.

"I don't think that was very kind," she told me, in the corridor. "Poor Miss Carter – she didn't know what to do. Messing around like that in lessons isn't funny; it's dead immature."

I was suddenly cross with her. Everyone else had enjoyed the joke; why couldn't she?

"You think you're so grown-up, don't you?" I flared. "You're always telling other people how to behave. You're such a goody-goody, you get on my wick."

Emma looked hurt. "So you know how to behave, do you?" she said. "You could have fooled me. Some friend you've turned out to be."

"Oh yes," I said, slowly and sarcastically. "And what a great friend *you've* been, telling Simon and getting me into all that trouble."

Emma looked baffled. "Trouble about what?" she asked. "What did I tell Simon?"

"Oh come on, Emma!" I was exasperated. "You know jolly well what. You told him what Mr Barnaby said about him, didn't you? And he told his parents, and they got cross and thought I was deliberately upsetting him and wrote to mine about it. Only I told them first, and when the letter arrived I got rid of it!"

Emma was shaking her head. "But I didn't," she said. "I didn't tell him. I'd forgotten all about what Mr Barnaby supposedly said. It was probably Laura."

I didn't want to believe her, although I had a sudden suspicion that she might be right. "I don't believe you," I said. I felt really fed-up and cross with her; it was the way she said 'supposedly', it sounded as if she thought I'd made the whole thing up.

I attacked on another front. "Anyway," I said, cruelly, "at least the right person is playing the concerto in the concert."

"Yes, and you're really pleased with yourself, aren't you?" Emma said, bitterly. "If you knew how hard I'd worked for it . . ."

"So've I!" I shouted. "They want *me* to play it because I'm better than you, and you just can't take that, can you?"

"You're not better than me!"

"Miss Quentin and Mr Owen think I am or they wouldn't

have picked me, would they? You wouldn't have played it in a million years, because you're *just no good!*"

"I am!" Emma choked. "I am! I'm understudying you, aren't I?"

I smiled; a knowing, nasty little smile. "Ah, but you're not playing it, are you? I am!"

Emma shot me a look of pure hate. "I thought you were so nice," she said. She sounded close to tears. "But you're just like the other two after all. You've turned out just like Laura and Simon. Well, I hate all of you!"

"And we hate you, too!" I yelled. "I don't believe you didn't tell Simon! You're a liar – and a thief!" I finished up.

Emma went white, and gulped. "I am not," she said, through clenched teeth. "I am not a thief, and I don't tell lies, and I never want to speak to you again." She blinked hard, to stop herself crying, and stumbled off down the corridor.

I steeled myself, and told myself I didn't care that she was upset. So what, I thought; I've been upset enough lately, what with her and Laura and Simon all mucking me around. It's about time someone else learnt what it feels like. But in truth, I felt dreadfully ashamed of myself for being so horrible to Emma and saying such nasty things; she hadn't deserved it, I knew that. Deep down.

But then the other side of me took over, a mean hard side. What does it matter, it said. She'll be all right. And who knows whether she actually stole those things or not? She hardly seemed to know herself, the other day; she'd obviously been so distraught by her brother's death she hadn't known *what* she was doing. And Laura did say the stealing had stopped once Emma had been caught. Anyway, she's not your friend; she said so. You don't care about her; you don't need her. You only need yourself.

In the meantime, I carried on disrupting lessons, egged on by Robert Wells and his cronies. I had discovered that making daft comments and generally getting on the teachers' nerves made my classmates laugh, and I enjoyed the feeling. I also like the feeling of living dangerously, of dicing with detentions; I had always been so well-behaved, such a goody-goody (like Emma), and this new me felt incredibly daring and devil-may-care. Of course, I carefully chose just whose classes to play up in; some teachers were safe, while others were most definitely off limits. I was beginning to enjoy myself again.

When I rang home to tell them the news about the concerto, they were thrilled to bits.

"Lizzie!" said Daddy, chuffed. "Oh, well done, sweetie! We're proud of you! Get tickets for us, won't you? I'm not missing your London début, not for the world!"

Then we got the results of the end-of-term exams, and I was amazed to find I'd sailed through all of them; I'd even got ninety-eight per cent in English, which was unheard of for me. I secretly wondered if my paper had got muddled up with someone else's, but no; when we got them back there was mine, marked in Mr Baker's round black handwriting – '98% – Excellent work!'

That lunch-time the conversation got around to our exam results.

"I only got twenty-three per cent in English," Robert Wells groaned. "Old Baker's got it in for me – my parents will go round the twist."

Laura picked at her salad. "That's because you're always mucking around," she told him. Her eyes slid sideways to me. "Like Lizzie," she added.

"I don't mess around in Mr Baker's lessons," I told her. "Anyway, I got ninety-eight per cent." They weren't as impressed as I'd hoped they'd be.

"Wow," said Tim Maynard, taking the tomato off Laura's plate, "a genius. Can I have your egg as well, Laura?"

"Yes," I went on, preening. "Actually, my father's a famous writer, so I suppose it must run in the family."

Laura scoffed. "He's not famous! I'd never heard of him before. Anybody'd think he was Jeffrey Archer." She started on her semolina pudding.

"Well, we all know you're illiterate. If you know what that means," I said, sarcastically. We glared at each other, like two cats on a wall, and the others exchanged glances, scenting a good argument.

"I'm not illiterate," Laura said, bristling. "But even if I was, that's better than being big-headed, like you. We haven't heard anything other than your brilliant exam results and your concerto for days."

"I'm not big-headed!" I was stung. "I've hardly told anybody!"

"Well, how come we're all sick to death of it then?" Laura looked round at the others for support. "Aren't we?"

Say no, I pleaded silently. Say you don't know what she's on about. Stick up for me – please. But a couple of them nodded their heads, and I shrivelled inside.

"You're just jealous," I muttered.

Laura laughed. "Jealous of you? You've got to be kidding."

I'd suddenly had enough of her. "You think you're so great, don't you?" I yelled, and there was a sudden hush in the dining hall. "Well I don't. I think you're a nasty trouble-making COW, and I wish I'd never got friendly with you in the first place!"

"The feeling's mutual!" Laura yelled back. "You're just a baby; a silly, childish, boring baby. You'll never get a boyfriend – you go red every time a boy speaks to you! Simon says . . . "

"Oh, *shut up* about Simon!" I was spluttering with rage. "I'm sick of him too. You two deserve each other! It was you who told him about – that *thing* wasn't it? It wasn't Emma at all !"

Laura sneered. "Yes, it was me, if you must know. So what?

What are you going to do about it?"

I had never been so angry with anyone in my life before. I stood up, aware of fifty pairs of eyes watching me with interest.

"This," I said, and I put my hand on the back of her beautiful blonde head and pushed her face squarely into the middle of her bowl of semolina. Everybody laughed, but as I stalked from the dining hall the satisfaction was spoiled by another less pleasant feeling.

That afternoon we had English with Miss Carter again. When she got into the classroom, she announced that she wanted us to act bits out of *Tess*.

"It's not a play, of course, but I think it will make it stick in your minds much better."

I immediately stood up. "Whizz," I said. "I'll be Tess, OK?"

Miss Carter looked dubious. "I don't know about that," she told me. "Perhaps somebody else . . . ?"

"Oh go on, miss," I pleaded. "I'll be much better than anybody else. Won't I?" I appealed to the class for support and they all murmured agreement, knowing I was likely to entertain them.

Miss Carter put her hands up, resignedly. "All right then. Just so long as you're sensible." But I could tell she wasn't sure; I could see it in her eyes, and the feeling of power I got was sudden and enormous. Just for a moment I thought I understood what made Laura act the way she did, trampling over other people.

Robert Wells stood up. "And I'll be Angel Clare," he announced. "As long as I don't have to kiss you." Everyone laughed, and Miss Carter joined in, to show she was a good sport, and of course she wasn't worried about what might happen, good heavens no.

Robert and I stood in front of the class. I put on my best Cornish accent.

The Mozart Concerto

"Oh Angel," I lisped, "I be so in love with thee!"

Robert tried to copy me. "Why, Tess," he said. "Thou be such a pretty maid, I don't half fancy thee. Get thy clothes off ..."

The whole class erupted with laughter, and Miss Carter stood up hurriedly.

"Come along now," she said, a worried look on her face. "You know that's not in the book. Do it properly, or you can both sit down and someone else can do it."

We looked at each other, thwarted. But then I had another idea.

"I don't feel right," I said. "I need to dress up." I looked around the room; there was a table at the back which had been used until recently for a display of Juniors' poetry, and it was still covered with a long white cloth. I took it off the table and wrapped it around myself, like a Roman toga. "That's better," I said.

"It's all right, miss," Robert assured Miss Carter. "We'll do it properly. Now, Tess," he addressed me, "go and milk thy cows."

I trotted obediently to a corner of the room, nearly tripping over the tablecloth as I did so, and pretended to milk a chair. I was getting bored; I really wanted to go and sit down at my desk. If I do something really stupid, something really beyond the pale, Miss Carter is bound to tell us off and make us sit down. So I stood up suddenly.

"Angel!" I bawled. "Thou art my heart's delight! I cannot resist thee any longer!" And I strode across the room and threw my arms around Robert. To my utter astonishment he kissed me on the lips, hard, and I felt myself go bright red with embarrassment as the class roared.

Miss Carter was horrified. "Robert!" she squawked, dancing around. "Lizzie! Stop that! Stop it, this instant, do you hear me!"

But Robert took no notice. "Oh Tess!" he groaned. He tipped me backwards and made kissing noises all round my neck. I was dead uncomfortable. "Oh Tess! I love thee!"

"Put me down," I whispered loudly. "Stop it, Robert, you're hurting my back."

By this time the class was laughing uncontrollably. Miss Carter was squeaking hysterically, and Robert was practically breaking my back. The din was monumental, and the classroom door swung open just as Robert dropped me on the floor with a thud.

"God's teeth!" boomed a man's voice. "What in heaven's name is going on in here?" It was Mr Baker, our usual English teacher.

Robert scuttled back to his desk, and Miss Carter burst into tears.

"It's these dreadful children," she sobbed. "Lizzie Oliver. She's been making a frightful exhibition of herself – kissing a boy in front of the whole class." She shuddered with distaste.

"But it was only . . . " I started to say.

"Only what?" Mr Baker barked furiously. "Only a joke? One that Miss Carter abjectly failed to see, clearly. Get up off the floor child."

I did so, nearly falling over the tablecloth again. I suddenly felt really sorry for Miss Carter.

Mr Baker looked at me, grimly. "What on earth do you think you're playing at? I've heard rather too much about your little jokes just lately; your fun and games in lessons. I think the time has come for you to visit the Director, don't you?"

I stared at him miserably. "But, sir . . . " I said. I tried to unwrap the tablecloth from my waist, but Mr Baker stopped me.

"No," he said. "Leave it on. I'm sure Mr Bishop would like to see your fetching frock." And with that he marched me by my shoulders from the room, leaving Miss Carter still sobbing behind us.

16

Facing the Music

I sat outside Mr Bishop's office quaking with fear; you only have to go and see him for the most awful crimes imaginable, and the only time I had ever spoken to him at school was at my audition. When I finally went in he sat behind his big leather-topped desk and looked dolefully at me over the top of his spectacles.

"Lizzie," he said, and shook his head sadly. "You have disappointed me. I didn't expect this kind of behaviour from you."

I looked at my feet and felt about two inches high. "I know," I whispered. "I'm sorry." I had expected him to yell and shout at me; his air of gentleness made me feel worse, somehow.

Mr Bishop looked at the piece of paper on his desk. "Let me see now; the catalogue of your crimes. Turning up late for lessons with no excuse. Cheeking teachers. Not handing in your prep. Telling Mr Blenkinsop you could hear the firebell, and persuading him to let the class go. Trying to drown somebody in a plate of semolina. Oh yes, and Miss Carter; she's complained five times about you. I see this time you were being particularly friendly with Robert Wells in front of the whole class." His eyebrows raised, and he looked at me. "I gather Miss Carter was in tears when Mr Baker persuaded you to leave the classroom and come and see me."

My head sank even lower. "Yes, sir. Sorry, sir," I whispered again.

Mr Bishop took his spectacles off and polished them. "Well, now," he said mildly. "Why don't you take off that tablecloth, sit down, and tell me all about it? Spare me no details – I'm extremely interested to hear why such a talented, well-behaved and polite young lady suddenly turns into a rabble-rousing hooligan."

I did as he told me, the first two things at any rate. The third was much more difficult. How could I tell him why I had behaved so badly, when I didn't even know myself? I dimly knew that it was all tied up with having fancied Simon and then gone off him, and being friends with Emma and Laura and then losing that friendship, and wanting to impress my classmates and have them like me. But I couldn't tell Mr Bishop all that; it was as unclear to me as it would surely be to him, and besides, it sounded petty even to my ears. What interest would Mr Bishop have in my stupid problems?

So I just sat there idiotically staring at my folded hands in my lap and not saying a word. After a while, Mr Bishop put his spectacles back on and spoke to me again.

"My dear," he said gently. "Don't you have anything to say? Miss Carter was extremely upset, you know; she says you've put her off teaching for life. I do hold a very dim view of baiting student teachers like that – it's very cruel."

Tears filled my eyes. I could feel all the events and emotions of the last few weeks churning away inside me, threatening to explode. I was afraid I would make a dreadful scene if I didn't keep it all under control.

I shook my head. "I don't know, sir," I said feebly. "I'm sorry if I upset Miss Carter; I didn't mean to. It was only a joke. We only did it for a laugh, Robert and me."

Mr Bishop sighed. "That's what I can't understand," he said. "We're used to that kind of silly behaviour from Robert Wells – we expect it, even. But I certainly didn't expect it from you." He looked at me closely, and I felt the old familiar blush creeping up my face. "You've let us down, Lizzie. But what's worse – what you're going to have to live with – is that you've let *yourself* down. Badly. It's a dangerous road, the one you've started to tread. Before very long people start treating you as just a clown, someone they can't take seriously, and they lose all respect for you. It's easy to get people to laugh at you, but once you've lost their respect it's well-nigh impossible to get it back." He said all this quite calmly, without any hint that he was telling me off, and somehow that upset me more than anything.

"I'm not like that really," I said urgently. I wanted people to take me seriously; I wanted them to respect me. "I won't do it again, sir. Honestly."

"I hope you're right," Mr Bishop said. He smiled at me, sadly. "Now, this isn't pleasant for me, but I'm sure you realize that we cannot allow this sort of thing to go unreprimanded. You have to be seen to be punished for your behaviour."

"Yes, sir," I said, worried at what awful thing he might come up with. "What – what's going to happen to me?"

Mr Bishop considered for a moment. "Well now, let me see," he said. "What's the worst thing you can imagine happening to you, here at Percy's?"

I didn't hesitate for a moment. "Not playing the Mozart," I answered at once. "Not doing the concerto at the QEH on Saturday."

As soon as I uttered the words I knew what Mr Bishop was going to say. He nodded slowly and smiled again, but it was an even sadder smile.

"Very well," he said. "I gather Emma Nash has been

understudying you. She will play the solo concerto instead of you. And I do hope, my dear, that you have learned something from all this."

I scarcely heard him. I felt as if someone had poured a bucket of cold water over me, and a loud wind roared in my ears.

"No!" I gasped. "No! It's not fair – she can't! I'm playing it. Miss Quentin said so. Please, no! Please!" I begged Mr Bishop, but it made not a scrap of difference. My fate had been decided, and what made it worse was that I had decided it myself.

The next few days were dreadful. I couldn't believe that I had been so happy at Percy's such a short time before. Now in the space of a couple of weeks I had lost my friends and my chance to play the concerto, and my whole world seemed to have crumbled. There was no more messing around in lessons; the word had gone round that I had had to see the Director and as a result my classmates hardly dared speak to me, as if even talking to me would tar them with the same brush and get them, too, into trouble with Mr Bishop.

I ached to tell someone about it, to confide in just one person, but of course there was nobody to tell. I was on my own. Not only that, but the really bad bit was still to come; I had to tell Daddy. He and Wendy were coming to London for the weekend for the concert, and were really proud of me. How was I to tell him I wouldn't be playing after all? What Mr Bishop had said about letting people down was right; I felt so ashamed.

I rang Daddy up two days before the concert with the vague idea of telling him then, but it was no good. There was no privacy by the telephone that evening and anyway, he kept going on about how everybody in Penwithin was sure I was going to be a world-famous violinist.

"We're so looking forward to it, sweetie," he told me, his voice bursting with pride over the wire. "Wendy's bought a new dress, and her parents are coming too. Ben's Mum and Dad are sending some flowers – whoops, I don't think I was supposed to tell you that! Only Mrs Polkerris was asking the other day if you like red roses, and I said I was sure you did. You do, don't you? And Wendy has strict instructions to bring back your autograph for half a dozen of the kids in her old class at school, isn't that sweet? I tell you, you're really famous in these parts – you'll be besieged when you get back!"

How could I tell him I wasn't playing the solo any more after that? I couldn't. I couldn't bear to spoil the pleasure he was so obviously taking in it. Him and lots of other people, by the sound of it; it seemed as though half Penwithin was rooting for me, and I was unbearably moved by it.

So I just made agreeing noises, only that didn't work either because Daddy asked me what was wrong.

"Wrong?" I said, unconvincingly. "Nothing's wrong."

"I hope you're not going down with something – you don't want anything spoiling your big day, do you?"

"It's nothing," I told him shortly. "I'm not going down with anything, Daddy – do stop going on about it."

"I expect you're a bit nervous; it's only to be expected, sweetie, after all it is an important occasion for . . . "

"Daddy!" I snapped. I couldn't help it. "Don't go on! I'm perfectly all right, I keep telling you. I'm not nervous; don't make such a *fuss*!" It was on the tip of my tongue to tell him that there was no longer anything for me to be nervous about, but I couldn't bring myself to.

So the telephone call ended with Daddy being puzzled and hurt, and me feeling awful. It's not fair, I kept thinking, bitterly; it's just not fair.

I was still playing in the concert, in the orchestra; we were playing an overture and a symphony, and of course accompanying Emma in the Mozart concerto, which meant I had to suffer the indignity of just being a common-or-garden member of the orchestra whereas before I had been the Queen Bee, the soloist. At the first rehearsal after Emma took over from me I had skulked in and sat at the back, hoping nobody would notice me and certain everybody was talking about me, nudging each other and telling each other what had happened.

It was a dreadful rehearsal. At least, the rehearsal itself was OK, but I felt dreadful. Afterwards I saw Laura and Simon go into a huddle; they were looking at me, whispering and giggling, and my face flamed as I bent over my violin case. I don't care, I thought furiously to myself. I don't need them. Everybody else ignored me; Teddie, Robert Wells, Tim Maynard, Bethan Williams; everybody.

Everybody except Naresh, that is. He went up and spoke to Emma when the rehearsal ended, and she smiled happily and looked slightly dazed. She had played beautifully, I couldn't deny that. Then Naresh spotted me, and came over.

"Hi Lizzie," he said. "I'm sorry about what happened – you know, not playing the concerto after all. You must be feeling pretty cut up about it."

I spun round furiously. "What's it to you?" I snapped. "I don't need your pity."

Naresh didn't bat an eyelid. "You're not getting pity," he said mildly. "Just a little friendly sympathy, that's all."

"I don't know why you're bothering talking to me," I said. "Nobody else is. Why don't you go back over to Emma and tell her how wonderfully she played, instead? Tell her I hope she enjoys herself." I heard myself whining and despised myself for it, but couldn't seem to stop it.

"Nope," Naresh said, cheerfully. "You tell her, if you want to. I'm not going to. And perhaps the reason nobody's talking to you is because you're not talking to them – had you thought of that?"

"Everyone's ignoring me," I told him. "They are, Naresh; people have been whispering about me all rehearsal. And look at Laura and Simon, over there – they're having a good laugh at my expense."

Naresh shook his head. "They're not talking about you. When I walked past they were giggling about something that was on TV last night."

"They weren't! They were talking about me, and – and *sneering*!"

"No they weren't."

"They were! They were! Everyone's laughing about me, and it's not fair. It was my concerto. It's just not fair!" I moved my hands helplessly, and Naresh stepped towards me.

"Keep your wig on," he said. "Nobody's ignoring you, or laughing at you – honestly. Emma's the only one who's bothered about what happened, and that's not exactly surprising considering it means a big chance for her, is it?"

"It's still not fair," I muttered. "It was my concerto – Miss Quentin said so – and Mr Bishop had no right to take it away."

Naresh raised an eyebrow. "He is the Director," he pointed out. "I guess that gives him the right to do what he wants."

"You've no idea, have you? You've no idea what it's like for me, having to play in the orchestra while everyone's gossiping about me."

"Look," Naresh sighed, impatiently. "For the last time, nobody's gossiping about you. Do you really think people have got nothing better to do than yack about you? I don't think anyone's that interested any more – apart from you, of course. OK, I admit it – I did feel sorry for you, having the solo taken away from you. But you can't say you didn't deserve it, Lizzie, the way you've been messing around just lately; you can't do that kind of thing and expect teachers to just laugh it off."

I glared at him and didn't say anything.

"But it's obvious you don't need anyone's sympathy," he went on. "You've got enough self-pity to last a lifetime. You want to stop feeling so sorry for yourself; who knows, you might even enjoy the concert then." And he went off to talk to Emma again.

I thought about Naresh's words as I lay in bed the night before the concert. He was right; I was feeling sorry for myself. But then, I thought, I had good reason to. Why couldn't anybody see how miserable I was? Why did they just seem to think I was sulking because I wasn't doing the concerto any more? Any why did nobody like me any more – what was wrong with me? A wave of misery washed over me and tears pricked my eyes and the back of my nose, like a sneeze. Even Naresh had lost patience with me, and he was usually so unmoved by things; I remembered how cool he'd been after the episode with Simon in Hyde Park.

I tossed and turned, feeling feverish and uncomfortable. My sheet was rucked up underneath me and I had a crick in my neck and a headache. Perhaps I *am* going down with something, I thought wildly; perhaps I'll be ill tomorrow and won't have to play in the concert tomorrow after all, perhaps I won't have to explain to Daddy, perhaps . . . but I knew it was just wishful thinking.

One of the other girls started to snore, and the sound irritated me. Shut up, I thought furiously; shut up and let me get some sleep. I hate sharing a dorm, I hate the lack of privacy; I hate this place and everybody in it, I hate it, I hate it, HATE IT! I clenched my fists and began to cry silently, hot painful tears that hurt so much because I couldn't give in to them for fear of waking the others.

Suddenly, from nowhere, a thought floated across my mind, so clear it was as if somebody had spoken. RUN AWAY, it said; my tears stopped instantly, as though switched off. Run away – but where to? I peered at the illuminated hands of my clock; it was five minutes to midnight. Where could I go at this time of night? Anywhere, came back the answer; just get out, get away, come on, get up, no time to lose, get up, get up, *RUN AWAY!*

Yes, I thought, yes, I have to, it's the only answer, and I was propelled almost despite myself out of bed and into some clothes. I paused to pick up Ben's sloppy letter, the photograph of Rufus and Fishpaste and my purse, and shoved them into the pocket of my jeans. Then I crept down the stairs, carefully avoiding the creaky ones, along the back corridor and out of the back door, which was on a Yale lock and easy to open. It was as simple as that. There was one nasty-ish moment, when I spotted the night watchman coming round the corner, but I stepped back into the shadows and he went past without seeing me.

I wandered through the streets and squares of Bloomsbury for a while, not really knowing what to do or where to go. It was a muggy July night, cloudy and threatening rain; all the fine dry weather of the previous weeks seem to have gone. I heard a rumble of thunder in the distance and yawned. After a bit I realized what a ridiculous idea running away had been, and that I would have to go back. Only when I got back to Percy's, of course, I couldn't get in; all the doors were securely locked, including the one I'd left by. I stood on the doorstep, yawning; the wind had got up, and a few drops of rain had started to fall. I supposed I would have to ring the bell and wake everybody up – the thought of the trouble I would get into for doing that horrified me. And what reason was I to give for being outside at that time of night? – 'Sorry, Mrs Nightingale, but I couldn't sleep and I fancied a stroll'? It was no good, I was locked out for the night.

Then I remembered Daddy and Wendy were in London that weekend for the concert, staying with Wendy's parents in Richmond. I would go there. It was the only thing I could do. I couldn't remember exactly where in Richmond they lived but I knew it was somewhere near the Park, and I didn't think it would be difficult to find.

The first part of the journey wasn't too bad. I caught the Tube at Russell Square, amazed at the number of people still around at that time of night and being careful to sit near the doors and not to talk to anyone. I was a bit frightened when a dirty-looking old man in a greasy hat sidled up to me at South Kensington, where I had to change trains, and asked me if I had a cigarette, of all things. I crossed my eyes at him and stuck out my jaw and babbled, and he went off muttering crossly about today's youth being allowed to stay up until all hours.

But when I got off the train at Richmond things got worse. For a start, the few drops of rain which had begun when I left Percy's the second time were now fairly heavy, and accompanied by approaching rumbles of thunder and flashes of lightning. Also, I realized I didn't have a clue which direction to go in. I wandered round vaguely for a while, hoping to see something I recognized, but it was hopeless; I had only been to Wendy's parents house a couple of times before, and hadn't really taken much notice of the surroundings. The rain had by now developed into a full-blown thunderstorm, and I was getting soaked – soaked, and cold, and tired and frustrated. What am I going to do, I thought frantically, what am I going to do? I dimly imagined myself wandering around Richmond for all eternity, like a modern Flying Dutchman.

Then I saw a wonderful sight – a cab, driving slowly past with its 'For Hire' sign lit. I waved my arms hysterically until it stopped, and the driver wound the window down and stared at me.

"Gor blimey!" he said. "You look a bit wet, luv - you better get in. Where to?"

I slammed the door shut behind me and sat there, shivering. "I don't know," I said, miserably. "I can't remember," and tears slid down my nose and mixed with the rain.

The taxi driver turned round and slid the partition window open. "Come on luv," he said kindly, handing me a hanky. "wipe your face and I'll see what I can do. It is clean," he assured me, and I did what he told me, sniffing. "Now then," he said. "What's the problem? Where are you trying to get to?"

"It's my stepmother's parents' house - they live in Richmond somewhere but I can't remember where, and I've been wandering round for ages in the rain, and I'm all wet, and I'm tired, and . . ." another sob shuddered through me.

"All right luv, take it easy. If you can't remember the road, what does the house look like? Can you remember?"

"It's big - it's near the park."

"Lots of those around." He pulled the cab up outside a telephone box. "What's their surname? I'll have a look in the directory."

"It's Bullock," I told him. "Mr Bullock's name is Gordon, if that helps."

The cab driver emerged from the phone box looking triumphant. "Gotcha!" he said, climbing back in behind the wheel. "Only one G Bullock in the phone book in them big posh houses near the Park. Soon be there, luv - you just relax."

When we stopped outside the Bullock's house - I recognized it once we were there - the taxi driver wouldn't take his fare.

"You keep it, luv," he said, shaking his head. "It was a pleasure to help a lady in distress. And don't you go wandering round the streets by yourself again at this time of night – it ain't safe."

. I was exhausted. I hammered on the front door for what seemed like hours, and Mr Bullock eventually opened it.

"What in heaven's name?" he said. "Don't you know it's two o'clock in the . . . Good heavens!" he suddenly realized it was me. "Little Lizzie! Come in, my dear, come in!"

My hair was in rat's tails, my jeans were sticking to my legs, and I was so tired I could barely stand up. Daddy was coming down the stairs tying his dressing-gown, a worried expression on his face. He looked even more worried when he saw me.

"Whatever's the matter, sweetie?" he asked me, anxiety and tiredness etched into his face. "What's happened?"

I hurled myself at him and flung my arms around his neck. "Daddy!" I choked into his dressing-gown, my legs buckling beneath me. "It's so awful! Don't make me go back! Don't make me go back!" And I burst into tears of misery and exhaustion and relief.

17

The Concert

Daddy looked slightly less alarmed once I'd stopped bawling. Wendy came downstairs looking serene and unruffled, and promptly took charge; she dispatched her parents into the kitchen to make me a hot drink, sent Daddy to find a blanket, and propelled me upstairs to take off my sodden clothes and wrap me in a pair of her father's old pyjamas.

Sitting downstairs again in the kitchen, sipping on a mug of Horlicks, with the blanket around my shoulders and Rufus on my feet, things didn't seem quite so bleak.

"But I'm not going back," I said definitely, still hiccuping slightly from the crying. "I can't – not now, I just can't."

"Just drink your Horlicks," Daddy said soothingly, as Wendy's parents discreetly slid away back to bed. "We'll talk about it then, and you can tell us what's been going on."

So I did, and it wasn't so difficult after all. I told them all about Emma, Laura and Simon; how they had been my friends, and how I had lost them, one by one. I told them about the trouble at school, how I had started off just by making my classmates laugh but it had gradually got out of hand, until Mr Bishop had finally told me I couldn't play the concerto after all (I carefully avoided looking at them when I told them that bit). And I told them how everybody had stopped talking to me after that, and had sneered and laughed about me behind my back, and Naresh had tried to cheer me up but I snapped at him, until even he got fed up with me and started ignoring me, and eventually I had become so miserable I couldn't bear it any longer "and I had to get away," I finished up. "I couldn't think what else to do. It was just awful, Daddy."

Daddy and Wendy exchanged glances, and Daddy put an arm round me.

"I can see it must have been. But sweetie, running away is never the answer; it doesn't solve anything, because the things you've run away from are still there, waiting to be sorted out."

"You mean, I've got to solve my problems instead of running away from them?" Daddy nodded, and I sighed heavily. "I s'pose I knew that anyway. It was just . . . it's hard. I always thought that life got easier as you grew up, but it seems to get more difficult."

Daddy thought hard.

"Not necessarily more difficult," he said slowly. "More complicated, perhaps; more responsibilities to people other than yourself. And you find out that other people don't automatically like you just because you're you – they can take against you for no apparent reason, and that can hurt."

"But why don't they? And why didn't Simon feel the same way about me as I did about him? I really liked him."

Wendy looked at me sympathetically.

"Sebastian House?" she said, and I understood what she meant and nodded. "Lizzie," she said. "You can love somebody like crazy, but you can't make them love you back. You invented the person you wanted Simon to be; he wasn't that nice caring person at all, you just wanted him to be like that.

That's why you feel so let down, because he hasn't lived up to your image of him."

Understanding why I felt so let down didn't make me feel any better, though. There were so many questions I wanted answers for, so many things I needed to know.

"Will boys ever like me – as a girl, I mean, not just as a friend?"

"Of course they will. Just be yourself, be Lizzie, and try to see them as themselves too."

"But why have I lost all my friends?" I asked. "Why doesn't anybody like me – what's wrong with me?"

Daddy took my hand and knelt beside me, and Rufus licked his face.

"Sweetie," Daddy said gently. "Nothing's wrong with you. Don't think that. You've had a bad time, and you're probably imagining people are talking about you when they're not at all. Naresh is right – people *are* usually far too preoccupied with their own problems to bother about anybody else's. Just go back to Percy's and be your usual cheerful friendly self; you'll find people soon treat you in the same way, and those who don't aren't worth bothering about anyway."

"But I can't, I can't go back. I've been so horrid to Emma, and I can't face Laura and Simon and all those teachers, and besides I've let you down. You were so looking forward to hearing me playing the concerto, and now I'm not, and I wanted to so badly!"

"It doesn't matter," Daddy assured me. "We still love you and are proud of you, whether you're playing the solo or are the lowliest and most insignificant member of the orchestra. When you go back you must decide for yourself the best way of coping with things – if I were you I should apologize to Emma and the teachers you were rude to, and to Mr Bishop too."

"I really wanted to play that Mozart," I said sadly. "It's just not fair."

Daddy spoke quite sternly, and I was surprised. "Come on now, Lizzie. Mr Bishop couldn't let you get away with that sort of silly behaviour," he said. "You must know that."

"Maybe," I looked at him. "But I still don't think it's fair."

"Life isn't fair, sometimes," Daddy told me, his face softening. "When you're a child you're protected from the bad things, and I sometimes wish I could go on protecting you. Every parent feels the same about their children – it's hard, watching them grow up and getting hurt by things. But I can't protect you for ever, and it would be wrong of me to try."

"There are good things about growing up too, Lizzie," Wendy told me, her voice gentle. "You'll discover some of those, pretty soon."

Daddy stood up decisively. "And now," he said, "I think you ought to go and get some sleep – you've a long day ahead of you, and you don't want to fall asleep during the concert. Let's all go to bed."

I stood up too, and for a long moment Daddy and I looked into each other's eyes. Then I smiled slightly.

"Yes," I said. "All right."

The journey back to Percy's the next morning wasn't as eventful as the one to Richmond, neither was it so worrying, although I was pretty apprehensive about what would happen when I actually got there. Daddy had rung after I had gone to bed to let them know where I was, and I thought Mr Bishop would be cross at having been dragged from his bed at such an ungodly hour. But he didn't seem to be cross when I went to see him, as soon as I got back; half-way through the morning, thanks to my mega-late night.

"Lizzie," he said, ushering me to a chair. "Your father rang and told me all that's been going on. I'm sorry you've been having problems. I do with you'd told somebody at the time – if not me then Mrs Nightingale, or another teacher you like and trust. Or did you not feel you could trust anybody?"

"It wasn't that," I said truthfully. "It was just I didn't think anybody would be interested. I mean, it sounds so stupid, doesn't it? – 'my friends don't like me anymore'."

Mr Bishop looked serious. "My dear, it's our job to be interested. That's why we're here – not just to tell you off, and stop you doing things you want to do, but to be here when you need us. For whatever reason. And if you feel you can't confide in us then that means we've failed. And if things get so bad you feel running away is the only answer, then we've failed badly."

"Oh no," I said hurriedly. "It wasn't your fault. Honestly. I know I shouldn't have run away, and I'm really sorry I was so rude to all those teachers. I won't do it again."

"I'm sure you won't," Mr Bishop said. "And I want you to promise me that you'll tell somebody if you have any problems in the future. No matter how silly you think they might be."

So I duly promised him, and as I did so I reflected that he wasn't so bad really. For a teacher. It did cross my mind, while he was being so understanding, to ask him if I could play the Mozart after all. But I didn't. I thought that was quite restrained of me.

Then I found Emma. She was in the day-room, standing by the notice board, and when I went up to her she looked at me steadily, with a spark of something I couldn't identify in her eyes.

"Hello," she said warily.

It was enough. "Oh Em," I sighed, touching her shoulder. "I'm really sorry about all those nasty things I said. I didn't mean them – any of them. I'm not a better violinist than you, and I don't think you're a liar, or – or anything else. I wouldn't blame you if you never wanted to speak to me again, but I wanted to wish you good luck for this evening. I hope it all goes well; you deserve it."

And I turned to walk away, but Emma caught my arm. "Thanks, Lizzie," she said, her eyes shining. "Thank you – that's really kind of you. I know how much you wanted to play the concerto, and it must be really mizz having to watch me play instead."

We stood and looked at each other for a while, silently. Then all at once we both smiled, and I felt a curious sensation of something lifting.

"It is," I confessed. "But I'll survive."

Emma pulled a face. "I'm sorry too – about what happened, I mean. All that trouble you've been having with Laura and Simon. Oh golly – you don't know about Simon, do you? He's leaving. We all found out this morning." She scanned my face, for signs that I was upset I suppose, but rather to my surprise I didn't feel upset; just puzzled.

"Leaving? But why?"

"He did really badly in his exams – failed them all, apparently. Only his mum and dad can't believe that the reason he's failed is because he never does a stroke of work, and they're saying that Percy's is no good and they're sending him to another school, up North. They're a bit odd about Simon – they think he's wonderful and can do no wrong." I thought about the letter they had sent to Daddy; with parents like that, I supposed it wasn't really surprising that he thought he was wonderful, too.

"Anyway," Emma went on, "he's going, I s'pose you'll miss him, won't you?"

"Only like you miss toothache," I told her. "You're glad it's gone. I know I used to be mad about him, but that's all over now. Besides," I said, thoughtfully, "all the trouble – with Laura, I mean – seemed to start when I started liking Simon. It's odd – she says he's just like a brother because she's known him so long, but she doesn't seem to like anybody else having anything to do with him."

"But she's like that with all her friends, not just Simon. It's as if – I don't know – she wants to be Number One all the time. Think about how she told us things about each other – she couldn't bear the thought of us being friends and leaving her out."

I stared at Emma. "I didn't know she told you things about me."

"Oh yes."

"What kind of things?" I wanted to know, although something told me I wouldn't like the answer very much.

"Oh, stupid things. Like how your friend Ben really fancied her, and told her he couldn't stand you. And what an awful house you live in, and how peculiar your family is."

I was furious. "She can't talk!" I spluttered. "With her weird family! Honestly, her brother is the creepiest thing on earth – he looks like a walking toilet brush . . . " I stopped, and Emma laughed.

"It doesn't matter, Lizzie – I didn't believe her. I know what she's like. And I bet she told you some pretty juicy things about me, too." I thought about all the times Laura had told me how wet Emma was, how dim and how stupid, and how she had made me wonder whether Emma really *had* stolen those things, and I went red. I really should have known better than to believe Laura instead of Emma, after all the nasty things she had said and done to me.

It was as if Emma read my mind. "Look," she said. "About that stealing business."

I stopped her. "It doesn't matter. You don't have to explain. I know you didn't do it."

"But Laura told you how all the stealing stopped once I was accused, and you started to wonder?" I went even redder and nodded, and Emma sighed. "It's true. It did all stop, and I s'pose that's what made everyone more sure it was me; it was almost the final piece of evidence. But it wasn't – me, I mean. Mum and Dad reckon that the real thief got scared when I was nobbled, and was put off by all the awful things that happened to me. Anyway, we'll never know, will we?"

"The trouble is, Laura can be so – convincing. When I'm on my own I can see sense; I can see she's lying. But when I'm with her it's a different matter." A sudden thought occurred to me. "Hey – you don't suppose *Laura* was the thief, do you? She only blamed you to cover her tracks – that would explain why it all stopped once you got the blame." I was surprised I hadn't thought of it before, but Emma was shaking her head.

"No." she said. "I did wonder that myself, when all the fuss had died down, and I mentioned it to my mum. But she said she doubted if it was Laura. She says that kind of stealing is done more for attention than for anything else, and that Laura gets enough attention. She picks on people like you and me to get rid of her unhappiness, Mum says, whereas people who nick things have sat on their frustrations and let them fester. So it almost certainly wasn't Laura, Mum says; although it would be much neater if it was, wouldn't it?"

I was silent for a while. "I'll never forgive Laura," I said eventually, "for stirring things like that – pretending to be my friend and then being horrible to me, and all the while saying nasty things and telling lies about me behind my back. She's – she's *evil*, like your dad says!"

Emma shook her head. "No she's not, She's just – well – not worth bothering about. Just ignore her – just don't talk to her any more. There's no law that says you have to. Just be polite, after all we have lessons with her, don't we, but don't get involved. You might find it easier now Simon's gone, and you don't have to stay on her right side to carry on talking to him." I blushed again – how well Emma seemed to understand.

"Anyway, I feel sorry for her," she said thoughtfully. "She's never going to keep any friends if she treats them like that all the time. I think she's quite sad really."

Afterwards I thought about what Emma had said. She was a much nicer person than me; much more forgiving. She was right, of course; Laura didn't seem to have any friends left, though doubtless she would soon find someone else to follow her about and hang on her every word, like I had done. I was through with her. But try as I might, I couldn't bring myself to forgive her for how she had treated me. I wished I was more like Emma.

At two o'clock that afternoon we had a dress rehearsal for The Concert in the Queen Elizabeth Hall. To my surprise, I felt a thrill of excitement; I hadn't thought I was looking forward to it, now I wasn't playing the concerto, but I was wrong. There was something very exciting about the prospect of a proper concert in a proper London concert hall. Emma and I had arranged to travel down to the QEH together, on the Tube, but she came rushing up to me during lunch.

"Lizzie," she said, looking distracted. "You'll have to go on without me – I forgot to bring my concert clothes. I've go to go home and collect them. I shouldn't be late, but could you explain to Sporanti if I am?" I assured her I would, and she dashed off breathlessly.

"Typical," said Laura cattily, from the other end of the table. "Some people would forget their heads if they weren't screwed on. Oh hello, Lizzie; I didn't see you there. Been for any nice moonlit walks lately?"

Don't take any notice, I told myself; I smiled sweetly, collected up my pudding bowl and left the table. A few people laughed, but not many, and I was surprised at how easy it was to ignore her.

The QEH was a hive of activity; members of the orchestra

getting out instruments and tuning them up, stagehands adjusting platforming and seats and Signor Sporanti's dais, Percy's orchestral librarian going round putting music on all the stands. The timpanist and Bethan Williams, the harpist, were already in their places, tuning up with that extra care their instruments require.

At last we were all seated; Sporanti stopped buzzing around, the oboist played an A and we all tuned again. Then I realized Emma wasn't there; Sporanti noticed at the same time.

He frowned. "Where is Emma Nash?" he demanded, making her name sound like one word – Emmanash, like ham'n'eggs.

I put my hand up. "She had to go home to fetch something, Signor," I told him. "She said she wouldn't be late."

"Well she *is* late!" he stormed, his brows beetling. Then he muttered something in Italian, and threw his hands up. "OK, we start with the Brahms until she arrives."

But we rehearsed the whole of the Brahms symphony, and there was no sign of Emma. Sporanti looked like thunder. We played the Mendelssohn overture, Fingal's Cave, that we were starting the concert with; still no Emma. By this time it was half past three, and I was worried .

"She's probably gone to the Albert Hall instead," Laura volunteered. "She's like that – she's always getting things wrong."

Signor Sporanti had stopped looking cross and was beginning instead to look concerned. He told David Springhof, the leader, to conduct us through the opening of the Mozart concerto while he went off to telephone. He was just hurrying up the aisle when the doors at the back were thrown open and a small dishevelled figure burst in. It was Teddie, and she looked in a right state.

"Signor!" she yelled, and although she was at the back of

the hall her voice rang out as clear as a bell. "Oh Signor, it's dreadful! Em's fallen down some steps and she's hurt herself, she fainted the pain was so bad, and a man called an ambulance and there were loads of people all standing round and staring, it was awful, and they took her off to hospital and Mummy and Daddy came and they x-rayed her arm, the doctors I mean not Mummy and Daddy, and anyway, it's broken. Her arm. She's broken her arm, and she won't be able to play the Mozart!" And with this startling piece of news Teddie flung herself at Signor Sporanti, who patted her rather gingerly on the back. The whole thing seemed somehow unreal.

Later, the members of the Central London School of Music Symphony Orchestra, me included, were standing backstage in various states of nervousness and clutching our instruments. We were all dressed in our concert-best of black and white and looked rather like a bunch of smart penguins. It was half-past seven, the time the concert was due to begin, and Mr Bishop, dressed in a dinner jacket, was standing onstage making an announcement.

"Ladies and Gentlemen," I heard him say. "Miss Emma Nash, tonight's soloist for the Mozart violin concerto will unfortunately be unable to play due to an accident." A ripple of concern went round the QEH, and I could imagine Mr Bishop raising his hands as he went on. "I am assured that it is not too serious an injury, and that Emma will be able to play as well as ever in a few weeks. In the meantime I should like to offer her my – our – condolences, and to inform you that instead of the Mozart, the orchestra will be playing Sibelius' tone poem, Finlandia." When Teddie had come rushing into the hall that afternoon, we had all been really concerned for poor Emma. Then, hot on the heels of my concern came another thought – *perhaps I'll play the Mozart after all. Who else can play it? I know it better than anyone else.* Then I felt ashamed at having such a thought, and when Signor Sporanti told us we'd be playing the Sibelius instead I started feeling guilty. Perhaps if I had gone home with Emma, if I'd been with her, she wouldn't have fallen and broken her arm, she would still be all right, she would still have been able to play.

I said as much to Teddie, who scoffed. "Don't be daft," she said. "You couldn't have stopped her falling. Nobody could – well, perhaps Superman might have done, but nobody else. She knew she was late and she went rushing down the steps outside the flat, and she tripped over a toy car the little kid in the basement flat had left out."

It seemed peculiar that, after all the bother surrounding the Mozart Concerto, neither of us were to play it.

The concert went well. Once we started to play I forgot that I was in the Queen Elizabeth Hall, forgot this was my first ever proper London concert, forgot everything, and just lost myself in the music. We played really well; at least, I thought we did, and Sporanti actually smiled at us at the end, a broad grin splitting his squashed tomato face and making him look almost human for once. And judging by the applause at the end, the audience thought we were pretty good, too.

When the house lights went on I looked out into the audience, and there they were; Daddy, and Wendy in her new dress, and Wendy's parents, all clapping and beaming and full of pride, and my heart felt swollen with pride too. And there beside them was the Nash clan, Mr and Mrs Nash, Emma with her left arm in a white plaster cast, and beside her Teddie and Theo. They were all clapping too, and looking at me and smiling, and I suddenly thought of the bouquet of red roses Ben and his parents had sent anyway, even though I was only a humble member of the orchestra. Suddenly, I realized that none of it mattered – Laura, Simon, playing the concerto, none of it was important. I somehow knew that there would be other concerts, other concertos even, and other friends and boyfriends, all waiting for me in the future, and I suddenly felt tremendously excited about that future. But what was important, here, now, and for always, was being true to myself; being me, and not being so influenced by other people as to try and change myself into the person they wanted me to be.

As I looked out once more into the audience I saw the audience all clapping and cheering, and it was as if they were doing it just for me. So I walked off stage, with the rest of the orchestra, to my future; I knew then that the people who truly cared about me would love and accept me for what I was, no matter what I did, and I felt lucky to be surrounded by such love. Really lucky.